MEMPHIS NOIR

MEMPHIS NOIR

EDITED BY
LAUREEN P. CANTWELL & LEONARD GILL

AKASHIC
BOOKS

Published by Akashic Books
©2015 Akashic Books

Series concept by Tim McLoughlin and Johnny Temple
Memphis map by Sohrab Habibion

The lyrics on page 127 are from the song "The Never Never (Is Forever)" by Tones on Tail.

ISBN-13: 978-1-61775-311-4
Library of Congress Control Number: 2015934037

First printing

Printed in Canada

Akashic Books
Twitter: @AkashicBooks
Facebook: AkashicBooks
E-mail: info@akashicbooks.com
Website: www.akashicbooks.com

MIX
Paper from
responsible sources
FSC® C004071

ALSO IN THE AKASHIC NOIR SERIES

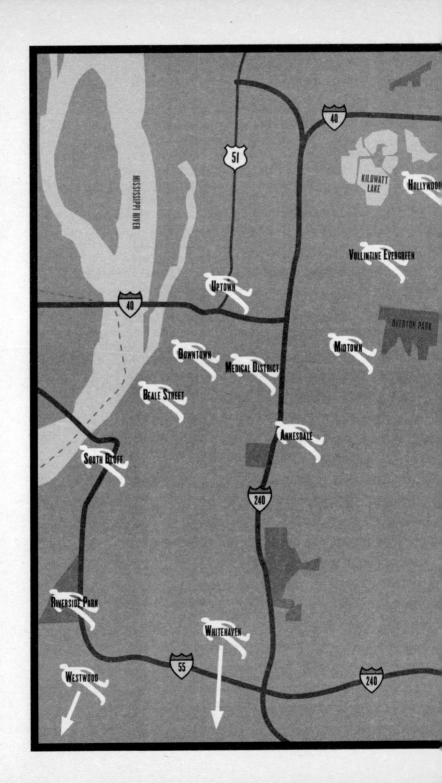

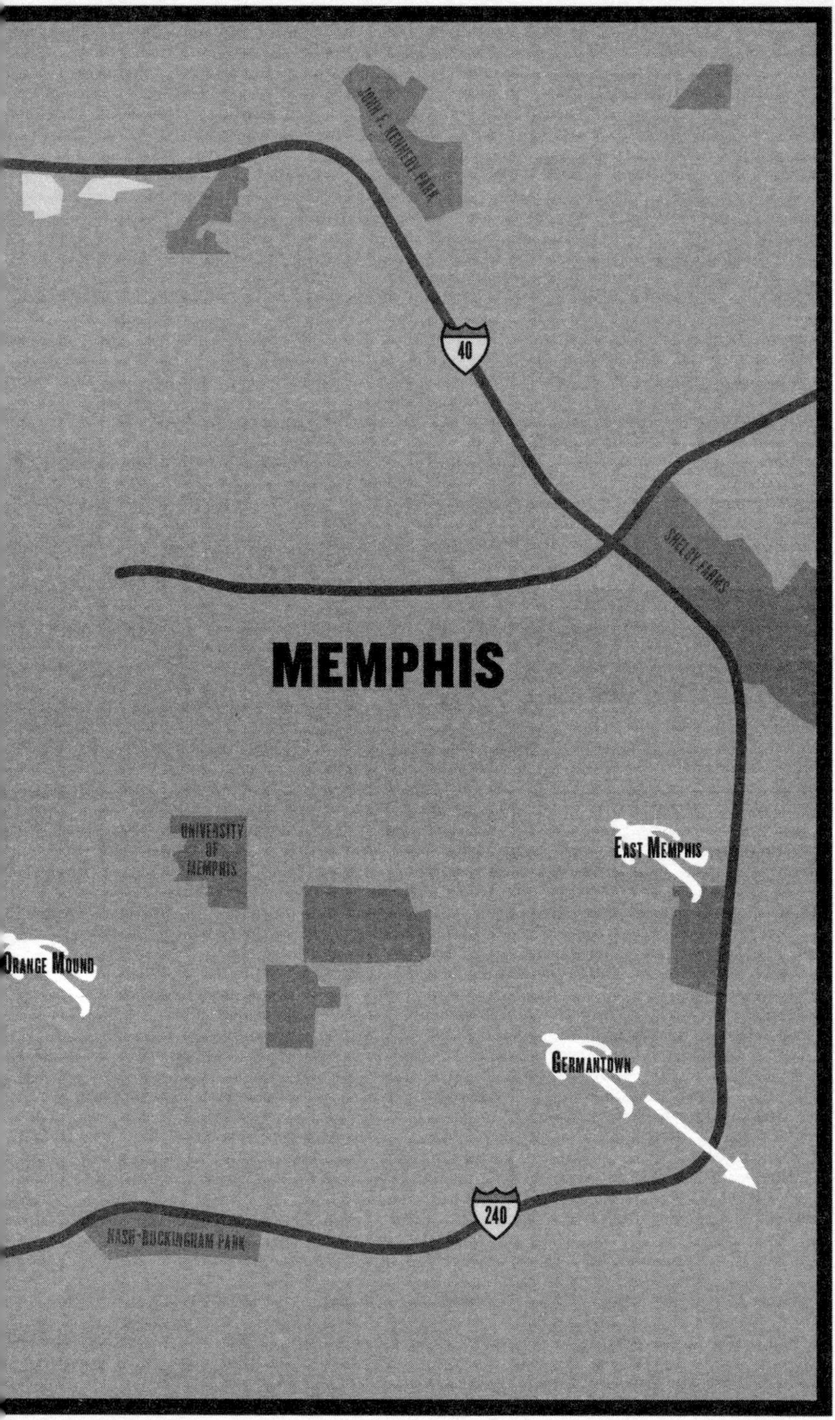
JOHN F. KENNEDY PARK
40
SHELBY FARMS
MEMPHIS
UNIVERSITY OF MEMPHIS
EAST MEMPHIS
ORANGE MOUND
GERMANTOWN
240
NASH-BUCKINGHAM PARK

To Mama and Jacqueline, for your love and support.
To John, for your nonstop encouragement, faith, and love.
To Leonard, Johnny, and the writers herein: thank you for making
this collection possible.
—L.P.C.

To Laureen, whose idea it was.
—L.G.

TABLE OF CONTENTS

INTRODUCTION
CITY OF MARVELS & MISFITS

A city equal parts darkness and hope. A scarred city. An often violent one. But a resilient city too. That's our Memphis.

Like many cities, we have a namesake—in Egypt, Mennefer became Menfe became Memphis, enduring and beautiful, on the banks of the Nile. Centuries later, another continent, another people, another river: Memphis, Tennessee, the soul of the Mississippi Delta, was formed. We are a place born of history, inhabited as much by memory as by the living—the past and present inextricably and inescapably linked.

What is the relationship between our city and the rest of the world? What does Memphis bring to mind?

We bet it's not that we had the world's largest mule market in the 1950s, or that we led the world in hardwood lumber and spot cotton in the late nineteenth and early twentieth centuries. No, it's usually the river. Floods. Music. Race. Yellow fever. And—of course—barbecue.

We also bet we've changed the world you live in.

Part of our resilience is survival against the odds—the Battle of Memphis in 1862 (which turned the city into a Union stronghold), seven yellow fever outbreaks and the flight of local wealth after the 1878 epidemic, political corruption, poverty, high teen pregnancy rates, high murder rates—we've definitely had enough going against us. Maybe even a lot worth hiding.

But lifelong Memphian Edwin Frank, Curator of Preservation and Special Collections at the University of Memphis, might ask you, "Why shouldn't the city be itself?"

In a city of deep and persistent tensions, the people of Memphis reside low in a delta, but sit high on the bluff. Remnants of slavery and sharecropping, of shifting underclasses (black *and* white), and of African folk traditions abound. Our popular culture works from the bottom up, built without the support of (but not so very far removed from) the sprawling plantations and aristocratic sociopolitical structure so often part and parcel with the image of the South. Instead, race and music, old endings and new beginnings, connect this city in webs spun deep in its very core.

R&B producer Ralph Bass could tell you of the impact of black radio stations like WDIA, the "Mother Station of the Negroes," in breaking down segregation in Memphis over unsegregated airwaves. Those airwaves brought black music to the white ears of a new generation and encouraged black clubs to add "spectator" tickets for whites, then "white nights," to become, eventually, a shared space.

Beale Street was built on black music and black commerce, and, for a time, it blurred racial distinctions—until Martin Luther King Jr.'s assassination brought tensions to a new level and urban renewal razed the music mecca and many of its landmarks. Decades would pass before Memphis, the "Home of the Blues," saw fit to bring Beale back, fitting for a city as rich in blues as in spirit—but not without its dangers.

Danger and music seem ever-entangled, like pit vipers in molasses: Richard J. Alley's contribution to this volume, "The *Panama Limited*," puts the reader inside a train car headed south for Memphis. So too in David Wesley Williams's "Her Better Devils," which takes us from floodwaters to the South

Bluff, in the company of a black blues singer, her white man, and the looming presence of an escaped criminal.

Adam Shaw and Penny Register-Shaw's graphic story "The Never Never Is Forever" takes hold of the tensions of love and oblivion in the city's downtown music scene in the '90s, with its constellation of alternative rock, abandoned buildings, drugs, and death. Just north of downtown, in Uptown Memphis, the folks inside Fat Red's underground club know good times and violence, and both collide in the gyrating crowd of Troy L. Wiggins's "Tell Him What You Want"— a tale evocative of Langston Hughes's poem "Beale Street Love," with fists and knuckles passionately engaged with lips, eyes, love, and desire. If Hughes's Clorinda had lived near Uptown, we have no doubt she'd have been at Fat Red's cooing, "Hit me again." Moving farther east, it's a matter of money and a loveless cage of a marriage in Suzanne Berube Rorhus's "A Game of Love," where a national tennis tournament serves as a backdrop to adultery—and murder—among the city's well-to-do, harnessing the faithlessness of lovers so often figured in the blues.

In the infancy of this project, Stephen Clements, author of "Battle," shared with us perhaps the most elegiac of summations: we had two kings, and we killed them both. "Battle" meshes Clements's experiences as a veteran, his love of the city of his birth, and his keen eye for redemption even in the darkest of corners, among the saddest of souls. "Heartbreak at Graceland" by Kaye George goes beyond heartbreak: a dark fascination with Elvis's place of death, his bathroom, leads to even darker revelations and little resolution behind the Whitehaven mansion's gates.

But leaving Graceland does not put the darkness behind. Sheree Renée Thomas's "Nightflight" captures the solitude of a brilliant woman at a time when the sun can no longer bear to shine on the soul of the Delta, which brings to mind another poem, John Townsend Trowbridge's "Memphis":

> At last he seemed to lose it altogether
> Upon the Mississippi; where he stayed
> His course at Memphis, undecided whether
> He should go back or forward. Here he strayed
> One afternoon along the esplanade
> And high bluff of the river-fronting town,
> To watch the boats and see the sun go down.

Spinning poetry, performance, past, and present into a tornado of a tale, Arthur Flowers highlights Memphis's hoodoo history with his special brand of prose in "There Is No Rest." "Mother," by young writer Ehi Ike, unearths the darkness at the heart of a nuclear family in the upscale suburbs, while Pulitzer Prize finalist Lee Martin, in "Chain of Custody," takes a slant approach to the commonplace: a party in Orange Mound leads to a shooting, which leaves police certain of their suspect but the suspect certain of very little.

And, no question, we are one of the most crime-ridden cities in America. Historically, Al Capone's Chicago had nothing on us; presently, there's hardly a negative top ten on which you *can't* find Memphis. Amid all the changes this city has seen, our crime problem remains.

Dwight Fryer's "Green-Eyed Blues" looks at our desegregated police force in the 1940s, the city's political power brokers, and the juxtaposition of love and lust, racial tension and murder. Shifting to the present-day: Jamey Hatley sets us squarely on the other side of the law, and takes us to Pussy Valley, in "Through Valleys," a story of conspiracies, fraud, and more—borrowed from local headlines and laid at the feet of city councilmen, state senators, the Memphis Police Department, and a librarian who isn't what she appears to be. The boarded-up remnants of a Midtown mansion sets the stage for the strange goings-ons in John Bensko's "A Shut-and-Open Case." Noir veteran Cary Holladay's edgy and eerie "Stinkeye" features not only Confederate general Nathan Bedford Forrest (from beyond the grave) but also the bizarre case of a Memphis medical examiner, a story imaginatively recast but torn from a front-page news story that garnered national attention.

Some might say it's the people who come here from elsewhere who often teach us most about Memphis, but—whether you're a native or a newcomer—there's no denying that the city has carved its place in history. Grasping our bottom-up culture, Sir Peter Hall's *Cities in Civilization* states, "What the Memphis story finally shows is that the music of an underclass could literally become the music of the world." In fact, popular song lyrics feature Memphis more often than almost any other city in the world. Whether you're sad or wistful, leaving or returning, walking in Memphis or riding the *City of New Orleans*, miles from or real nearby, thinkin' 'bout Elvis or honky-tonk women . . . you're singing about us in a bittersweet way. George A. Norton knew the moody, muddy echoes of the city well:

> *Hear me people, hear me people, hear I pray,*
> *I'm going to take a million lessons 'til I learn how to play*
> *Because I seem to hear it yet, simply can't forget*
> *That blue refrain.*
> *There's nothing like the Handy Band that played the*
> *Memphis Blues so grand.*

Oh play them Blues.
That melancholy strain, that ever haunting refrain
Is like a sweet old sorrow song.
Here comes the very part that wraps a spell around my heart.
It sets me wild to hear that loving tune again,
The Memphis Blues.

Somewhere between our blues and our kings, our fevers and our rock 'n' roll, our history has transformed yours—our Piggly Wiggly began the self-serve grocery businesses; our FedEx changed the way you do business; our Holiday Inn brought you *your* Holiday Inn; and our music has been the soundtrack to your life. Its wild beat has rocked your world. And our struggle against our own darkness has kept us in the headlines. Memphis is marvels and misfits—two-faced and unabashedly so.

And no, we are not Atlanta, or Chicago, or Nashville; we are not Austin or New York, Detroit or Los Angeles—and we shouldn't try to be.

We are Memphis, and this is our *noir*.

Laureen P. Cantwell & Leonard Gill
Memphis, TN
August 2015

PART I

BEALE AND THE BLUFF

HER BETTER DEVILS

BY DAVID WESLEY WILLIAMS

South Bluff

1

She sat on the top step of the porch, watching the rain, and he stood in the doorway, watching her. "It's not the end of the world," he said, and she said, "I think the end of the world's been called on account of rain."

They said no more for a spell, her watching the rain and drinking what was left of the gin and then switching to what there was of rum, and him watching for some hint or sign, from her or from the heavens.

It had rained for weeks, first as a few plump drops and then as a steady drench. Then it almost stopped and the sun almost shone, but only almost, and then came the rain again—from great oaken buckets it sloshed. And then it did stop, as if in its own muddy tracks. It stopped for a full minute, and he said, "Finally. I think the rain's run out of ways to fall." She said, "Just wait, you," and watched with a kind of wearied bemusement as it rained a hail of bullets across the land. She might have been using her drink stir as a baton, to conduct all this doom.

This lasted all of one day and the night that followed—not that day had one dim bulb on night, these days. Then it was one endless drop. It spanned town blocks and country miles and days of the week. The rain became time, place, law, religion, and the arts. The rain was myth and legend and tomorrow's headlines wrung from the morning rag. The rain was all. There was only rain. Then the wind joined in. The wind howled hymns and chants and ghostly blues. It all seemed terribly biblical to him.

And she sat watching it, and he stood watching her. "You're going to catch your death," he said, "or get religion." She said, "You really think anything happens when we die but that there's one less soul in the world, and what's one less soul, unless it was one who made a difference, like—" She leaned back against the front porch beam and sighed. She was thinking. She said, "Well, I guess there must have been one or two in there somewhere who made a difference." She looked for something, some new bottle, to slug. "All right. I'll give you Lincoln, and the Reverend Al Green. Don't say I never gave you anything."

"Soul," he said. "You said one less soul, not one less person. There's hope for you yet, Mrs. Flood."

But still there was no hint or sign that he could see, except that the rum was gone and it was whiskey now—sour mash and the lightest rain yet, too soft to even call it falling: a veil upon the land. But rain is rain, and so the land sank further into itself.

The land swallowed deep, and the river body rose. The riverbanks swelled, and the river god crept closer.

He sat beside her on the top step of the porch. She had a fresh whiskey. She had bare feet and toenails painted blue the shade of dark in the usual way. He ran a finger along the barbed-wire-shaped scar on her left knee, the scar the color of midnight against her skin the color of dusk. It was her lucky scar, she said. She'd gotten it falling from the sky during a dream. He said that didn't sound very lucky, and she said there were all kinds of luck. She said you could hang from luck; you could drown in it. "Anyway, it happened," she said. Or anyway, that's the story she told him that night, the night they met, on the bluff in Memphis. Three days later they were married. *Three years next month*, he thought now, *river god willing and the world don't end.*

"This is a soggy river town," she said.

"Most river towns are," he said, "if it's any kind of river at all."

This seemed to cheer her some, for him to be the bearer of such news. She wagged her drink stir at him; it was a wand now. She sipped the whiskey. She poured him a glass and leaned in. She knocked him a kiss. He ran his finger some more along that barbed-wire scar and then considered her legs at great length. He admired their shape and sheen in the blue dark; he hoped for a lightning bolt, illumination, for better to see her skin, that scar, the full dusk of her. The power was out from Lower Grace to the big river, or else he'd have turned on the porch light.

"Well, well, well," she said.

He considered her toes, kissed and even counted them.

"All there, Mr. Flood?" she said.

Now the sky spat, and the wind sighed; they seemed to be having a conversation about the end of it all.

He ran a finger the length of her shin, up and down, up and down. He settled on up. He bypassed that barbed-wire scar.

Said the sky to the wind, "You think it'll ever stop raining?"

He stopped at the hem of her dress, and then he didn't stop. "Ahem," she said, and sipped whiskey through a hairline crack of smile. It was her favorite party dress, blue-flowered and drink-stained with a couple, three Lucky cigarette holes. She wore it that night, the night they met, on the bluff in

Memphis, as a three-piece band played the electrocuted blues and the Saturday-evening sun painted the sky purple with mischief. He thought they could use a bluff about now.

Said the wind to the sky, "Don't think so, no."

He ran a hand up under that blue-flowered dress, between the soft tatters of fabric and the cold sheen of dark skin. She turned on him, threw a leg over, and so now they rolled on the porch of the small country house as husband and wife, trying to save their marriage as the great sky fell and the river god rose to meet it.

"All there, Mrs. Flood," he said.

This is a true story, made up and written down. This is a fable and a good cry, a cautionary tale, a murder ballad.

This is the story of rain and more rain, high water and the search for higher ground—Beulah Land, or that bluff in Memphis. God is high up in heaven, watching, with silver flask and furrowed brow.

This is the blues, played on a single strand of broom wire.

This happened, just not yet.

They lay on the porch, after. She reached for the bottle of sour mash. Kentucky bourbon was her preference—sacrament, she called it—but she liked the label on the Tennessee sour mash, black the color of her scar and on it the face of some silver-bearded ancient with eyes wild like Moses on a bender. "A pint of Old Testament, my man!" she'd tell the counter man at the package store in Brownsville, and the counter man—born again, or claimed he was—would look at her with his best scold and say, "God'll get you for that, Mamie Flood." Then he'd look away, lest she—or God—see his smile.

She took the next-to-last sip and offered the last to him.

He drank the sip—it was, he thought, a little like a sacrament, the way she drank—and then she kissed his lips for a taste of those last traces.

They sat and watched the rain some more. It was a billowing sheet now, spread over the weary, spent body of land. Land was fast becoming memory; there was little more of it than the rise on which the small house sat, and beyond it only half-trees with limbs like arms trying like hell to swim their way out of the great muck. He tried but couldn't remember it not raining, and then he did: the night they met, that night in Memphis, the bluff there. It didn't rain that night. It didn't rain that whole summer. There was only hot breath and sweat, smoke and neon. They danced as that blues band played "Ramblin' on My Mind" and then "I Feel Like Going Home," and she shouted, "Make up your damn mind, you!" then took the stage herself and sang "I Can't Be Satisfied." The way she sang it, dirge-slow, you'd have thought satisfaction had drowned that very day. She'd get that way. Moods would strike her down, and evil would gather around, a flock at her feet. Her better devils, she called them.

But by night's end, that night, anyway, she was leading a joyful clamor. Horn players materialized, and jugs were passed; satisfaction walked on water, that night in Memphis.

The stories they told about her—that she killed a woman, upstairs in a Memphis bar that once was a brothel, late of a Saturday. Killed her with a railroad spike, some said, though not how. No, it was poison, or pistol shot, kitchen knife, guitar string—there were as many versions as there were storytellers. They agreed about as much on the why, though the smart money had it that this slain woman, known as Cheatham's woman—Beatrice was her name, though it died too, from

disuse—had been, briefly, her lover, but that she'd gone running back on threat of death from Cheatham. "That's the
why," they'd say, and someone would always ask, "Then why
kill her and not him?" And were told, always, "Don't you see?
She found a way to do away with the both of them and only
had to kill the one. Ain't it like her to do twice the harm with
half the work?"

He'd heard the stories, versions of them, after he married
her. He only said, and then only to himself, "Then why didn't
the police come? Why was she walking free and free to marry
and no more haunted than she is?"

And then, not even saying it to himself, not even thinking
it, really, but knowing, somehow: *It's not like she'd deny it. She
doesn't lie. It's her one virtue, even if she wields it like a vice. She's
incapable of telling a lie. It's why I don't ask.*

Anyway, it was a town for tales, Memphis. As for truth,
well, it was murdered nightly and back the next morning, a
little woozy, was all. The truth? Ah, you could get that however you wanted in Memphis, like you could get your pork
shoulder chopped or pulled, your ribs wet or dry.

Even so, he suggested they move to the country, and she
said, "I reckon a woman with a new name could do with a
fresh start altogether. Pack the bottles, husband."

How they met and married, how that all happened:

His work brought him to Memphis. He came to look for
ghosts and found a live one. He was a folklorist, a university professor from "Up North," which is to say, Kentucky. He
collected old stories and songs, saw folk art and deep mean-
ing in found items, in NuGrape bottle caps and broken plow
handles and hand-lettered signs that spoke of Jesus, sorghum,
tamales, and $2 covers. Splinters of crosses. Vials of dirt. An

eleven-foot cotton sack said to have been dropped by Muddy Waters the day he walked off Stovall Plantation—the shroud of Clarksdale.

Saturday night on the South Bluff. The air thick with the smell of summer heat and pig meat. Beer sold from a trailer and stronger stuff from behind a tree, buck a shot. That blues band in a tin-roofed gazebo, playing songs about homemade sin and juice-head women.

He saw her from across the way, the big river to her back, talking to some woman's man, swaying as she did, telling some long-legged tale and laughing—a cackle, really, that carried across the way and struck him so hard his knees buckled. He wondered if she could sing. Then she did, and that was it.

So that night in Memphis, after the band and the dancing, when it was just the two of them on the bluff and the moon in the sky and the devil off somewhere, and God too, the both of them soused and near to sleep—that night, the first they met, he asked her to marry him.

"Marry me, see if I care," she said. "Marry the hell out of me."

Later, in some fit or funk, she'd accuse him of collecting *her*, a gone black woman of song. He'd say, "But I loved you. I love you still. You must have loved me too. Or else why—" and she'd just shrug and say, "Who was I, white boy, to deny you the one wild thing you'd done in your life?"

2

They sat on the porch and drank—it was moonshine now, her dead uncle's handiwork. They passed the bottle, back and forth, back and forth, her taking swigs and him sips, until there was nothing left, only a drop, and she said her uncle told her that was a devil's tear, that last drop, and never to drink it.

"The devil's tear," he said.

"I always figured that was the only thing could make the devil cry—the sight of a near-empty bottle. But my uncle, he said it all had to do with bad luck, you know."

"Yeah," he said, sounding more like her by the sip, "I'd sure hate to break this winning streak we've got ourselves on."

She laughed one of those laughs of hers, not the cackle but another: husky with a deep bottom, a gallows laugh, a gutbucket number almost like the blues she sang the night they met, that night in Memphis, on the bluff there. It was as close as she came to singing, these days.

"My granddaddy, one time he died," she said. "I mean, one time he died and came back and told about it. That's what he said. I don't know if he really did die, but I do know he was gone a good while—I was there beside his bed, a girl, watching him, his dead eyes, his not breathing—and when he got back from wherever he went, he, by damn, had some fresh stories to tell. He told me them. He said he'd seen angels of the flesh and silver-winged hounds, and he'd seen the night sky peel away like old whorehouse wallpaper to reveal God on His golden throne, surrounded by a burgundy-robed choir singing 'Sinner You Better Get Ready' and 'Get Right Church.'

"He just told me, not the others. He waited for the others to leave the room. He said the others would think he'd gone full mad, lost what scraps were left of his mind. But me, he liked. He said I had a little of the devil in my eyes. That made me interesting to him, I think. Or anyway, I was a good audience. I was ten, something like that. I was a girl. Devil in my eyes—I'd been told it before, and I'd be told it again. I was told it all through my growing up, but all the rest, my mama, aunts, my sisters, this one boy I liked, they said it like just a little of the devil, a drop, a tear, was enough to taint whatever it touched. Like I had just a little of the devil in me, and just in my eyes, but I was lousy with him, still and all. Spoiled and ruined. *Spoilt* and *ruint*—how they said it.

"Fine, I was evil, then. So I scared my sisters, which I liked doing, and I scared that one boy I liked, which bothered me at first, but I warmed to it. He would have robbed banks for me. Hell—*churches*. But my mother and aunts, they prayed for me, pitied me. I could hear them talking, late at night, wondering could I be saved? Like saying, would the devil let loose of this girl? And me, five, eight, ten, twelve years old, and hearing this."

He just waited until she started up again. He wanted to ask how wild she'd been, but he just looked at her. She knew, though.

"I wasn't that bad, really," she went on. "Only a little. I was more contrary than anything. I was just working up to really bad, I guess. I didn't mind what I was told. Ever. Just for sport. I didn't care when they said they'd whip me. They whipped me until *they* were sore, and begged would I say the word so they could stop. But I wasn't sorry. Hell no. And I'd disappear at odd hours. I'd slip out at night, go nowhere but down to the creek. I'd sleep there. They'd ask where I was, and I'd say Hot Springs or out to the juke, or Memphis, looking for a man. They weren't lies—I was there, in my head. Memphis was my favorite place to want to be. Heaven sounded like a sentence, and hell was just some place they made up to scare us all. But Memphis. Shit, Memphis was real. City upon the bluff, like in the Good Book, only not like that at all. That white stuff wasn't salt, and the light was pure blue neon. Dreamed of that place. I mean, dreamed hard and woke up spent.

"And then liquor came into it. I figured out if I poured out some of a bottle of my uncle's hooch, they'd think I drank it.

I hated to pour it out—that was the only sin I saw in it. And then I didn't pour it out. I was twelve, something like that, when I started drinking. I'd been smoking for a year already. I lit up in church one day. I shouted *Holy hell!* when it ought to have been *Hallelujah!* That's about the time they quit taking me to church, see."

"They pushed you to all that, your mama and aunts and the rest."

"They didn't have to push hard, husband."

"Well," he said.

"And anyway, now it's me, all me, full-grown, sitting here. A ruint black woman in the rain at the end of the world."

He stood to go inside, to gather their things. It was time. There was an old johnboat out back of the house, left by the previous owner. She said she wished it were a steamboat, white with a big, red paddlewheel and draped lights on the bow, couples dancing on the deck to a little combo playing the "Beale Street Mess Around." She said she'd drink too much and put the make on Mark Twain. She sighed. She said, "But I'd settle for a rusted party barge and just a devil's tear to drink, and you, my man, to put the make on," and he said, "Well, it's just a johnboat, but I guess we should at least be thankful for that much."

"Thankful," she said back to him, as if it were rotting fruit at their feet.

He turned to go inside, and she turned to watch the rain. It was pure noisy spite now. There was no reasoning with it; it would not respond to batons or wands. It did not fall from the sky but rather seemed to be flung from it. And she sang, for the first time in ages. She sang snatches of Charley Patton's "High Water Everywhere." She sang, "*I was going to the hill country, but they got me barred.*" And she sang Kansas Joe Mc-

Coy and Memphis Minnie's "When the Levee Breaks." She sang, *"Cryin' won't help you, prayin' won't do no good."*

From inside the house he heard a sound like music, singing. He turned and listened but then went back to his gathering. He figured it to be the wind.

When he reappeared in the doorway with a peach crate of their things, he said, "Well," and she said, "Did you bring your Bible?"

He just looked at her.

"Because a Bible, they say, is handy in hard times, and particularly in a flood."

Still he just looked at her.

She stood, took the crate from him, and set it to the side of them. She kissed his neck, draped her skinny, long arms over his shoulders, weightless as shirtsleeves. She kissed his lips. She pulled back and said, "What you do is, you put that Bible on the ground where you're standing, and then you stand on it. A Bible's a good inch thick, what with all those books inside it, all those plagues and prophets, and their scoldings, all those tall tales and God sightings, and the revelations, *oh*, and the lamentations, *oh*, and the miracles, *oh*, and Jesus Christ Himself, and Queen Esther too, and *Thou shall not this* and *Thou shall not that, either,* and the proverbs and the psalms and the odd parable, and some true stuff too, even, I guess. So, anyway, like I was saying, you stand on that Bible, a good inch thick. It won't save you, like you're taught it will," and she kissed his forehead, "but it'll buy you ten whole minutes from the rising water while you think of something better." She stepped away, looked down at her bare feet and toes all there. "That's what little I believe," she said. "Lucky for me you believe enough for the both of us, huh?"

But it was as if he hadn't heard a word of it. He was grinning still, eyes shut since she kissed him. But when he came to—it was like coming to, like he'd been knocked out, blissfully dead, there for a moment—the grin had been washed away as if by the rain or blown off by the wind. Then the rain did stop. Finally. The rain had run out of ways to fall. And so now the sun shone on all the rain had wrought. The sun shone like some vengeful god, mean streaks on the memory of land.

There was little left of the rise on which the small house sat, and those trees were up to their middle fingers in muck.

"We'd best go."

"Yes."

They boarded the small boat and began to row. It was that or pray.

3

They rowed until they collapsed and then let the currents take them. They lay on their backs and listened to the river swish like choir robes at a funeral; they swayed to that burgundy sound. And they floated, a one-johnboat procession across the river of land. It looked about like land you could walk across, that river of land being the color of mud, dusk, and her skin.

The sky was scarcely any color at all; gray would not have claimed it as kin. The sky was all plummet and regret. The sky rued the day.

She closed her eyes and began to hum. He closed his and listened. She became, for him, that choir. The deep thud of her voice, the thrum of her hum.

It was "I Got to Cross the River of Jordan" and "Creep Along, Moses" and "Glory, Glory, Hallelujah." He said, "They're beautiful. Those songs." And she said, "Furry Lewis sang about glory, but he sang about jellyroll too. They all did, those old blues singers. They sang about crossing the River Jordan, but they sang about getting in your wife's drawers too. They sang about the Memphis strut and that Tennessee crawl. Sang about jive and knives. Sang those dirty blues and then turned around and cut a gospel record—piss off God and the devil, both. But shit, who am I, telling this to you, Professor White Boy?"

"They were torn," he said. "Conflicted."

He had written scholarly papers on the subject, old blues singers who sang smut on Saturday and every other night, and then shouted praises, come Sunday and some other mornings.

"The hell," she said. "Those ol' boys were just selling records. And those church ladies, they got needs too."

He looked at her and smiled. The busthead talking, saying the damnedest things. She took a swig of her dead uncle's shine and said, "You don't know the half of what goes on up under those choir robes, husband."

4

Somewhere in West Tennessee, on a day without a name under a cast-iron sky:

"Will it be wicked when we get there?" he said.

"If it's not already, yes," she said.

5

There came a newsboy on a skiff, waving the bulldog edition out of Memphis, shouting headlines.

"Cheatham escaped! Baddest man in three states!"

"What about the flood?"

"Old news, ma."

"I ain't your ma, boy."

"I ain't your boy then. I sure as shit ain't his."

She gave him the back of her hand and sneered. He shrugged and grinned.

"What's all that about Cheatham?" she asked.

"Oh, baddest man in three states."

"I heard all that. What's he supposed to have done?"

"Bulldog edition run you a nickel."

"Play ball with me, boy."

"All right, all right, ma. He was in the pen, account of a murder he said he didn't commit. Falsely tried and wrongly convicted's what he said."

"What they all say."

"I ain't saying either way, ma. I ain't God or Judge Harsh. Just a newsboy on a skiff at the end of the world."

"Cheatham," she said carefully, precisely, as if the word was a fish hook she was removing from her finger.

"Yeah, see, ma. It's like that, ain't it? Just *sound* guilty. *Cheat 'um,*" the newsboy said. "He knew it too. Stood up at his trial, said it was all on account of his name. Ha! And him, with a record long as my nevermind. But a man got to try. So he did. Said if his name was Work or Church or Goodpasture, something like that, they never woulda made him for it. He said it was a woman who did it. Said she killed her and then framed him. Said a woman killed his wife, all because . . ."

"Because what?"

"Got it all in the bulldog edition," he said. "Got funnies in there too. Show me some coin or something else, big mama. I'll show you my . . ."

She looked at her husband to see what he was making of it all. But he was asleep, or acting it.

"Well, that's all real tragic there, boy," she said. "But what about this flood? What's that Memphis rag of yours say about that?"

The newsboy unfolded the newspaper and held it at arm's length from his face. He scanned it up and down.

"Cheatham escaped!" he shouted. "Baddest man in three states!"

6

They made Memphis on a Sunday with a sky the color of bourbon-barrel char; the neon looked all the better against it.

They made the South Bluff, welcomed there by an old man in a stovepipe hat who said, "There is no hell. There is, however, a Memphis, and it's here the devil lives in relative pain and ease like any man."

"You him?" she asked.

"Nah, devil's up in the big house, playing cards with the mayor. Mayor already lost City Hall and Central Station and Nathan Bedford Forrest's grave."

"There any word of what's his name?"

"You got to be more specific, ma'am. Boss Crump? The Reverend Green? Ol' Chief Tishomingo of the Chickasaw Nation?" The man in the stovepipe hat smiled and tipped that hat, and from it a crow flew. He watched it climb the sky and then looked disappointedly into the dark of the hat, as to wonder why it was just the one.

"You know who I mean. Cheatham, they call him."

"Oh, him. Well, you know."

"Know what?"

But the man was deep in the task of fitting the stovepipe hat back upon his head. When he had it just so, he said again as he had said before, "There is no hell. There is, however, a Memphis . . ."

She made for the gazebo, the band there. She took a bottle

from the horn player and a swig from the bottle and then licked her cracked lips. She looked out upon the crowd of dancers on the dried-mud yard they called a dance floor, and began to sing. She sang murder ballads and gospel novelties about Jesus in an *air-o-plane*. She sang "Sweet to Mama" and "I Got a Gal." She dedicated songs to God and the devil and the chief of the Chickasaws, to the Reverend Green and the ghost of Furry Lewis, and to her good man there in the crowd.

He watched from the wings, thinking, *And I married her. Me, who had never done a wild thing in my life.* She closed her eyes as she sang, threw her head back, and shouted whispers. That's how it seemed to him, when she sang. And he was mesmerized, as ever. Maybe that's all it had ever been, he thought. Maybe she was right—it was not love, never had been. Maybe he collected her, the living ghost—or, more like, he thought, had been collected by her. Company for her better devils.

After, she asked the horn player, Tippo Jones, "I miss anything, Tip?"

"Never known you to miss a thing, Mamie."

"You know what I mean."

"Oh, all that."

So he told it, how Cheatham broke out of the pen and came back to Memphis, like they all knew he would. But he knew they knew, and so he was careful as a desperate man could be. There were bulletins out, his face on the radio. He was said to be armed—"Wasn't but a shiv," Tippo Jones said— and dangerous. He was that—took that shiv to a former crony, for the sole crime of telling him what he knew and it not being what Cheatham wanted to hear:

"Heard she took to livin' out in West Tennessee. Heard she died out there, on account of this flood they got going."

"Where in West Tennessee?"

"*Out near Lower Grace, how I heard it. Lived with her husband. Good man, they say. They say he married the hell out of her, you know, but way I heard it, there was some left.*"

"*Ain't that sweet.*"

"*Just tellin' you what I know, Cheat. They say she married this man—all but a stranger to her. They say he heard her sing and that was it. Couldn't help himself. He was from Up North. Kentucky, I think it was. White boy too. White boy name of—*"

Tippo Jones said the crony told Cheatham the name, that last bit of everything he knew, and then Cheatham stuck him with that shiv anyway. So he was a killer now, if he wasn't one before. And they caught him, like he had to know they would. Because he was more desperate than careful, and he was getting to be more crazed than desperate.

They caught him on the railroad bridge, or anyway, had him all but caught. He climbed over the railing and was making more noise than a train would've, they said. Ravings of a madman, saying a woman named Flood had been the ruin of him, and he'd ruin her if he had to go to the bottom of Big Muddy to find her.

Tippo Jones said Cheatham shouted a few more words on his way down, but nobody could make them out. Nobody tried, he said; ravings of a madman and all.

Then he laughed; it was a deep and mellow tone, like you would expect from a horn player. That laugh was like silk had taught bourbon to sing. Then he was gone, off to play an after-hours gig at the big house for the new mayor.

And Mamie Flood, she went to find her good man, ready to tell him if he was ready to know, to ask. He was. She could tell by the way he stood waiting for her.

But he held her first, and they began to dance. It was their anniversary, after all. Well, more or less. Hard to know, for the days had become one. So they danced. Some music would have been nice—and then it came, just fell from the sky.

The rain was song. It played mad piano rags on the tin roof of the gazebo, funeral marches on the dance-floor muck. They danced, no matter the rain. They danced, and she sang it to him. It's the one way she could tell him, the one way he could hear it.

HEARTBREAK AT GRACELAND

BY KAYE GEORGE

Whitehaven

J ed waited until I got out of the car, but not long enough. My scarf got stuck in the door, and I turned around to yank on it. He didn't notice, started up, and down I went. When I began hollering, he slammed on the brakes and flew out to help me.

"What the hell did you do, Izzy?" He stared at me, sprawled in the street, my shoulder resting on the curb.

"I tried to get my damn scarf out of the door."

He helped me up with one hand. He's a big guy.

"You okay?"

"No, I'm not okay." I massaged my right shoulder. Man, was it sore. "I hurt my shoulder and I think my scarf is ruined."

He turned around and released it from the car door. "Yeah, it's pretty much shredded."

And greasy where it had been caught.

"I better get goin'," I said, gritting my teeth with pain. Li'l Darlin' Diner opened in about twenty minutes.

"Give me your keys." He took my elbow and unlocked the restaurant's front door.

Sometimes I liked it when he treated me like a helpless Southern belle. After all, that can be worked. But mostly I didn't, since I wasn't one. He insisted on staying, until he saw I was going to be able to work. Jed's a one-in-a-million guy. I got lucky the day I found him.

Larry, the cook, and Agnes, the owner, showed up, so Jed decided he could leave.

"Gotta run." He gave me a peck and took off. He worked at Graceland, down the street, his dream job, even if it was only opening the front doors for the tour groups. He was born loving the King. He didn't look much like Elvis, even with the pompadour and the sideburns, but he could sing a lot like him. Played guitar pretty good too. He even used to want to act, he said. After letting groups into Elvis's mansion all day, he would come back here, eat a bite, and take me home.

When I first got to Memphis, I'd taken the Graceland tour and met him in the Jungle Room. We were both staring at the stone waterfall on the wall. He was taking the tour as part of his training. I wanted to see the place Elvis had built for himself, and where he had died so dramatically.

I was bummed that the tour didn't include the bathroom where he died, because that would have been the highlight for me. Gruesome, I guess, but I'm always interested in how people die, especially celebrities. They die more interesting deaths than normal people, seems to me.

Jed asked if I'd have dinner with him after that tour. I kinda shrugged him off. I mean, I was new in town and didn't give a shit about a guy I'd just met. But he leaned close and started singing, soft, *"Don't be cruel . . ."* He made me laugh, and that counted for a lot right then. I didn't know anyone in Memphis, and I needed a laugh. So I went out with him.

Anyway, in spite of the fiery pains shooting through my shoulder, my day was beginning. Larry flipped the sign to *Open* and people started coming in.

The day rolled on like any other, except for that damn nagging pain in my shoulder, until dinnertime. *Diner* was in our name, but we were a small neighborhood bar and grill, really. We got a few tourists and lots of regulars. I liked my job, even though I went home with sore feet.

That night, a couple came through the door and caught my attention. From their conversation, I knew they were going on the tour of the mansion. From the looks of their clothes and her jewelry, they'd probably gotten the Platinum Tour. I could be wrong though. Sometimes people with a ton of dough don't like to let go of it.

They weren't old enough to be "original" Elvis fans. That's what Jed calls people who were alive when the King was hot shit. Okay, she wasn't old enough. He might have been. I knew I looked younger than I was by the way the male customers always stared at me. I was smart enough that I didn't look back—not if they were with a gal. I always gave the little ladies a big howdy with a smile and just flicked a glance at the guys.

If you give the guy too much attention, as any female member of the waitstaff profession can tell you, the woman will make sure you get a bad tip. If you butter *her* up, though, you stand a better chance.

This gal wasn't a looker. Her nose was too long and hooked. She put in a lot of effort with the makeup and hair, but hadn't gotten herself a nose job. Thinkin' on that, I decided they weren't that flush.

The guy was drop-dead. I mean drop-dead. I didn't dare give him more than two seconds for a look over. That was enough to start my heart pumpin' overtime.

As I took their drink orders, she fluttered her overloaded eyelashes and simpered, "I just can't decide, Eustace. You pick for me."

I made a mental bet he'd pick a chard.

"Look, Jory, this is the same little white wine you had

last week. You liked it. Remember, baby?" Bingo.

"Oh, I surely do. I'll have that." Her long red fingernail stabbed the cheapest chardonnay on the menu.

Eustace picked a single malt for himself.

Sure, you good-lookin' bastard, I thought. *Spend the money on yourself.*

While I waited at the bar for the drinks, it occurred to me that I knew who they were. He was Eustace Rage, the famous playwright, and she was Jory Rage, formerly Jory Cay, the star in his first play. *The Rabid Night* had gone on to Broadway, then was a popular movie. It was supposed to be full of literary symbolism. I saw it with a theater student I dated a few years ago, in another town, another life. It was a huge money-maker, he said.

Right after I brought their drinks, a young family came in. I sat them across the room from the couple so if the baby started hollerin', they wouldn't pick up and leave. Our place wasn't big enough to get too far from a squaller.

I was working my regular shift, ten to five, breakfast through early dinner. I liked that shift the best. My day got over early, but I was there for some of the dinner crowd. God knows I could use the bigger dinner tips.

Jed and I scraped by, but I wished he had the dough to get me the baubles that Jory woman wore. This was unlikely since he worked at Graceland during the day and played in an Elvis cover band at night. Not a lot of money there.

The young family ordered their meal at the same time as the drinks. I brought some crackers and a cup of ice for the baby, a cute, chubby kid, about a year old.

"Thanks so much," gushed the baby's mom. "Henry can get restless in restaurants."

Business had been slow for an hour or so, but it started

picking up and soon I was rushing around from kitchen to dining room with plates stacked up my good arm. I usually used both of them, but with the throbbing today, I was afraid I'd spasm and drop everything if I used my bum right arm. Eustace, that good-lookin' sugar daddy, waved me over at the least convenient time. I had five plates on the pass-through ready to serve. I didn't want them to get cold.

"Miss, could we move to that corner table? I'm thinking of getting up a card game."

The big round six-top in the corner was empty, so I gave him the go-ahead. "No problem."

The place encouraged poker games. The card players usually drank enough to pay for keeping the tables out of circulation for a few hours.

As soon as Eustace started shuffling, a young guy joined the couple. He'd been sitting with a gal I knew named Kandy. She worked at the Peabody. Kandy seemed to run through a lot of guys. She got up to join him, and I caught her on the way over.

"Who's the latest?" I asked, curious. She was a good kid, a regular at our place, and I hoped she'd find somebody one day.

"His name is Wes." She held her hand next to her mouth, all confidential like. "He's from Texas. Isn't he cute?" Her nose scrunched up with her giggle.

"Not too bad." I hurried on to collect the tab on the table nearest the door. They looked like they were about to ditch without paying.

Kandy went over to stand behind Wes's chair. I kept an eye on them, trying to see if the guy was a loser or not. He carried a spit cup, set it on the table next to his cards. I hate the things, but Agnes had a dad who chewed, so she never said anything about them.

Eustace did a slight double take when Kandy showed up, then turned away like she wasn't even there. I'll bet you money he knew her. Probably slept around on his wife. Eustace and Jory wore matching rings, so it looked like they were still married.

When Wes introduced himself and Kandy, Eustace gave them each a polite nod. Jory batted her incredible lashes at Wes, although he was way too young for her.

Baby Henry's dad craned his neck to see what was going on across the room. When he saw the cards, he perked up and sauntered over. "Mind if I sit in?" he asked.

Eustace nodded him to a seat, and the game started.

I kept an eye on Henry's mother. Their meal was over, and the couple had been splitting a dessert. The baby was starting to get fussy. After five or ten minutes, she picked up Henry and jiggled him on her way to the poker game.

"Aaron." She spoke loudly. I could hear her from the kitchen door. "What the hell do you think you're doing?"

"Bea, don't talk that way in front of Henry," he answered. His voice was nasal, prissy.

"You promised me you were done with gambling. You haven't played in six months. Come on back to the hotel."

"You go ahead, angel. I'll be there real soon. Just a couple of hands."

Bea took Henry back to their table and chowed down the rest of the Bigga Hunka Chocolate Cake, stuffing it in with such angry jabs of her fork I was afraid she'd cut her lip.

When Jed showed up to take me home, I glanced at the card game. The three guys were intent on the cards. Aaron (whose wife and son had left ten minutes ago) had that hunched, tense look of an addict. Kandy had taken a seat next to Wes and seemed bored. I predicted this one wouldn't last any longer than the others. Jory wasn't playing, but fluttered around the table from guy to guy, stopping to give Aaron a brief shoulder rub.

I thought he probably needed one, the way he was holding his shoulders almost up to his ears.

When I looked more closely, I saw that Jory was giving signals to Eustace. Cheating, I'd bet anything.

"Looks like a serious game," Jed said, helping me on with my jacket. A tortoiseshell guitar pick pinged onto the floor. He shed those things like feathers.

I whispered back, walking to the front door with him, "I almost want to stay and see what happens. I think it might be exciting."

"Wanna have a drink at the bar?"

I kinda did, but I was dead tired from being on my feet for eight hours. "Let's go to bed."

He grinned that lopsided Elvis sneer he had. I liked it. "You got it."

He held the door for me, and we walked out into the cool of the evening. As summer swung into Memphis over the next few weeks, that cool would evaporate into hot, steamy nights. Those were about a month away, so I enjoyed our drive home with the windows down while I could.

Jed gave me the usual foot rub, plus a nice shoulder massage that night, among other things, and I felt a tiny bit better.

I was off the next day, but Jed had to work. I often snuck in on a tour, because Jed would let me in free. Today I was going on a tour, but I had an extra-special plan this time. After I slept in, shopped a little—picking up some Icy Hot for my shoulder—and puttered around the apartment, I set out for Graceland.

I'd try to get on the last tour of the day, so we could leave for home after that. Seeing him all in command like that, opening those big, grand double doors, turned me on.

I went to the ticket window, and Sally handed me the ticket Jed had left for me. I got my headset, although I never listened to it—I knew the tour by heart—and sauntered out to the shuttle bus, following the group that was next. Two older women were at the back of the group. They were having a contest to see who could name the most Elvis songs. I'd never heard of "Smorgasbord."

It was after I got on the bus that I noticed from my seat in the back that the tour group, about twenty people, included the whole table of card players from the night before! Including the couple with Henry. Henry's dad, Aaron, looked like he'd kept on drinking long after I left. His wife, Bea, sat beside him, staring straight ahead, probably disgusted with him. I know I sure would be.

Kandy was still with Wes. In daylight, I realized he was older than I'd thought. Too old for her, in my opinion. Damned if he didn't have a plastic spit cup with him.

A group of six or seven dark-haired people sat right behind them. They all had cameras around their necks, and they were chattering like grackles. I wondered if they were all related.

There were Eustace and Jory. Last night I thought he was too old for her, but I wasn't sure now. Her makeup didn't hide the cracks and valleys as well in sunlight.

The air sparked with tension. I wondered if Aaron and Wes had found out about Jory and Eustace cheating at poker. Well, they were all alive, at least. But why in the hell were they all on the same tour?

Kandy and Wes were sitting across from Eustace and Jory,

with the guys on the aisle. They'd been talking back and forth, getting louder.

Wes leaned out toward Eustace but looked past him. "You," he said, pointing at Jory, "you're the bitch that fed him"—he jabbed a finger at her husband—"the cards. That's why we both lost. You two are filthy rotten cheats."

Eustace stood up, getting ready to answer Wes, just as the bus stopped at the entrance to Graceland to let the gates open. The bus jerked and knocked Eustace back into his seat.

"You keep your mouth shut," he said. It would have come out better if he'd been standing since Eustace was taller than Wes. "We did no such thing."

Aaron, a couple of rows back, paid attention to the whole thing, frowning and squinting. Maybe Wes and Aaron were after Eustace to even up the score after he'd cheated on them.

The bus stopped, and the driver called for us all to exit. Eustace and Jory stayed away from the other two couples.

When we got to the front doors, Jed, dressed in his cute jacket, threw them open for us. He greeted the group and told them where to start the self-guided tour. He watched the people file in, a frown forming on his face when he saw the card players. I was last, and he bent toward me to whisper, "What the fuck? Did they stay all night and then come over here?"

"I don't know what's going on," I whispered back. "I'll stick with them to see."

Tailing them might derail my personal, secret plan, but I could always put it off another day. What I wanted to do—had always wanted to do, but hadn't had the guts for—was sneak upstairs and see the bathroom where Elvis died, lying in his vomit. Like I said, I was fascinated with seeing where famous people died. Something weird in me, I guess. I got to go to Ford's Theatre once, where Lincoln got shot, and it was a thrill seeing the place Kennedy was ambushed too.

I gave a longing glance at the staircase that led to the upstairs, to Elvis's bedroom and the infamous bathroom. The stairway was forbidden to visitors. I always thought they could charge a bunch of money for people to go up there; they'd make a killing.

The group, guided by their headsets, entered the first room. Everyone, even Eustace, got wide-eyed at the white furniture in the living room.

"Did you ever see such a big couch?" Jory said.

Eustace gave her an indulgent smile, like she was being stupid or naïve or both. She fluttered her eyelashes at Wes. He returned a sexy, quirky smile. She fluttered again. Eustace didn't seem to notice.

Kandy, though, looked like she'd about had it. She lifted her chin and moved a couple of steps away from Wes.

Staying behind them, I didn't think they'd noticed me. I wanted to hang back and see what was going on. Was Wes here to keep track of the card sharks? Maybe Aaron was doing that too.

By the time we got to the Jungle Room, the one with that waterfall on the wall, the temperature around all three couples was dropping fast. Were none of them getting along? Even little Henry was squirming in his mother's arms. She handed him to Aaron, and he took his baby, but gave Bea a dirty look. *Bastard*, I thought. *It's your kid. You can hold him.* I hoped Jed wouldn't be that kind of dad.

The group trooped down the stairs to the game rooms, but when we got there Wes had disappeared, spit cup and all. I wondered how the hell he had gotten past me. There was an outside door, so maybe he'd left that way.

Eustace and Jory were ignoring the well-stocked liquor rack behind the bar and talking softly to each other, their noses almost touching. I thought it didn't look friendly, but I couldn't really tell. I inched closer to hear what they were saying. I hoped there were enough people on the tour to shield me.

Before I got to where I could hear what they were saying, Jory spun away from him. Eustace turned abruptly too, and started talking to Kandy, who had been just behind him.

Now I had to inch closer and see what those two were talking about. Eustace was smiling at her, and she was returning a wary look. Kandy spotted me.

"Hey, Izzy, what are you doing here?"

"I could ask you the same thing. You been here as many times as I have."

"Yeah, well, Wes wanted to come." She looked around. "Hey, where is he?"

It had taken her long enough to notice he wasn't there. But Jory wasn't in the room anymore either. Jory and Wes? Stranger things have happened.

Or maybe Wes was waiting somewhere to waylay Jory and teach her a lesson about cheating. You'd think he would want to teach Eustace too, but Eustace had height and weight on Wes.

The group started to move to the billiards room. When Eustace and Kandy headed that way, his arm around her waist, I put my plan into action.

Bea and Aaron seemed to have made up. Henry was sound asleep in his daddy's arms, and his mommy was beaming, touching shoulders with her husband. *Nice that someone's getting along,* I thought.

I hurried up the stairs, through the Jungle Room, kitchen,

dining, and into the living room, then stopped. There were voices in the front hall. One was Jed's, but I didn't recognize the other. No, others. There were two more people there. I flattened myself against the living room wall, willing them to leave.

"See you later," said a female voice as she headed for the living room—where I was!

I scrambled into the dining room, then through to the kitchen where I crouched in the corner by the ancient security system, which was a couple of small TV screens and wall phones. My palms were itching. I opened my mouth so my nervous breathing couldn't be heard. I knew they didn't like tourists wandering around alone all over the place.

I heard steps moving to the Jungle Room.

I started to rise, then heard another set of steps coming from the Jungle Room. They continued out of the kitchen, and I started to get up again. Yet another set of footfalls came from the Jungle Room. I ducked.

What the hell was going on?

I waited a good ten minutes, then stuck my head out. No one was there. I made my way back to the front hall.

This time I heard angry male voices.

"How did you think y'all would get away with it?" That accent had to be Wes.

"Here's the deal." This nasal voice was Aaron. "Give us back what you stole last night, and we let you get off without a beating."

There was scuffling, muffled protests, then I heard them go out the front door.

Should I go after them? See if I could help? The hall was empty. It was now or never. I wasn't about to let my opportunity pass. I took a deep breath for courage and tripped up the carpeted stairs as fast as I could, my heart racing. I got to the top and stopped. I had no idea where the bathroom was. I tried a few doors until I found what looked like it might be Elvis's bedroom. It was dominated by an oversized bed. Some clothing was strewn about, maybe the same things that had been there the night he died. Was it being preserved as a shrine?

A door led to, I was sure, the bathroom. I grinned. This was it. I was going to see the place poor Elvis died after taking all those drugs that fateful night. I crossed to the doorway. I turned the knob, psyching myself up, and nudged the door open.

I had read somewhere that the bathroom carpet was red. That must have changed, because the floor was tile now. Sure, they would want the carpet changed, after the vomit that Elvis landed in.

I pushed the door open more, inch by inch, savoring my anticipation. I glanced behind to make sure nobody was about to shoo me away. Turned back to the bathroom.

There it was. The black porcelain toilet. The one Elvis had fallen off, to his death.

There was something else too.

A woman knelt at the toilet. The lid was up. Her head was inside.

After a moment of shock, I knelt beside her and pulled her head up, out of the water. When I lowered it to the floor, her head flopped at an unnatural angle. One of her eyelashes floated in the bowl alongside a shiny brownish object. Her left arm, which had been tucked under her, fell to the floor, her rings clanging. Her face was badly bruised, but it was Jory, for sure. And she was dead.

"What the hell are you doing here?" a deep voice said behind me.

"I, I just found her like this. I was trying to see if—"

"Stand up."

I stood, and a large man in a security uniform took two long strides to reach Jory. Water ran from her ruined hairdo onto the hard tile floor. Her eyeliner was all smudged, and her thick makeup clumped on her face. None of that would bother her now.

The man felt for a pulse and shook his head. He spoke into his radio, and another security person was there in less than a minute.

Water and blood dripped off her face onto the floor, blending with a few brown spots.

"What did you do to her?" asked the large one.

"I just lifted her head to see . . . to see if she was all right."

"No, I mean what did you do to her before you dunked her in the toilet?"

I took a step backward. "You think that I . . . ? I just found her."

"What're you doing here?"

The second guy, a short redhead, was calling 911.

"It's been a goal of mine for a long time," I started to explain.

"To kill someone in Elvis's bathroom?"

"No! To see this room. She was here when I got here."

After the cops arrived, I was handcuffed and taken out the front door, past Jed. The way my arms were wrenched behind me like that killed my poor shoulder.

"Izzy! What's going on?"

"They think I killed Jory!"

"Who's Jory?"

There was no sign of Wes or Aaron.

The cop hustled me to his car and shoved me into the backseat.

"I'll be right there!" Jed yelled. "I'll come to the station!"

Later, he told me he had come right away, but I was in a small, stuffy room being questioned for hours while he waited. I fell into his arms in the reception area. The whole night remains fuzzy to me to this day. I was so scared I couldn't stop shaking while I was being hammered with stupid questions. Not that I mentioned they were stupid questions. I'm not dumb.

Jed took me home, and I had a hot bath and a couple of cups of tea, laced with bourbon. It's not bad in a pinch. Even with all that, my shoulder was still on fire. Morning came real soon. I called in sick. Agnes raised holy hell, but I told her I couldn't come, I'd been in a wreck and spent the night at the hospital. No way was I going to tell her I'd been in jail, being accused of murder.

Jed called in sick too, and we spent the morning racking our brains, trying to figure out what the hell had happened. He brought me an ice pack for my shoulder.

"Look, Wes left before she did," I said. "I thought they were gonna meet up somewhere. She was on the outs with her old man, far as I could tell."

"Did you tell the cops that?"

"Of course. But I don't know his last name, or anything about him. Except that he was upset about the card game and was hanging out with Kandy. I gave 'em her name."

"Uh, she's not gonna like that."

"You're right. She'll never forgive me. But what was I supposed to do? Anyway, it looked like she was through with him."

"Was everybody breaking up with everybody during that tour?" Jed asked.

"It looked that way. They were arguing about the card game too." I took off the ice pack.

I told him about hearing people come through the kitchen while I hid there and the threats in the front hall.

"Were they threatening Jory?"

"I don't know if they'd have time to do that, then kill her before I got upstairs. I wonder if they were threatening Eustace. Maybe one of them had already killed Jory. I think I should talk to Kandy."

"Will she be at work?"

"Not sure. Sometimes she works the night desk."

I called the Peabody, and Kandy answered.

"It's me, Izzy. What time do you get off?"

"Izzy! What happened? No one would tell us anything."

I told her I'd spill everything after her shift. She met us at a little dive bar near where Jed and I live, and the three of us got a booth in the back corner.

As I told her about finding Jory's body upstairs, her eyes got wider and wider. "How awful for you. What do you think happened? Did she slip and fall?"

"Considering how beat-up her face was, I doubt it. I think her neck was broken too. It flopped all funny-like."

"Somebody killed her?"

"The cops thought I did."

Kandy shook her head slowly.

"Kandy, I have to ask you. About Wes. He left the tour, then Jory left."

"And that older guy too."

"Eustace? Jory's husband?"

"Yeah, right after I noticed you missing, he was gone. It was weird, everyone leaving like that."

"Did you think Wes might be meeting up with Jory somewhere?"

"In the upstairs bathroom?"

"Well, more likely the bedroom. That would be sacrilegious, but maybe they don't care."

"Wes told me they had a thing once, but it was a long time ago."

Jed and I glanced at each other. Did Wes and Jory meet up, quarrel, and he kill her? Then come downstairs and threaten . . . Eustace?

"Wes could have told her he wanted to talk to her, maybe say they were going to rekindle their old flame," Jed speculated. "Then, when she showed up, he told her how angry he was over the card game, and they fought."

"Maybe," I said. "Did you see Aaron leave?"

"They both left," Kandy said, "to change the baby. He had a poopy diaper. Stunk to high heaven."

Something about the scene in the bathroom was still bothering me. Those brown spots. Were they tobacco juice? Had Wes been there and missed his spit cup? Or tipped it while they fought—or rather while he beat the shit out of Jory?

Maybe. But something else was nagging at the back of my brain. I couldn't dredge it up.

"Look," Kandy said, "I should tell you about those people. It's complicated. You know Eustace is a playwright, right?"

"I figured that out. Eustace and Jory Rage."

"They came through here a few years ago and stayed at the Peabody," she continued. "Jory was drunk a lot and flirting with everyone, including the bellhops. Eustace and I, well . . ."

"You fucked him?"

"Just a few times. It wasn't recent. But do you know about Wes?"

"What about Wes?"

"He had a bit part in that first play, but got dropped from all the productions after that."

"And he fucked Jory, right?"

"Well, those people do that a lot, you know."

I held my head in my hands. "There are tons of motives floating around here."

Kandy shrugged. "I suppose so. I'd better go. I have to get to work early tomorrow."

I wondered if that were true. Did *she* have a motive?

That night, I tossed and turned until Jed said I could go sleep on the couch if I kept it up. I stayed as still as I could, but my mind spun with motives and suspects.

Jory was dead. Someone killed her. It wasn't me.

Was it Wes, her old lover? Was that his tobacco spit on the floor of the bathroom?

Was it Kandy, wanting to get back together with Jory's husband?

While I was huddled in the corner of the Jungle Room, other people had traipsed through, moving toward the front of the house. It could have been Kandy. It could have been Eustace. Bea and Aaron left the tour. Wes had already left it. I was putting my money on Wes.

In the morning, before I left for work, I called the police and told them my theory about the brown spots and Wes. I also gave them the background I'd learned from Kandy.

They let me talk to a detective working on the case. "We've gone into backgrounds on everyone involved. The substance you saw wasn't tobacco juice. It appears to be soap that dripped on the floor."

There went that theory. The soap on the sink was brown.

"Is there any evidence anyone else was there?"

"Besides you, you mean?"

Yes, that's what I meant, you moron. I didn't say that. I wasn't stupid.

That's when a lightbulb went off. I figured out what was bothering me about the murder scene: the thing floating in the toilet.

Later in the day I asked Jed if he'd ever met Jory Cay. He'd acted like he hadn't before.

Now he clenched his jaw and closed his eyes. "It's not a good memory. Eustace hired me for a part in *The Rabid Night*, kind of a big part. He was excited about me. Then Jory"—he bit down on her name—"scotched the whole deal. I wouldn't sleep with her, and she got me fired after three rehearsals."

"What part was it?" I got a cold feeling in my chest.

"Kondo, the supporting male part." His eyes glinted. I'd never seen him so angry, so bitter.

The guy who had played Kondo had gone on to ever bigger and better things and was now a top box office draw.

I took a short breath and swallowed my inclination to pull away. I reached out to touch Jed's arm. "Aw hell, I'm really sorry about that."

"So am I." He poured himself three fingers of bourbon. No tea.

The TV news carried the story the next night. Eustace Rage was arrested and charged with the beating and drowning of his wife. On the screen, he looked like he'd been beat up bad. Aaron and Wes? The reporter said Eustace had admitted that his jealousy flared up when he saw his wife getting back together with Wes, the man he'd gotten rid of all those years ago. She'd had other affairs over the years, but nothing like the one she'd had with Wesley Stark. However, Eustace insisted he hadn't killed his wife. He loved her.

No one ever mentioned the guitar pick in the toilet.

By bedtime, the fire in my shoulder went away. The cold in my gut didn't. I looked at Jed after he was asleep, trying to decide whether to turn him in or leave him come morning.

THROUGH VALLEYS

BY JAMEY HATLEY

Westwood

for Katori Hall

I am not a librarian. I don't hold the proper degree, and librarians are very particular about titles. Nevertheless, I am efficient and tidy and quiet. Exactly what you would expect unless you are actually *looking* looking. In this tiny library in the hood, I am a ghost in old-ladyish shoes, disappearing down an aisle with a cart full of books. I nestle them in perfect order so that *Sula*, *Their Eyes Were Watching God*, and *Eva's Man* are there right when you need them.

"Here comes lunch," said Miss Anne, the legitimate librarian and branch manager.

No one delivers over here, where boundaries are messy—Westwood, Walker Homes, Valley Forge, even Whitehaven. Still, for a week or so, a skinny teenager in a wifebeater and sagging shorts arrived with enough food to feed a small family. Crumpy's hot wings. Fish plates from Kimble's Fish Market. Barbecue from A&R. Steaks from Marlowe's. Pizza from Exlines'. Each day I tried to send the food back. Each day the teen refused.

"Trey sent this. This from Trey." Trey never introduced himself to me, but I knew exactly who he had to be.

Trey had come into the branch right before closing. He was gesturing at the copy machine, pointing at it like he might be trying to shoot it with his finger. I appreciated the regulars, getting to understand what people want, what they need, but each stranger feels like a potential catastrophe. I try to brace myself for them, prepare. I spray perfume in the crook of my elbow so that I smell it when I shelve. I pilfer pills. I wear underwear in lurid colors under my shirtwaists from the Midtown or East Memphis Goodwills. Spike my thermos of coffee. Neaten. Straighten. Order.

I kept my face closed and glanced at the big clock right over his head. I didn't answer him, but headed toward him. When he saw that I was on the way he let out a huge smile. Tribulation worked its way through me.

"Mane, I done fucked off all my lil' change on this here machine," he said.

I shushed him and gestured over my shoulder. "Do you see those children?"

He glanced over his own shoulder, stretched to his full height, and then leaned down to me and lowered his voice. "My bad. I don't mean no harm, ma'am, but those kids probably curse worse than me," he said. I could smell the Black & Mild smoke and mints on his breath.

"They are prolific cursers, but that is beside the point," I said. The diamonds in his ears were at least a karat.

"You got jokes?"

"A few. Let's see what you have here."

He handed me the papers and explained he just needed to take a signature off so he could replace it with his own. *Fantastic.* A bit of petty forgery right before close. I once watched a nearly blind little old lady in a crooked wig forge a document for Social Security. I usually chastise the younger ones, but all I could do was admire the work she had managed by typing with just two fingers. Who am I to judge?

"I'm in a fix. I need some help. Just a little help? Please."
"Please?"

His hand brushed mine and let loose something quivering inside me. I went to work: ruler, scissors, Sharpie, correction fluid. Library forgers probably keep Wite-Out in business. When I was done, I pulled the newly blank form off the glass and handed it to him.

"I need an extra copy of that, if you please," he said.

He signed the form. I made the copies.

"Let me thank you. Take this." He was holding out a twenty.

I waved him away. "It's my job," I said and went to the back. Neaten. Straighten. Order.

The next day, the lunches started arriving.

I love being alone in my library. I sent Miss Anne on to choir rehearsal and got the shipments ready to go out to other branches. I had a cousin who once drove the van that delivered the books from branch to branch. It tickles me to think of my big, burly cousin being the book delivery fairy. He moved on to other things, but I'm still here. As soon as I stepped outside, I saw him. Trey was leaning against his Escalade. He had parked in the farthest space. I suppose this was to keep from spooking me, but I jumped when I saw him. He held up his hands like I was holding a gun on him and started walking toward me.

"Look, I don't mean no harm," he said.

"I don't have any money."

"Damn. You think I'm a robber?" He shook his head, trying to shake off the insult. "I just wanted to talk to you for a minute."

He approached me slowly, like you might approach something wild. I held my keys in my fist like they teach girls to for protection.

"You know, I love me a gal with short hair. You just my flavor of Kool-Aid."

I smiled in spite of myself. Just a little smile, but it was enough for Trey. I have been holding myself together very carefully since my mother died. He recognized my tiny surrender. I was ready to be disturbed. I leaned back against the hot metal of the library door, and he put his hand on it, over my head. With his free hand he traced my jaw line and collarbone. He rested his hand over my heart, traced my nipple with his thumb. Traffic flew by, but we were invisible to the people getting off work, going to work, hurrying elsewhere.

I turned and unlocked the door. He pressed against me. He was already hard.

He lifted me up on the counter where we label the books. *Mystery. Thriller. Romance.*

Trey peeked inside my dress like he was looking behind a curtain. You don't get to see actual shock often. People know too much these days. Think they have it all figured out. See what they are already planning to see.

"You 'round here with this sexy-ass bra and no draws on?"

I opened my legs, and he pressed his lips on me, gently, almost tenderly, but not. I trembled so much I was embarrassed. He slipped his fingers inside me, working me until I came. The tears were a surprsie, something in me unlocked.

He lifted me off the counter and bent me over the bins of books awaiting pickup. With less to prove, he made quick, vigorous work of fucking me. I was floating somewhere above us, converging, dismantling, becoming.

"Tie me back up," I said when it was over.

I watched his big hands fumble to get the bow just right. Zipped him up.

"Shit. Look what I done found in PV. My gal in the Valley. Valley. Val."

He claimed me, just that quick.

Once upon a time I did everything I could to keep from being marked by PV—"Pussy Valley." There was a time, but this was now.

I set everything right. Tidied. Wiped things down while he watched. I unlocked the door, startled by the bright sun. I locked what we had done inside and turned to him.

"Don't ever come back here again. Ever."

"Let me drop you off."

"My ride is on the way," I lied. "You should go."

"You gone do me like that?"

"You should go."

He was riding an Escalade with illegal tint. The paint looked black, but the job was custom. It had an iridescence that made the paint blue, purple, green, depending on how the light caught it. He walked toward the Escalade, stopped and looked back at me.

"Go. Please." I put on my sunglasses and lit a clove.

He finally got in the Escalade and pulled off. I watched myself disappear in its inky sheen. I stared until the car balled up Third Street, headed downtown. I waited, collecting my nerves and watching to make sure he didn't double back and follow me. When the quivering finally subsided, I started for home.

Trey didn't stay away. He would show up at lunch or at the end of the day. Each time I would tell myself that I would send him away.

I did not send him away. I would suck him off in the Escalade or let him finger me until I was hot and glistening. For those brief moments, I felt like a roiling river in a rising storm. I was being reset, realigned. Every time, he would beg to take me somewhere else, to give me a ride home, and I would say no. This, I could say no to. I kept us contained.

"Val, why you do me like this?"

"This is your window. Don't make me close it."

"Window?"

"Right now. Right now is your window," I said. I didn't bother to point out that he was married, since he hadn't even bothered to take off his ring.

"Do you see this shit?"

I looked at where Trey was pointing. Traffic was just starting to pick up, headed south toward the Tunica casinos. But strutting down the sidewalk was a magnificent peacock. It was a beautiful beast. The bird spread the fan of its tail feathers, and I was entranced. I remember when my mother first pointed one out, right here in the middle of the city: "He better get away from that chicken house there before they fry him," she said and laughed. Peacocks have been my familiars ever since.

I watched the bird strut across the street, almost get hit by a car, and then hop the fence to the big tumbledown house on the hill. Missing my mother got tangled up in Trey's beautiful body, that dimple in his cheek, the sharp lines of his goatee, the glimmer of gold in his mouth.

"It's your lucky day," I said.

He raised his eyebrow at me and smirked. Rubbed his hands together. "Is that right?"

I hit the dash and pointed the way out of the library parking lot and up the street.

"Pull up right here." We had gone less than a mile.

"You can't be serious."

Again, shock. It was refreshing. I got out and walked over to the gate and waved him through, then locked the gate behind him. I felt the tribulation in my spirit, but I was aching for something to happen to break me from my grief, to make me real again.

"I didn't even know this was back here. You live here? In this fucking mansion? It's a whole fucking Graceland tucked off in the cut. Pink Palace or some shit."

It was my turn to raise an eyebrow.

"Oh, 'cause I'm from that North-North you think we didn't go on no field trips? Please."

The house is impressive. The property sits up on a hill, right in the X that Horn Lake and Third Street make. Like a woman crossing her legs, Mama used to say. That's where the power's at. The property has become so overgrown since the owner died that you can barely see it from the street. There is a wide stone porch with steps leading up to it. It looks like someone dropped a Mediterranean villa down in the middle of South Memphis. There's even a fountain lit from underneath. I still get startled by the creepy shadows it casts. Up on the hill you can almost forget that pawn shops, strip clubs, fast food joints, and gas stations are your neighbors. A private Eden.

"All of this shit right up here by PV."

Even though the housing project has been demolished for years now, L.M. Graves Manor is still the major landmark of the area, but no one I know ever called it that. Everyone calls it PV. Pussy Valley. Shorthand for fast-tailed girls and mannish boys (women and men too), but only the girls ever carry the weight of that shame. When I was doing my library training, I looked up Dr. L.M. Graves and found a grainy black-

and-white photograph of him standing at a microphone. The photograph was from the dedication of a housing project. I squinted at the caption and connected the men (Edward F. Barry, L.M. Graves, Walter Simmons, H.P. Hurt) to their legacies: Barry Homes, Graves Manor, Walter Simmons Estates, Hurt Village. A village of hurt? A manor of graves? Those names—the stuff of Memphis fairy tales. Or nightmares.

Trey started walking toward the big house. I grabbed his hand.

"We are going there." I pointed to the little cottage down the hill from the big house.

"Okay," Trey said.

I made him a drink, and we sat on my patio with the big house hovering over us. Every now and then Trey would glance up at the house with an expression that looked like longing.

"Do you really want to be a librarian?"

No one had ever asked me that before. It wasn't the sort of thing people questioned. "I don't know. Maybe. I like keeping order."

"I noticed."

"Do you want to see my place?"

"You told me to enjoy my window."

"You're behind the gate now. Might as well."

I gave him the nickel tour. He looked around, opened my fridge, and seemed to be surprised to find food there.

"So you cook?"

I slid my hand into the waistband of his shorts. I went down on my knees and smiled up at him. He was such a gorgeous mistake. My cousin Leslie keeps telling me that I need to make more mistakes.

"You think I don't eat unless you feed me?"

"Are you for real?" he asked. His hands were on my scalp sending shivers all through me. I was electrified, ready to take flight.

Afterward I made us Old Fashioneds with homemade bourbon cherries. Warmed the rib eyes and creamed spinach and scalloped potatoes he brought with him.

"A nigga could get used to this."

"Don't get used to this," I said to him, to the both of us. Just then the lights turned on at the main house. We were out on my patio, the sky turning purple. I was curled into him on the chaise longue. I nuzzled into his thick neck and inhaled.

"Who lives up there?" he asked.

"My father owned that house, and he never claimed me," I said, listening to his heart. "He never lived in it while I was alive, but my mama used to work for him. The big house was willed to her, but it didn't work out like that. None of his real family even want to live out here. All out in East Memphis or gone from the South completely. One last old-lady cousin still in the house, too mean to die."

"For real? You ought to let me put my lawyer on it."

"I don't know. This little place is mine. Free and clear. See them try to sell it with me here. Sometimes this is my favorite place of all. Sometimes I hate it."

We strolled along the property, and I imagined that we were elsewhere, some other place, some other time, some other selves.

"Look," I told him and pointed. About half a dozen peacocks were gathered in a little grove.

After I told Trey about the house, he kept coming up with schemes for me to get my due. He had experience in these matters. From what I could gather, Trey owned a string of car detailing operations that likely laundered money. These schemes ranged from the mundane "Sue them tricks!" to complex schemes involving fraud and violence. Trey's obsession exhilarated and disturbed me. I would egg him on and then beg him to just let it be. We both needed a distraction, so I let him talk me into going to a fight party together.

He waved me over to make introductions.

"Big Lo, this is my gal."

"Val," I said and extended my hand.

"Val?"

"Like valley," I said. I had let the name settle on me. It made it easier to keep the me I was with Trey confined to its own territory.

"Hey Trey, let me holla at you for a minute."

Big Lo and Trey stepped away, and I pretended not to pay attention. The other guy kept his voice to a low grumble. He lifted his eyes toward me and then back to Trey.

"My girl good, mane. A librarian. Don't nobody know how to be quiet better than her. Can you believe that I found that over by PV?"

"She don't look like the girls I used to mess with in PV," Big Lo said.

I pretended not to know what they meant and let them enjoy their joke. As director of the health department, Dr. L.M. Graves once coauthored a report blaming the poor health of Negroes on their immoral behavior. I wondered what he would make of the housing project named after him being renamed Pussy Valley. Prophecy? Proof? What about the unnamed namers of PV? Was the naming a rebuke, an epitaph, a shame, or something trickier? When I was a girl, I would have taken not appearing to be from Pussy Valley as a compliment. But that was then. I know now that closed legs and proper talk won't save you. And there are Pussy Valleys everywhere, even if they aren't called that.

There were about a dozen men and half as many women or girls there. My dress, though it was one of the scantiest ones I owned, could make three of theirs.

We made our way through a crowd that seemed to be a mix of above-board and underground dudes. This seemed to imbue the atmosphere with an illicit vibrancy that happens when boundaries get crossed. The undercard match of the fight blared in surround sound. I was overstimulated already. I just wanted to get out on that balcony to get a glance at the Mississippi.

Then, a man—tall and handsome. He wasn't kitted out in ill-fitting Greg's menswear suits or sagging jeans. This dude was wearing immaculate white jeans, a crisp black linen shirt, tortoiseshell glasses, and shiny oxblood loafers.

"Trey, good you could make it out."

"Fo sho, fo sho. Hey, this is my gal, Val."

"Val?" he asked.

"Valley," I said. He was curious, interested in the kind of unnerving way that powerful people can have.

"It's a family name," I added, and leaned back against Trey.

"I'm Nile," he said.

"That's a lot of name," I said.

"So it is. Please, help yourselves to anything you wish."

"Baby, hook me something up. Hook Nile up with something too," Trey said.

"What would you like?"

"Surprise me," Nile said.

I nodded, happy to be unmoored for a moment. There was a bored-looking young woman behind the bar.

"Do you mind?"

We switched places, and I checked the selection. Nice. Folded a napkin down. Scooped ice into a glass to chill it. Sliced a little citrus. Got things set. The girl was mesmerized.

"You look so familiar to me," she said.

"I get that a lot," I said.

"I could swear that I know you from somewhere."

Memphis is a really big small town, and the last thing I needed was for someone to report to one of my remaining relatives that I was hanging out with low-level riffraff.

"Don't think so. I'm Val. It is very nice to meet you."

"I'm Shelby. Like the county."

I mixed Trey's cocktail. An Old Fashioned. His usual. The men at this party were higher up on the food chain than he was. I didn't want the name of a drink to trip him up; he was clearly trying to impress them. I dispatched Shelby-like-the-county over with his drink.

Next I turned my attention to Nile's cocktail. *Surprise me.* This was the kind of man Leslie kept telling me I should date, not that what Trey and I did would be considered dating. Maybe by Shelby-like-the-county, but not by me. This one I mixed and delivered myself.

"Enjoy," I said.

He took a sip and nodded. "A Manhattan."

I nodded.

"Excellent. Quite excellent."

"Enjoy," I said again. I walked away and resisted looking back.

A roar went up among the other partygoers. The underdog in the undercard fight snuck in a sucker punch, and the undefeated champion went down.

It wasn't often I got to see the city from this high up, so I wanted to take full advantage of the view. I was also tired and wanted a bit of air. Trey would want something soon. Maybe Nile would want something too.

"Hey, hook me up one of them dranks," said a tall light-skinned dude. It wasn't a question.

"I am Val. What's your name?" I said, and held out my hand to shake.

"Mane, I didn't even ask you all that. I just need you to hook me up a drink." He was drunk and towering over me.

"Could you give me a minute?" I asked, hoping to stall him. I turned to go back into the party, and he grabbed my arm.

"Bitch, just make my drank," he slurred, and flicked a bill at me. A hundred-dollar bill seemed to float in slow motion to the ground. I took a step back again, and he stumbled toward me.

Trey appeared and pinned the guy against the balcony.

"Mane, forget putting your hands on her, you speak another word to my gal—naw, you fucking look in her direction—and we gonna have a problem."

He was punching the guy, and I had a vision of them both going over the balcony wall. Trey threw him to the ground.

"Take your little red punk ass on up out of here," he said, punctuating each word with a kick.

"That's enough, Trey! Stop! That's enough," I said.

Big Lo and another man had the guy by both arms and were pulling him out of the main room of the suite. It didn't take much, considering how drunk the guy was. Big Lo's blazer was open, and I could see the gun in its holster under his arm.

Trey was sweating, furious. He turned to me, lifted up my chin. My eyes filled with tears. I hadn't even thought of crying until then.

"You good?"

I nodded.

"I will be right back."

"Maybe we should just go, Trey," I said.

He looked over at the TV. The main event was starting.

Nile came forward. "I want to apologize to the both of you. Please stay."

I nodded. Trey left the suite. Told me he would be right back.

I found the bathroom to freshen up. It was one of those huge marble affairs. I stared in the mirror and contemplated just slipping out into the night. Wondered if it would be possible to just disappear. There was a knock at the door.

"Val?" It was Shelby-like-the-county. I let her in. She shimmied up on the counter. "Don't worry about him, Val."

I started to fix my face while she talked. My eyeliner was a little smudged, but I like it like that. Usually can only get it after I sleep in my makeup, but then only I get to witness my smoldering.

"Who? He's already forgotten," I said, and shook my head to make it true.

"Half the dudes in there police."

"*Really?*"

"Tony's dumb ass gonna end up at 201 tonight. Off some bullshit. Your dude was 'bout it, though."

"He was, wasn't he?" I said and laughed. I took out my makeup bag and Shelby gasped.

"Wait! A Céline bag? And you got the whole NARS store in here!"

"I have a hookup," I said and winked. "You have your eye on anybody out there? Even if it's just for tonight?"

"Well," she giggled, "the one with the good hair. I seen him on TV. I danced for him once. He doesn't remember, though. At a bachelor party."

The young politico. Of course.

"Why don't we go make him a drink?"

"How did you learn all the drinks and stuff?"

"A book. A bartender's guide. Give me your address, I'll send you one." I held out my makeup kit. Told her to pick something. "You know what, Shelby? Too bad about Tony going to jail tonight. All he had to do was ask."

I checked my reflection in the wall of mirrors again. I looked a little savage, a little untamed, but a little more alive too.

I worried that it was a mistake to venture out beyond this tiny territory with Trey. It's dangerous at the border, and something had shifted, perhaps permanently. Ours was a fragile, reckless thing that needed to be contained. Trey couldn't get away as often. Said he was working on something important. Something big. Without his steady agitation, I began to sink back into a haze of grief. I needed a moment to get myself together. I needed to adjust my energy.

I did the things my mother taught me. Cleaned the house from top to bottom, front to back. I wiped down the walls and floors with Van Van oil. Tended to my altar. Burned sage. Dressed and lit a candle for my mother. Watered my rosemary plants. What my mother called the old ways. Knowledge. For this my alleged father's family accused my mother of many terrible, ghastly things, up to and including murder. Every black woman on this here earth better use everything she got to survive this world, my mother said. She also said she wouldn't abide a man who didn't choose her of his own free will.

Leslie told me to make sure I don't let Trey "Bigger Thomas" me. I said I would "Teacake" him first. We both let out a boisterous laugh. Leslie and I were cuzzies. First cousins. We had called each other cuzzy since we had language.

* * *

When Trey showed up again, he started right back in on the schemes.

"We can talk to my dude Nile about your paperwork, lock this down." He gestured out toward the big house. "And until then, I got a few ideas. Look, I'm working my long game for us. This is just the short game."

"Long game? Like what?"

The party was a success for Trey. He told me they had a foolproof plan with people at every stage of the game. From police, judges, lawyers, politicians, document clerks. It sounded like something from television. They even had somebody on the property room in case evidence needed to disappear.

"All that money gonna flow through me. Splish splash."

"Trey, this is too much. I don't know about this."

"That's for me to handle, for the future. I wouldn't get you involved in that. Look, I hate how they treating you. You shouldn't have to live small like this. Don't you want something bigger? I want to give you that."

"Let's talk about something else," I said.

His phone buzzed, and he held up his finger. He walked a bit away from me, and I stared up at the house.

It wasn't like I hadn't considered that the house was oppressing me, that I was stuck on this little no-man's-land.

"I said I was on my way!" he yelled into the phone. "Just think about it," he said to me, and departed for his own province.

I sat and watched the house above me and let the night descend around me. Up on the hill, the lights at the big house came on.

"The house will be empty for the Fourth of July." I regretted saying this almost immediately. He had been away for about a week. I started to imagine a peaceful disentanglement. Independence Day. Freedom. A cliché, yes.

"For real though? That might be the perfect time for our little plan." He was still getting antsy with whatever his life was when it wasn't here, and so was I.

"I don't know, Trey. It's not so bad. I have a good thing here. They are family, however twisted. They could have just sent me on my way."

Something loud and heavy hit the roof.

"The fuck?"

We jumped out of bed. Trey pushed me back and motioned for me to get down. He grabbed his pistol and edged toward the door. He opened it the tiniest bit and peered out. Quickly, too quickly, he flung the door open and stepped outside.

"What the fuck. Val, come out here."

"What is it?" I pulled my robe together and stood at the threshold of the door.

"Come on out. You got to see this shit to believe it." He was waving me out, laughing. There was a huge male peacock on the patio. I stepped toward Trey, and the peacock stumbled over.

"Did you hurt him?" I asked.

The peacock righted itself and took a few swaggering steps.

"Hell naw! This lil' nigger bold as hell. Watch this." Trey rushed toward the peacock who stood its ground.

I started laughing. "He's drunk."

"Drunk?"

"It's the peaches. The fruit falls to the ground and ferments." When I first moved here I had a standoff with a drunk opossum, but never a drunk peacock.

"Didn't you say they was lucky? Can't get luckier than a drunk-ass peacock." Trey rushed again toward the peacock. The peacock just stumbled backward a bit, but still held his ground.

"Leave him be," I said, and we went back into the house. "What would we have to do?" I asked.

That night in bed, Trey told me how it would work. Candy from a baby, he said. He figured it would be best to just file an insurance claim, and then we wouldn't even have to fence the stuff. He had somebody who could file the insurance paperwork and a police officer to make the report.

"No one would even notice. This is a high-crime area. You deserve it."

Once it was decided, both of us were more settled, calmer. The wildness was one we made together, that we were constructing. Just as I was about to drift off to sleep, a fact about peacocks invaded my thoughts. I remembered that wild peacocks, like the ones on this property, stalk and eat snakes, even poisonous ones. The thought of a snake infestation unnerved me, so I didn't sleep the rest of the night.

Trey's insurance lady told him we would need photographs to backdate their files to make it look like the policies were not brand new. I hadn't seen him in such a good mood since that day I first let him behind these gates. I felt excited too. Like something was beginning again for me. He showed up with a huge box of fireworks from down at the state line and a big box of chicken from the Dodge store. Spicy fried chicken wings.

"Should we get something to drink down here?"

"Let's drink high off the hog up there," I said, finally getting in the spirit of things.

He draped his arm over my shoulder. And we walked up the wide steps of the house through the front door.

"This is a real-deal house right here. Shit, we should be living like this all the time."

"Better," I said.

"You getting crunk. Loose. I like it like that."

I pressed play on the remote for the stereo, and music flooded the room. Told him where to put the food.

"Damn, your old ladies be listening to Gangsta Boo?"

"You'd be surprised at what they do. Let me show you my favorite room in the house."

"It better be a bedroom."

"Better. The library."

I lingered at the doorway and let him press against me, pulled his hand under my dress.

"I want to give you the world. I want to make that happen."

"I want that too," I said, and reached down for him, sliding my hand in his waistband. Hungry, eager.

Just like that, the gun was in my hand.

Easy.

The door flew open, and in an instant they descended on him, Big Lo and some others. It is best not to know.

"Val, what the fuck. What the fuck is going on?"

"Val, Val, Val. That is not my fucking name." I shook my head and took my place by Lo, though I never called him that. Not ever. "Big Lo? Your crooked cop in your pocket. Low Down Leslie Brown is what they called him when we were in high school. Bussed out of PV for academics." I pointed to myself. "Valedictorian," I said, then pointed to Leslie. "This one, salutatorian. My first cousin." I could feel myself rising, becoming, claiming myself.

"Bitch, I'm gonna kill you and your whole family," Trey said.

Leslie hit him on the head with the butt of his gun. Trey let out a yelp like a dog.

"Doubtful," I said. I poured a bourbon for Leslie and one for me. "And you, with so much to gain, ran your mouth to me. Names, how the whole con worked. Folks who ain't even got nothing to do with this. What happens when the feds come? Think about it. What do you really know about me?" Trey couldn't answer; they had gagged him by then. "You should have been trying to impress him instead of me. All that info you thought you knew? Wrong, wrong, wrong. All a part of the test. You hungry, cuzzy?" I asked Leslie.

"I could eat," Leslie said.

"Clearly you failed," I said to Trey. The organization was full of Treys and Tonys. Hungry with ambition, good to launder money or act as muscle, but never to be let into the inner circle. Pawns to sacrifice when necessary.

"Gentlemen, take care of my lightweight. Give him that lake view he can't shut up about," I said.

Leslie showed them out while I fixed our plates with Trey's chicken wings.

"Some Jo-Jo's in there?"

"Yep."

"You had to bring up the salutatorian-valedictorian thing."

"But I beat you fair and square."

"By one-tenth of a point. I was playing football while I was doing it."

"I was at every game too. Homecoming queen. Potato salad?"

I was happy to get back into my full kitchen and opened the big stainless-steel fridge. The little house was my studio space mostly, but a good device to gauge intentions.

"Was the Gangsta Boo too much? Clichéd?"

"Cuzzy, you always did have a flair for the dramatic."

"What do you think about marble in here?"

"Thought you said you wanted that new Viking range."

"We will see. Insurance all set?" I had life insurance policies going to Trey's wife and a baby mama I located in addition to the policies coming to me. I had everything I needed from that first moment at the copier.

"So, cuzzy, you use some old ways on him?"

I shrugged. Snagged another Jo-Jo. "Mostly, he saw what he wanted. A few lights on a timer. Scared schoolgirl routine. Hard to get. You men love a damsel in distress."

"Right, right. That nigga was so sprung, he could not shut up."

"Good thing he was talking to me."

"Yes, indeed."

"Wait, before I forget." I went up and got the salt and pepper.

"Yeah, you still keeping up the old ways. Mama would be proud."

"When does she get out?" Mama and Auntie both went to jail for insurance fraud, identity theft, and other miscellaneous charges. Mama had an extra charge for practicing medicine without a license. She died in prison, away from home, but when Auntie got out, she would have a place right here.

"Pop quiz: so what's this for?" I asked as I went to get the broom.

Leslie's face clouded over, trying to recall. He's had his size and his strength, so he didn't need to lean on the old ways like me.

"Sweep salt and pepper after somebody you don't want back. Not that we need to worry about this one," Leslie said.

"Better safe," I said.

"Better safe."

PART II

MEMPHIS BLUES

THE PANAMA LIMITED

BY Richard J. Alley

Beale Street

He was mesmerized by the way the brown liquid moved from side to side like a metronome in the highball. It left traces on the glass, and he'd heard these traces were where the term "spirits" came from. They caught the light that flashed through the windows in time to the *click-clack, click-clack* of the wheels on the rails.

"This normal? This swaying?"

The man behind the bar of the club car only shrugged, the light from the windows gleaming on and off the midnight black of his bald head.

"Just seems to be listing over to port more than usual is all," said the one they called Mort.

"Navy?"

Mort nodded.

"Normandy," the bartender said, and raised his glass in salute before adding, "Ghosts."

"How's that?" Mort looked at his glass again, at the spirits there. He glanced around the club car, but there was not a soul in sight. It was around midnight, and he figured everyone else on the *City of New Orleans* had dozed off from a combination of the train's rocking motion and the late hour.

"They say it's ghosts pulling her from side to side like this, trying to turn us over. We're all doomed." At this the bartender tipped his head back and laughed.

"Ghosts? Who says that?" Sweat trickled down Mort's neck and into the collar of his shirt. He'd never been scared a day in his life that he could remember, but something had happened to him recently. Something profound, he'd say to whoever might be close, usually a waitress at a late-night greasy spoon or a whore being paid to listen.

Again, the bartender shrugged, his merriment having been put on the shelf with a cork in it along with that last bottle. "Porters. Conductors. Those what knew them."

"Knew who?"

"Jackson LeDuc. Ma'am Toussaint."

"They haunt this line?"

"Not in any chain-rattling way. They ain't specters floating through walls and such. But their spirits are here, be sure about that."

Again, Mort looked into his glass. "Spirits."

"They was pure fire, those two, and you can't just close a coffin lid on that; burn you up. You believe in ghosts, young man?"

Mort shook his head, but even his glass could tell his heart wasn't in it. The bartender didn't notice, fixated as he was on his customer's empty glass. He refilled it, and the light passed through the pour like a haint. Beyond the windows it was all ink through the cornfields of middle Illinois, as flat and dull as day. Mort wondered at the flickering light and where it came from.

"Where you say you served, young man?"

"Didn't say."

"Might you?"

"Okinawa. Guadalcanal."

The barkeep sucked on his back teeth as he put the bottle back in its slot. "Seems to me anybody spend time on them islands don't believe in ghosts must be one his own self."

"Tell me about this LeDuc and the lady. What's her name?"

"Jael Jean-Baptiste Toussaint. Beautiful girl. Musicians both, she was a singer and he played trumpet better than anybody around. Better than Miles. Better than Booker Little. Better than Dizzy." The man leaned over the bar, his own whiskey breath between them like train steam, and whispered, "Better than Pops Armstrong."

Mort didn't know shit about jazz, but he'd heard those names, everyone had. "They're both dead now?"

"He is. She . . . well, ain't no telling. Disappeared."

"But they both haunt this train, you said. He's on this train now?"

"Believe that."

"Floating up and down the aisles, between cars?" Mort was agitated now, his voice rising with the train's whistle. He was on his way out, heading down to New Orleans and then . . . what? He thought he might catch a freighter to a tropical clime, or maybe he'd just sink into the underbelly of that city and disappear from society and himself altogether. Either way, he was out. This one last job, and then he was done. He'd had enough of the life and was starting to see those ghosts, those spirits, everywhere.

"What? No, mister, he in a coffin, nailed in and resting there in the porters' car." The bartender gestured away with his dirty bar towel. "He's what you call, ah, *in state*."

Mort gulped his drink, his hands shaking now; he squeezed them to make it stop. "Why don't you tell me about him, huh? We got a long ride, why don't you tell me who he was?"

"Musician, like I said. Come from Nova Scotia by way of Winona. This train here'll pass within a donkey path of where he grew up, though he won't be getting off there. No sir. His body'll be off at Elmwood Cemetery in Memphis, Tennessee. Grew up just down the road in Miss'ssippi, though, and came of age on this train right here. Spent his early days ridin' these rails, raisin' Cain, playin' shows, and carryin' on. Then he met Jael, and he was humbled, tried to go straight, and that's when they say he got good. Channeled all that love and fire and jealousy into his horn. But I don't know too much about all that. I'm just a barkeep on a train."

The liquor was calming him again, and Mort took pleasure as it burned through his chest. He focused on that. "Can I buy his records?"

"Nah, you can't find that brother's records," said a new voice. "Couldn't be slowed down long enough to record."

Mort hadn't heard the man approach due to the rattling of the train and the trumpet from the whiskey. It's why he knew he needed out—his instincts, his senses, were diminishing. The new arrival, a pianist working his way south, threw a quarter on the bar, and the bartender poured him fifty cents' worth of gin.

"You knew him?"

"Got to know him in Memphis where he'll be laid to rest." The man winced as the good gin washed over his teeth.

"How did he get from Nova Scotia to Memphis?"

"Wagon," replied another new voice—a rumpled, graying man, unshaved and with a stoop to his shoulders, had appeared on the other side of Mort. The ends of his fingers were ink-stained. Newspapermen, they could be spotted a mile away. "Came down south when he was just a boy, one of six brothers and sisters. Mama died in childbirth, daddy got tired of the cold. Can't say I blame him. The old man was French-Canadian, and his mama was the daughter of escaped slaves,

God bless 'em. He was dark, but could pass for Mediterranean if needed."

Mort was unnerved by these bookends, the way they'd crept up on him like, well, spirits.

The two new men and the old bartender fell into laughter. The hack continued his story. The LeDucs left Nova Scotia in 1910, piling all of their belongings, including the mother's upright piano, onto a wagon, and began the slow march south from frozen lakes into the rich, warm soil of the Delta. They followed the very line these travelers were on—the *Panama Limited* it was called then—as it was being built, feeling the climate change in their very bones.

Papa LeDuc was a blacksmith and took work along the way in the railroad camps, forging rivets and repairing tools. They'd often stay in the camps for a week at a time. The LeDuc children would play that piano and sing—ten-year-old Jackson blowing his trumpet. The laborers, stinking of sweat and cinder, worn from a day's work and drunk from a night's drink, would laugh and howl and throw coins at the feet of the children, grateful for any diversion from the monotony of laying rails in a straight line for miles at a stretch.

"The railroad bosses noticed LeDuc's work," the newspaperman explained. "They offered him a piece of land in Mississippi, right near a new yard they were planning. All he had to give them was five years of service. He had his sights set on New Orleans, but he'd never had his own land before. Another thing Jackson told me: his grandma's name, his mama's mama, was Winona."

Jackson grew up in his father's forge, his back and shoulders broadening, his nights spent working on his trumpet. On trips to Memphis, he would hear W.C. Handy play and watch the people who flocked to see him. In New Orleans, where his father would take his children to be near the water again and to talk to men on the docks in his native French, Jackson heard stories of Buddy Bolden. His head became filled with the smoke and voodoo, the vibe and music.

He saw the train speeding past his home in Winona as a lifeline to music and went to work as a porter when he was barely seventeen. He spent his days and nights slinging luggage, spending his off-hours on the train smoking dope and playing along with other would-be musicians in the porters' car, sitting among the bags and trunks of the travelers.

"That's where he coupled up with the music for work," said the younger man on the other side of Mort.

"You were there?"

"Mhm, yes sir." He drummed his fingers on the bar top, a piano man in an eternal state of play. "I was there, and it's the first time I heard that sweet horn. He jumped down on the tracks that day at some stop or other between here and there. Played as though his goddamn life depended on it. Told me later he heard one of the porters' brothers needed a trumpet to round out his 'tet, and old Jackson had it in his mind to audition wherever that boy might be. I was a boy myself, waiting at the depot with my mama's hem in hand. Never heard nothing like it. Mama and me, we got on that train that day, followed him to Memphis, and I'm following him there now, I suppose. I'd've followed his horn anyplace."

"Did he find the porter's brother and round out that 'tet?"

The pianist shrugged and nodded at the white-gold liquor set in front of him. "They found him. They all found him in time."

"And the girl?"

"I was there that day." A porter had now slipped into the car and sidled up next to the bartender, pouring his own finger of fun. "I was working that train. Still working that train by the looks of it. I was in the luggage car that day knockin' a few back, listening to a band—what they call *impromptu*—keep time with the clicking and clacking of the wheels, when this vision walked in. How she made her way back to the porters' shitty car, I don't know, but she brightened it as soon as she entered. A face like suede, she had, with emerald-green eyes and tight ringlets of hair. She was an angel, or looked like one. And then, if the wings and glow wasn't enough, she started to sing with them boys. LeDuc's horn was something else, but you ain't never heard an instrument like hers. The clicking and clacking stopped right there. I think, and you can't tell me different, that we floated there above them tracks."

"LeDuc heard her?"

"He was outside, between cars lighting a cigarette. Waited until she was finished, scared it was a vision that might evaporate before he had the chance to lay eyes. It was the first time I'd seen him in his silky suit and watch fob. All that material, though, them shoes and pinky ring, couldn't make up for the fact that the boy was ugly. Small and square, he had one eyebrow to speak of, and skin didn't know if it wanted to be French or swamp black. Goddamn ugly. Nose set off-center on that head of his, looked like it'd been broken a couple or dozen times, maybe once that very morning."

The porter said he'd never seen anything like what happened then between Jackson and Jael. Said that instant was like lightning striking.

He played his trumpet for her, blew it soft so it rolled around her curves, pushed all that suede the wrong way and then smoothed it over again. And she sang for him, hummed at first before it became words so he could get a foothold and climb aboard.

She had nowhere to be, no particular destination, so he brought her to Memphis where they took a room above Pantaze Drug Store, just across from Central Station on South Main.

"Where'd she come from, though?" Mort asked. "What'd she want? Who the hell was she?"

Mort lived his life in the shadows on Chicago's South Side, willing to live and let death do the rest. Maybe the slivers of light from the lives he'd touched and snuffed had finally broken through to open his eyes and show him what life might be. Yet all he'd seen there through the bleariness and haze were the ghosts that run amuck.

There were five in the car by then, a proper quintet, looking into their glasses for an answer to the newest age-old question: who was Jael Jean-Baptiste Toussaint? That's when a woman's voice said, "She was trouble."

Heads turned to see the middle-aged beauty who'd just entered the car. She wore a cocktail dress, and her hair was in curls that fell to her cheeks. She stood with one hand on the Pullman's door and the other on her hip, and as she walked to the bar, it seemed that the car's swaying subsided in deference to hers. "Sextet" always did have a nice ring to it.

"You knew her?"

"Mmm, I knew her. I played piano behind her several times. How you, Harold?"

The two pianists greeted each other, and the bartender said hello by way of a pour of vodka. The newspaperman sipped his drink while the porter tried his best not to stare at the woman's décolletage.

"I'm good, Miss Lil. You?"

"Getting by. What y'all talking about Jael Toussaint for?"

"Weren't," the newspaperman said. "Talking about LeDuc. Toussaint's just a by-product."

"Shit," the woman tapped out with her lithe espresso fingers on the bar. "Ain't no Jael, ain't no Jackson."

"Tell about her," Mort said, mesmerized by this new arrival.

Lil slipped a cigarette from a studded case and put it to her lips where it was greeted by four lighters. She took the flame from Mort's dented Zippo. He felt some satisfaction as it snapped shut. "She was seventeen," Lil breathed out with a stream of smoke.

"Daughter of a whore born outside Baton Rouge and raised in Storyville. Passed around from auntie to neighbor to stranger alike. She told me once she and her cousins would play hide-and-seek among the raised gravesites of the city's cemeteries. Her daddy? He was absent . . . ain't so many? A fireman on trains, she'd been told. Not on any as well-appointed as this—" The woman looked around and seemed to wrinkle her nose at the men in front of her. "But freight trains on the long haul north and west."

Jael Jean-Baptiste Toussaint would learn to hustle early, making her own way among the whorehouses as she had the cemeteries of her childhood, learning when to hide and when to appear for the taking. The first man left her with a handful of coins. She stood naked that morning, staring down at her palm as though it held manna from heaven. She was thirteen. She'd decided right there that she loved the money more than the man, and set her own course. The money she made after that was mostly taken by pimps and her mother on those rare occasions she was sober.

At fifteen Jael was spirited away by a mulatto who'd told her to sing while she sat astride him. He'd been so surprised by what he heard that he'd gone limp, made the sign of the cross, and took her back to East St. Louis to sing in his saloon.

"She stayed a month," Lil said. "Nearly drank that old

fool out of business and scared off customers with her fits and squalls. I was there for a weekend's worth of shows, first time I come to know her, and I thought this was a voodoo priestess brought up from the bayou. Louis thought she was great, reminded him of home. He even gave her money for the train and showed her to the depot. That little girl told that swooning husband of mine that she was gone to look for her daddy. Word has it she never found a man fit to be called such and has been riding the rails ever since."

"She here now?"

Lil shrugged and held her empty glass out to the bartender without looking in his direction.

"Day Jackson found her, she looked worn down," the porter offered, his elbows on the bar and chin resting in his hands as though his big head held all the thoughts of the world. "Looked older than her years, but when she sang . . ." He rubbed his hands over his face. "Ooh-wee, there was that spark. Something was touched off like your Zippo, and it lit up that whole dank luggage car. Jackson must've seen it from under the door as well as heard it."

Jackson LeDuc would take her, not only into his arms, but into his life. He put together a band just to back her, a quintet of the highest order; the voice that would make them all rich.

Jackson and Jael grew close, played some gigs, and tried to make a home in Memphis. But Jael still hustled. She hustled, because it was in her blood. She hustled the way a shark has to keep swimming, never stopping for fear of death. Jackson had professed his love right there on the *Panama Limited* that first day, and he professed it every night to the city below as he sat in the open window above Pantaze and blew his horn for her. Jael might be right there in the room with him, or she might have been at the Beetle down the street drinking and carrying on. Some nights, as the train rumbled by on the trestle so close Jackson might have reached out to touch it, he knew she was in one of those luggage cars again, smoking dope among the porters and wandering sidemen.

"There was tender moments too, now, don't you take everything a newsman says to be gospel, young man." Lil produced another cigarette, but the slick piano man beat Mort this time. "Even the hardest woman goes soft from time to time and needs to be held."

There were those late nights when he'd wrap her up in his arms after making love, and she'd sing him to sleep with the nearby train and street musicians keeping time. Those nights she'd sing only for him, lullabies her mother had sung to her. He'd run his fingers the length of her back, raising chills on her skin, the color of cream coffee, as she twirled his thick chest hair around her fingers. They would watch the moon through the filmy windows, confess to dreams and fears. It was those moments that kept Jackson going, along with the nights onstage when he would watch Jael from behind, all swaying silhouette in the spotlight and smoke-filled room. He would wish into his horn, hoping that it would find her ear, that their affair would never end.

"When it did end, it was on this very train," the bartender said, working his towel on a wineglass like it was the slide on a trombone.

"Why did it end?" Mort asked. "Sounds like they could've made a go. They had music and love."

"They had no money, and that's what she wanted more than anything. Loved money more than man, remember?"

"They used to play up and down Beale," Lil went on. "That was the place to be, baby. It started with Jackson walking the cobbled street, weaving in and out of those revelers, glad to be out of the cotton fields, happily marinating in whiskey juice, and into the saloons and pubs to ask if they were in need of a band. Back then, though, when it was the place to be, you couldn't hardly swing a cotton sack without hitting a bandleader, and Jackson LeDuc was sent on his way more often than not.

"The club owners took little notice when that ugly-ass man stopped to play his horn right there at Beale and Main. But when Jael joined him, baby, those club owners raced to host this beauty and her beast.

"Regular work would come fast and easy. It wasn't long before more than the club owners and music lovers took notice. By then, Aldo Venotucci, from his de facto office in the Hotel Men's Improvement Club at Beale and Hernando, had taken notice. His purview was Beale, from the mansion to the water, and not much happened without his say-so.

"Told Jael Jean-Baptiste Toussaint later that her voice made it up to his office window and that he practically floated down to Sunbeam's place just to meet her. More than likely he had his boys meet her at the stage door and drag her fine ass up to him, but there's no poetry in that, no rhythm, and Beale was all about rhythm in them days.

"Venotucci put her under contract. It was more money than either Jackson or Jael had ever seen, and they couldn't help but say yes. Had no choice in the matter anyway. The Italian took a healthy 60 percent, and the quintet was guaranteed fifty-one weeks of work from Memphis to New Orleans and back up to Chicago.

"But something else happened, and the old Italian fell in love with the young chanteuse. He'd go to one of the clubs he backed, something he rarely did, and sit to the side of the stage just to watch her sway and hear her sing. That was the effect she had on people, on both men and women—they couldn't turn their eyes or ears from her.

"He'd have her up to his office where she'd sit in an uncomfortable chair sipping a cocktail by the window, watching the action on Beale below with the sun on her face while he tended to his work. She heard people come in and plead their cases, asking for money or time. Sometimes he'd grant it, mostly not. She grew to fear him despite the tough life she'd led so far, and he grew to love her more despite the life he'd led.

"Venotucci didn't interfere with LeDuc and Toussaint; he wasn't going to stop that money pipeline. She still went home to the room above Pantaze at night, though sometimes straight from another room Venotucci kept in the hotel, and she still traveled extensively along the *Panama Limited* line. Sometimes he'd show up in New Orleans or St. Louis. The quintet would take the stage, and there would be old man Venotucci sitting to one side, a thimble of grappa at his knuckles. On those nights, Jackson knew he might not see Jael back at the hotel until late, maybe not until the train ride home, and it made his heart ache.

"There were other nights, dark nights on the road when she might disappear on her own, without Jackson or Venotucci. Those nights Jackson would stay up, wailing on his horn until the hotel manager beat down the door to appease the other guests. Those were drunken nights, frenzied and awash in jealousy and uncertainty. Nights when Jael's past peeked from behind the thin curtain of lace that separated it from her present. It was a night like that that would end it all."

"Ended right here on this train," the bartender reminded the assembled gallery.

"Last night."

"Last night," Mort repeated, and the corner of his mouth ticked up in the semblance of a knowing smile. Not so that anyone noticed, yet he played it off as thirst and looked toward the bartender. He needn't have. That old man was moving around the bar like the minute hand on a clock face.

The pianist nodded. "Killed."

"Who did it?"

He shrugged, deep. "Don't know. Could be somebody on this train. Could be somebody in this room."

There was a beat, two beats—*click-clack, click-clack*—before everybody laughed. Some easier than others.

"How?"

"Knife, so it was close," the newspaperman reported. "Happened as this here train pulled into Union Station, deep underground like it does. It was dark, hot, and it gets loud when brakes start to squealing and the porters start slinging that luggage before she even comes to a halt. Happened in that dark time and poor old Jackson LeDuc bled out, running deep like the Chicago River."

"They didn't even take him off the train," the porter chimed in, lighting the cigarette he'd held behind his ear. "Brought a doctor in, declared him dead as St. Paul, and brought in a coffin too. Only difference seems to be there's an empty seat in coach and a full one in luggage."

All bowed their heads. Mort watched them. They shook their heads from side to side, swaying with the travel in a moment of silence for their old, dead friend. Mort let them have it for three beats, four. Then: "And Toussaint?"

Their heads snapped up, thankful for the reprieve.

"Gone," Lil whispered, and everyone's swaying went to nodding.

"Gone?"

"Like the wind, baby."

"She escaped?"

"Shit. Weren't no escape to it. Jael Jean-Baptiste Toussaint done been gone. She lit out months ago. That's why LeDuc was on this train."

"Where'd she go? Why?"

The younger pianist shrugged, so the older kept on: "She wanted out."

"Of the quintet?"

"Of the contract. Too much involved, too much expected. She was singing all night then hustling off to the Italian's room then back to Jackson. Too much. But she couldn't just break that contract, could she? She couldn't just buy it out, ain't enough money on Beale for that. So what'd she do?" Lil looked around the car for the answer. Men always have the answers, don't they? She faced blank stares through the smoke and gulped her liquor. "She told Jackson LeDuc to kill that dago."

This brought mumbling and murmurs of assent to the surface. Men may not have the answers, but they cotton to violence like a dog to a bone.

Lil continued, "Jael left the club that night, summoned by Venotucci, and then back to Jackson. She oozed the old Italian and tasted him on her tongue, and it made her sick the way it always did, the way it had since she was little. She'd had enough and had thought about crushing his skull with his own cane that very night. But she was tired. She was tired from a hard life of hustling and lying and drinking and fucking. That night, as Jackson held her in his arms, ignoring her scent and the stale sweat on her neck, she sang to him. It was soft and it was sweet and it ended the way it never had before. *Kill him,* she breathed.

"She promised her undying love to Jackson if he would

free her. She promised to sing only for him. Without a thought, without a plan or a weapon, he went to Beale and up to the office of Aldo Venotucci on the third floor of the Hotel Men's Improvement Club and told him, *It stops now!*"

"What'd he say? The dago?" The younger pianist was on the edge of his seat now.

"What you think he said, baby? Told that ugly old Frenchman to get the hell out of his office."

"And then?"

"And then Jackson LeDuc, he picked up a typewriter off that big oak desk, one of them heavy Remingtons, you know? Old one. And he beat that old man to death with it. They say teeth scattered across the room like a child's set of jacks. They say blood was on the ceiling, and you know the ceiling's ten feet high in that place. They say—"

"Who say?"

"Never you goddamn mind who say! But they say that old typewriter ain't never gonna work again . . . LeDuc fled the scene. People reported back to the Hotel Men's Improvement Club that they saw the Trumpeting Troll—that's what they called Jackson LeDuc—up to his elbows with blood and running his way past Third and Second, up onto Main, and back south, still running between them trolley tracks, all the way back to Pantaze.

"When he got there, though, the room was empty. Jael Jean-Baptiste Toussaint was gone. There wasn't a stitch of clothes, wasn't a stitch of song in the air. It was as if she *had* been an angel, and she'd gone back up to heaven."

"Or down to hell," the bartender offered. But he didn't offer a drink. He was putting bottles away, death has a way of killing a party.

"Jackson stood in the doorway and listened to all that silence, the creases of his fingers stained by blood and matter. He wanted to scream. Opened his mouth to do so, but all that shattered that quiet was a train whistle as it pulled out of Central Station and across that trestle."

"So close he could almost touch it," the newspaperman said.

"Been riding these rails ever since," Lil said. "He rode them down to New Orleans, asking after her at every stop along the way. He rode them clear up to Chicago and back twice. Some say they seen him through Texas, up across Dakota, forget which one, and back down California. Some say it's love, heartbreak. Some say he's running."

"From the law?" Mort ventured.

"Shit. Law the least of that boy's worries. Got no worries now, I suppose, rest his soul. Aldo Venotucci had a man, a stone-cold killer, a ghost some called him because ain't nobody ever seen him. They say he moves in the shadows; they say he hails from up north someplace. They say he don't use nothing but a knife. Know how to use it too. Mean, hateful, loathsome, they say."

"Who say?"

"Never mind who say! Aldo's people, they put a hit out, and that man, whoever the hell he is, is the finger of death. And that's who LeDuc was running from, if he was running at all."

"What *do* you think he was doing?" Mort asked, thumbing his Zippo in the hopes she'd need another light. "Running from or running to?"

"You got a lot of questions, ain't you? You a curious sort." She did it then. She pulled another cigarette from the studded case and put it to those full, plum-painted lips. Nobody's to say, but she may have done it just for her new friend Mort, just to see his flame jump up in his hand. "Love. That's what LeDuc was after. He'd had it, and once you've had it, there ain't nothing take its place. Not drink, not music, nothing."

The party, such as it was, was still going when Mort took his leave. He shook their hands in turn, and Lil obliged him a kiss on the cheek. He took his hat and thanked them for the drinks, for the company, and for the story.

Walking down the passageway, feeling the car as it swayed slowly like the tide coming in, he reflected on what he'd learned. Mort had killed many, and never asked for their stories either before or after, but this one fascinated him. He was intrigued to learn that Beale was a street. *Always figured Beale was a man,* he thought. *"Beale needs this, Beale needs that," they'd tell me.*

Cold as he may be—and Lil was right: "stone cold," as many perceived him to be—Mort was surprised to find that he appreciated the story of love and loss. He'd never realized he had the capacity for anything close to reverence.

He found his way to the luggage car and sat on a suitcase, took off his hat, and placed it on the long pine box in front of him. He lit a cigar, the *clink* of the Zippo's lid breaking the silence, and watched the smoke drift over the coffin. He held the lighter up in front of his face and watched the way it caught the light that flickered through the windows like a film projector; life blinking past at thirty frames per second.

"Hell, I ain't never been in the navy, Jackson. Navy don't know nothin' about me. Shoot, I never left Chicago before today. Didn't plan to leave at all, but once the train started moving, once you was dead, figured I might as well stay on. Might as well see what's out there."

There was no sound as he placed the lighter next to the

drink and knife already on the pine box like a still life. "Figured the GI I killed last week didn't need this no more." He blew a tired stream of smoke over the coffin. It looked like incense at Mass. "She out there, Jackson?"

He'd decided, somewhere between the drinking and the storytelling, to find Jael Jean-Baptiste Toussaint himself and see what it was in a woman that would make a man kill and roam the country. She had sounded like a dream, and he aimed to find out on his own if she was one. He was paid to kill her, but this one would live, he'd decided. He just wanted to know her.

He'd get off the train in Memphis, tag along at the back of that long and winding funeral procession from the station, past Pantaze, to Elmwood Cemetery, if only to hear the sad blues played beneath a canopy of oaks. Then he'd board this train again for New Orleans and those cemeteries where it was said that Jael Toussaint was known to hide.

GREEN-EYED BLUES

BY DWIGHT FRYER

Annesdale

On a hot Saturday night in 1948, Aaron Washington sat at the Club Hippodrome bar. He looked in the mirror at his fine blue suit and down on his shiny tan and white Stacy Adams. He touched his military mustache and cleft chin.

The bartender said, "Officer, more black coffee?"

Aaron nodded.

"Who'd a thought Memphis'd have Negro police?"

Aaron shrugged and said, "I got to get out of here; you seen Mae?"

"She left with Sol, but said she'd be back."

"Damn," Aaron said, "I told her to leave Sol alone."

"Can't nobody tell Mae nothing."

Cab Calloway was introducing his next song. "I think I'm in Harlem and not Memphis. What a good-looking crowd!"

The audience, filled with brick layers, carpenters, garbage men, and maids, applauded and cheered. These folks were out for a night on the town and dressed to the nines. The liquor flowed.

Cab said, "Everyone, do something for me. Sing after me the *hi-dee-hi-dee-hi* and the *ho-dee-ho-dee-ho*." His band played, and Cab twisted around the stage. Then he arrived at the microphone to croon the opening words: *"Hello, folks, here's the story about Minnie the Moocher . . ."*

"*Hi-dee-hi-dee-hi-dee-hi, ho-dee-ho-dee-ho-dee-ho,*" the crowd sang along. Some stood, danced, and swayed. Here they mattered. Officer Aaron was smiling wide, laughing aloud, and clapping too.

When the bartender answered the ringing phone, he handed it to Aaron.

Aaron said, "Washington." He frowned. "Tell the sergeant I'll be right there." He hung up the phone. "Duty calls."

"What is it?" the bartender asked.

"They found a Negro woman dead on the Riverside cobblestones between Beale and Union. Tell Mae she needs to get another way home. Gotta go!"

Aaron weaved his way through the crowd and out the rear entrance of the Hippodrome to his Hudson Commodore 8. He drove west down bustling Beale Street, and he passed the cotton bales lining Front, until he arrived at Riverside, near the banks of the Mississippi.

Aaron parked on the cobblestones leading down to the river. Then he recognized a familiar face. "Withers, they called you on this too?"

The man said, "Yeah, for traffic and crowd control. That's all Jim Crow thinks we can do, but I brought my camera." Ernest Withers offered a big smile and gripped Aaron's hand.

"How long you been taking pictures?"

"I got the photography bug in the Pacific."

"I served in Africa and Europe."

"Glad you made it back," Ernest said, gripping his camera with both hands.

"A miracle anyone could live through that."

"I'm not used to operating in hostile territory without a gun. You think they'll let us carry soon?"

Aaron shrugged, patted his pockets to discover his pistol was missing.

They reached the onlookers and policemen at the bottom of the cobblestones. Waves lapped at the rocks and mixed with the crowd noise. A tugboat growled, and its floodlight flashed.

Aaron and Ernest glimpsed the body through the crowd. She wore a red dress. Aaron edged forward; Ernest followed.

"Where you boys going?" a white officer asked.

Ernest showed his badge and said, "We're police."

The white cop said, "Forgot you boys joined the force." He handed Aaron a pink compact. "Give this to Sergeant Smith; he's right up there. Might have something to do with the case."

Ernest trailed Aaron through the crowd to where the body lay facedown.

Aaron whispered, "Lawd God have mercy. It's Mae."

Ernest moved beside Aaron. "What did you say?"

"Mae."

"Mae who?"

"Mae Clark, my neighbor from Euclid Avenue. She works for the Carters and sings at the Hippodrome."

"When'd you see her last?"

"This evening at the club."

Ernest put his hand on Aaron's arm and whispered, "Sergeant Smith got eyes on every porch, in all the kitchens and back alleys." He squeezed Aaron's arm. "Be truthful when he asks."

Sergeant Smith squatted next to Mae's body. "Withers, get over here and snap some pictures."

Ernest moved forward. Aaron put the compact in his coat pocket and followed too, while reflecting on how his evening started.

* * *

As the Hudson turned west toward Beale, Aaron gazed into his rearview mirror at his backseat passenger, then out the window at the Hunt-Phelan Home; the redbrick mansion glowed in the dark.

Mae Clark giggled from the backseat. "Aaron," she purred, "I ain't ready. Park over there."

He downshifted from third to second gear, and the engine purred too.

"Grandpap said his daddy shined boots for Grant out back of that house while the general planned the attack on Vicksburg."

"Officer, you shining any shoes tonight?" Mae tossed her powder-blue maid's uniform aside and pulled a red satin dress over her head. She sprayed perfume on her bosom, neck, and arms. The flowery smell filled the automobile.

Aaron shook his head and flashed a smile. He enjoyed watching and listening.

"Them white dogwoods and azaleas make that place look spooky." Mae pulled the nylon stocking above her right knee and attached it to her waiting garters.

Aaron laughed, one eye on Beale traffic and the other on the twenty-year-old Mae.

"What happened to that sweet gal from Euclid who wrote me all those letters during the war?"

Mae put her left leg onto the middle of the front seat, adjusted the stocking.

"She grew up, waiting on you to come back from the war. What it feel like to be one of Memphis's finest?"

He adjusted the mirror. "It was time for somebody Negro 'round this town to be a policeman. My number just came up."

"Huh, just like in '42." She extended her leg, almost

touching the Hudson's ceiling. Then she rolled the stocking from calf to knee and beyond.

"Girl, you putting on quite a show back there."

Mae giggled again and wiggled across the backseat. She put on her shoes, opened her pink compact, and pouted into its mirror. She clipped on dangling white earbobs. And she put on a pretty smile.

"Officer, you wasn't the only person drafted during the war. You struggled 'gainst white folks over there; my problems come from the big house in Annesdale."

"Now, we can't talk like that about the fine Carters."

Laughter erupted from Mae's lips. She patted powder onto her chin, cheeks, and forehead. "Officer, don't make me mess up my makeup." She pressed the ruby lipstick to her mouth. This last touch completed her transformation.

Aaron said, "You sure know how to go from housemaid to singer."

"What you expect from Queen Mae, opening act at the Club Hippodrome on Beale Street?"

"We gone get our money's worth tonight."

"You bet y'all will."

Aaron shifted the car's gears and drove. He pulled into an alley toward the rear of the club. Mae reached out and touched his shoulder. Her thumb stroked his cheek.

"Aaron, stop the car."

Chauffeur and new Memphis policeman Aaron Washington complied, like always for dignitaries.

"You gone drive me home when I'm through?" she asked.

He turned toward her. Her hand slid to the side of his face. She ran her fingers over his close-cropped hair.

"Mae, you burning yo' candle on both ends and the middle too . . . ain't you?"

Mae looked a little sad. "One of these days," she said and her smile returned, "I'm gon' be free, like them white folks y'all liberated."

"What's Sol gonna say about me driving you home?"

"He ain't got nothin' to say. Besides, I'm leaving town soon."

"Sol thinks he's got a say about everything regarding you. Where you heading, and where'll you get money to go?"

"I got to get out of this hateful place, the whole South. I, I'll get my money same place you got this Hudson."

"This car was Stephen Carter's idea, not mine. He doesn't like what he doesn't think of."

Mae nodded, looked into his eyes. "Till I leave, officer, I jus' need you to drive me home some nights. Ain't that the real reason yo' sponsor, Mr. Stephen Carter, Esquire, sold you this fine car?"

Headlights appeared behind them. Aaron turned forward, shifted gears, weaved his way around the building corner and through the tight parking lot to the back entrance.

"Mae, my mama told me my name means 'light bringer from God.'" He turned to look at her. "I'll be right glad to radiate you tonight."

Inside the screened porch of her historic home in Annesdale, Esther Stein Carter hung up the phone and returned to her knitting. Her son, Prosecutor Stephen Stein Carter, stood nearby.

"Who was on the phone, Mother?"

"Anna Jean. She will work the party tomorrow."

"Good ole Cousin Anna Jean. Our former maid is coming out of retirement and to our rescue from Queen Mae."

Mrs. Carter frowned.

Stephen said, "After all, Father and Anna Jean did have

the same great-grandpappy. Now didn't they?" He laughed and slurped his bourbon.

"Somebody sure needs to save us."

"Mother, please."

"Why did she name that child after me?"

Stephen did not reply. He stirred his drink with a finger.

"Has Emily returned?"

"No, my wife headed off to her mother's."

"Perhaps you should go there and console her."

Ice clinked against the sides of Stephen's glass. "Mother, I am not in a consoling mood."

"Is she coming back for the event tomorrow?"

"Of course, my wife wouldn't miss Boss Crump and Senator McKellar."

"Did you let that girl go, like I told you?"

Stephen laughed. "You and I know this is not the time to release Mae." He stared at her. "I did fire Solomon Cooper, and he's on notice to not cross me again."

"So, you think your wife is going to continue to allow her to work in our household, now that she knows?"

Stephen sipped from his glass. "Why not? Isn't that the Southern way? Besides, Mae wants to move west. Solomon Cooper is the problem, not Mae. The little black weasel should have kept his mouth shut."

"Have you lost your mind? Let her go. I am glad your father is not here to see this."

"Perhaps, Mother, but I am not doing anything Father and most of his cronies didn't do."

"Stephen, you're drunk."

"Mother," he laughed, "I shall leave you in the peace between your Jewish and Protestant Sabbaths while I work on my campaign and get drunker."

"There'll be no need for that if you don't handle this."

He downed his drink and walked into the parlor and toward the front stairs.

Mrs. Carter put her knitting aside, turned off the lamp, and rose to her feet. She pulled her shawl around her small shoulders and grabbed her purse. The seventy-year-old walked into the parlor, headed to the kitchen, and retrieved the automobile keys from the hook beside a cabinet.

Sergeant Smith held up a pistol by a pencil in its barrel. The slender white man wiped the sweat from his forehead and dried his hand on his shirt. "Dr. Walls, looks like this short .38 is the murder weapon." He handed the gun to a man in a white coat with *Coroner* stitched on the pocket.

Dr. Walls removed his glasses and adjusted his comb-over, which had wilted in the humidity. He bent over the body. "Shine your flashlights on her. Black powder. She was shot at close range. These two bullet wounds in the back appear to be the cause of death. I'll autopsy her first thing in the morning."

The coroner handed the gun to Aaron.

"Boy, hold it by the pencil!" the coroner barked, then turned Mae's body over.

Aaron grasped the pencil and stared at the gun.

Smith said, "Somebody roughed her up, but she's a pretty colored gal . . . dressed mighty fancy too."

Ernest Withers's camera flashed.

"Anybody know her?" Smith looked at Aaron.

Aaron squatted beside him. "She's Mae Clark and works with me at the Carters. Mae grew up in my neighborhood."

"When you last see her?" the sergeant asked.

"Dropped her off at the Hipp just befo' I saw you in the Peabody alley. Got back in time to catch her last two numbers.

I was supposed to drive her home, but the bartender told me she left with her boyfriend, Solomon Cooper."

Both stood, and Sergeant Smith looked up at the six-foot-two Aaron. "I heard you had a fight with Sol out back of the club earlier this evening."

Aaron said, "Yes sir," and handed over the pistol.

"I got eyes all over this town."

"Then you ought to be able to help me find out who killed her."

"Washington, I know you been unofficially helping Prosecutor Carter with his cases, but this town ain't ready for colored cops to investigate murders." He removed his cap and ran his fingers through his oily black hair. "Solomon Cooper, I locked that boy up befo'. Ain't he from over there in South Memphis?"

Aaron stared at Mae's body and nodded.

Smith said, "I'll send a car to pick up Solomon. Meet me back at the police station by two."

In the glare of the flashlights, black pools replaced Mae Clark's beautiful brown eyes. The camera flashed. Aaron Washington put his hands in his pockets and moved through the crowd across the cobblestones.

"Mae, Mae, whoever did this is going to pay." He pulled out and opened the pink compact. Its mirror was broken. And Aaron thought back to earlier that evening . . .

Solomon Cooper paced back and forth behind Club Hippodrome, a cigarette hanging from his lips. His anger rose with each syllable Mae sang. He turned when he saw Aaron Washington striding through the parking lot.

"Policeman, you working for Mista Whitey tonight or you here for personal reasons?"

Aaron slowed but kept moving.

"Ain't you heard me, Mista Police Chauffeur?"

Aaron turned and closed on Sol. "Boy, don't get hurt tonight."

"Don't be wolfing me. I can handle things if the white man and his toy police stay out of my business!"

"Sol, I walked the black forests in the Ardennes alone. Keep yo' damn mouth shut," he pointed into the man's dark face, "or get your 4-F ass ready to go to war."

Sol drew back to take a swing at Aaron, who blocked the punch before it was thrown, grabbed Sol, and slammed him to the ground.

"You got enough, or you want some mo'?"

Sol moaned.

"I'm gonna whip on you till you say we done."

Solomon breathed hard. "We done . . . we, we, done."

Aaron adjusted his suit and turned toward the Hippodrome's rear door. Inside, Queen Mae was singing "Don't Sit under the Apple Tree."

Solomon Cooper put his hands on the ground to get up, and his left hand closed on something. He slipped the pistol into his pocket with a smile.

Across the parking lot, someone inside a shiny black Lincoln watched and waited.

Solomon Cooper was picking gravel from his clothing and his hair when Mae stepped through the rear door of the Club Hippodrome.

"Mae, what's going on?"

"Nothing, Sol. Just waiting for Mr. Calloway to start his show." She pointed at Sol's bleeding hands. "What happened to you?"

"Colored police brutality."

"What you and Aaron into it about?"

Sol looked at Mae and answered her question with one of his own: "Can you take a ride with me?"

"I don't know, Sol. I want to hear the show."

"We need to talk 'bout that move you want to make." He flashed a roll of bills.

Mae smiled. "Why can't we talk tomorrow?"

"'Cause I want to talk tonight, right now."

She pulled out a Lucky Strike. Sol obliged with his lighter, and Mae exhaled that first big puff. "Where's your car?"

Sol offered his arm and led Mae to his '39 Ford.

Emily Carter sipped the last of the Double Cola. Her companion took the bottle, and it rang against the whiskey when he placed it in a brown paper bag.

Emily said, "My husband and I used to come down here, back when we were lovers."

The man said, "Well you here with a better lover now." He pulled her close into a long kiss. "Mrs. Carter, no more talk about the prosecutor." He kissed her again.

Aaron used his key to enter the shotgun house on Euclid.

From the middle room, Miss Anna Jean Washington called, "Aaron, is that you?"

"Yes, Mama, it's me."

"Good, guess I can put my pistol back under the pillow."

"Where and when did you get that .25?"

"Miss Esther had Mr. Stephen give it to me while you were at war. He bought 'em for his black mama, his white mother, and his wife."

"What did he get his black wife?"

"A cute red baby."

They both laughed.

Aaron said, "You know how to handle that thing?"

"Old womens knows all kinds of things."

Aaron hugged her.

"What time is it?"

"Three thirty a.m. Mama, I got bad news."

"Mae dead, ain't she?"

He sat on her bed. "How you know 'bout it?"

"My phone started ringing two hours ago. Tried to tell Mae to slow down, but she wouldn't listen."

"Mama, looks like Solomon Cooper did it."

"Have they arrested him?"

"Yes ma'am, and he's been placed at the scene with her."

"Did he say he done it?"

"They roughed him up pretty good, and he admitted to killing her. They found his fingerprints on the gun."

"What Sol doing with a gun?"

"He got if off me in a fight this evening."

"Boy, when you get a pistol?"

"This evening. Mama, I'm a policeman, and I need a gun out there."

"Maybe you need to quit the force."

"Well, I haven't, and now Mae Clark's dead."

"Aaron Washington, I told you not to fool 'round with that gal. She got a baby by Mr. Stephen, and now this fool Sol done told Miss Emily all 'bout it."

"How you know that?"

"Miss Esther done called to tell me."

"How often you talk to that old hag?"

"She calls eve'y day."

Aaron laughed. "I told you the Carters wouldn't know what to do after you retired. Did you talk to Miss Esther this evening?"

"She awful upset. That woman talked and talked and talked 'bout how mad she is 'cause Mae named her daughter after her."

"Three years later and she's still having a fit. And the judge is probably turning in his grave over at Elmwood."

Miss Anna Jean laughed. "I had to work somewhere, and he just happened to be kin and white. Son, they're good folks. But I'll never get the twisted ways that makes a person mad about your only grandchild being named after you. It's a sickness that takes a long time for even the Holy Ghost and Jesus to cure."

Aaron said, "Mr. Stephen came to the police station this evening."

"How was he?"

"Shook up, angry, really mad. He plans to go for the electric chair."

"Huh, that young gal done put a spell on him."

"Wonder what'll happen to Mae's daughter now."

"Her grandmama'll keep on raising her."

Aaron walked to the front room, disrobed, and lay down on his bed. "Mama," he called through the door, "she wrote me all those letters while I was away."

"Aaron, I know you cared 'bout Mae. I cried when I wrote to tell you she was with child by Mr. Stephen."

As Aaron lay there, Mae's face flashed before his eyes. Just hours ago she was alive and in his life. His breathing slowed. The memory of her voice reverberated.

"Mae dedicated her last song to me, 'The Very Thought of You,'" Aaron said as he drifted off to sleep, remembering how he got that revolver . . .

When Aaron pulled the Hudson into the alley behind the

Peabody Hotel just before nine, three Negro workers stood in his headlights. Cigarette smoke rose in the night air, and their banter echoed across the brick, mortar, and paved urban space. Aaron killed the lights and motor.

One of the men pitched two dice against the wall, then said, "Watch out, boys! Here come the colored police."

The group laughed, but stopped when Aaron walked around the car and stood over the man. Aaron pulled a pack of Camels from his pocket, thumped out a cigarette, and placed it between his lips. Another porter popped open a lighter and kicked the flame to life. Aaron leaned into the man's hand and inhaled.

The dice shooter stood and looked up into Aaron's piercing brown eyes. Aaron blew smoke into the man's face, opened his palm, and the man placed the bones into Aaron's hand.

"Yeah, I'm the colored po-lice." He took another drag on the Camel and pocketed the dice. "If you boys want to spend a few days in jail, keep on in this alley." He found the eyes of each man in the dim light before bursting into laughter.

One by one, the four men shook hands.

Another worker, dressed in a red jacket, spoke: "You working tonight?"

Aaron said, "That's a fine thing for the Peabody's Duck Master to ask. It's Saturday night, and most of us coloreds, including us police, is working." He found their eyes again. "And y'all be careful 'cause a bunch of them white-boy cops out here too!"

A car sped toward them from the west end of the alley.

Aaron said, "Here comes one right now."

A black-and-white cruiser came to a stop next to the men. The policeman spoke through the window: "What you boys doing out here?"

Aaron spoke up: "Evening, Sergeant Smith."

The white cop leaned through the window. "Washington, didn't recognize you, boy. Everything all right wit' this group?"

"Yes sir, everything's top shelf."

"Ain't you posted at the Hippodrome this evening?"

"Yes sir, getting ready to head back over now."

"See you do that right away." He looked at the other men. "You boys get back inside the hotel. Wouldn't want y'all doing something y'all might regret."

Smith hit the side of his car and zoomed away. The men watched his brake lights turn red at the end of the alley, then the cruiser turned north onto Third toward Union.

One of the porters adjusted his bow tie and white jacket. "How you work for that dude?"

Another in identical garb replied, "Officer, le' me answer that . . . The same way we do for that fool inside."

The four men laughed. The two porters walked away.

Aaron turned to Edward Pembroke, Duck Master. "Ed, you got it?"

Ed looked around before pulling a revolver from his pocket. He handed it to Aaron who kicked open and spun the bullet-filled chamber.

"Thanks, man. Colt Detective Special .38. Where you get it?"

"Found it on the hotel roof, next to the duck pens."

"Sure enough," Aaron said. He snapped the gun closed and put the pistol into his right front pants pocket. "Now I'll have some help out here. How you like teaching those ducks to march?"

"It's a lot better than raising cotton."

They both laughed.

Edward Pembroke said, "Who's at the Hipp tonight?"

"Queen Mae's opening for Cab Calloway."

"Whooo, that pretty gal and Mr. Hi-Dee-Hi-Dee-Ho."

"I better get back befo' some fool lose his mind."

The sun was already hot at nine thirty a.m. on Sunday when Aaron and Miss Anna Jean stopped a block east of their shotgun at the home of Sallie Clark, Mae's mama.

Miss Anna Jean said, "Look at all those grandchildren."

Ten children ran back and forth, chasing a ball, pushing an empty bicycle rim with a stick, playing jump rope, or digging in the dirt. One looked to be around three. Her sandy-brown hair was thick, curly, and moplike. She had skin that was a golden tan, too light for black and too dark for white.

Aaron said, "Think Mae's baby knows yet?"

"Thank the Lord she too young to understand."

A ten-year-old approached. "Hello, Miss Anna Jean! You come to see my grandma?" He stood on the passenger-side running board. Several of his cousins joined him. Mae's daughter squeezed between the boy and the front passenger door.

Miss Anna Jean said, "Hello, Stein, how are you? You have the prettiest green eyes."

"Thank you," the child responded. "Do you know my mama? Grandma says she went to heaven last night."

"Yes, Stein, your mama sure did," Miss Anna Jean said.

Aaron got out of the car and reached into the backseat for the box of Miss Anna Jean's fried chicken.

Miss Anna Jean whispered, "Stein, I've seen eyes like yours but on another face."

The young child's eyes widened and she smiled. "My mama says my other grandma's eyes are just like mine."

She and her cousins scattered when Aaron opened the passenger door to help Miss Anna Jean from the car. She paused to look at Aaron. "Son, looking at that baby gives me the green-eyed blues."

"Emily, where were you last night?"

"Why do you care?" She brushed her thick auburn hair.

Stephen exhaled. "We got a house full of guests arriving. Much is riding on this event."

"I was at my mother's last night."

"Yes, but you were not there at one thirty a.m."

"So, are you acting as prosecutor, judge, or loving husband?"

"I drove by on my way to the police station to interrogate Sol. Your Lincoln was not there."

"So you're tracking me by my Lincoln . . . guess that's why you begged your mother to purchase one for me, you, and her. I bet you and Solomon had a great visit."

"There wasn't anything nice about it. I am charging Solomon with first-degree murder and going for the electric chair."

"That ought to help you win the white *and* black vote while avenging poor little Mae."

"You act like such a bitch."

"The most skilled bastard in Memphis taught me how."

Stephen jerked the knot into his necktie and put on his suit coat. He reached for the door.

Emily asked, "What kind of gun killed our Queen Mae?"

"Probably the .38 found at the scene."

"How sure are you?"

"Emily, where were you last night? Why do you care what gun killed her?"

"Stephen, I couldn't sleep last night and went for a ride along Riverside Drive. Parking on the cobblestones is amazing, especially at night. You weren't with me so I took my .25

automatic for security . . . You used to drive me down there in the cool of the evening, didn't you, Stephen?"

"What are you saying, Emily?"

"Ask your mother. See what she tells you." Emily laughed and threw her hair about her shoulders. She moved toward her closet.

Stephen approached and grabbed her. He shook Emily. "Don't play games with me."

"When I was at the cobblestones, a car drove onto the lot and parked near the water. It was Sol Cooper and Mae. I couldn't tell what they were saying, but I heard shouting. He hit her about the head and face. Mae jumped from the car. Sol started to follow her, but another car pulled up so he drove off. Then the car pulled up to Mae."

Emily squirmed, and Stephen released her.

"Stephen, it was your mother. Mae was in her face through the car window. I heard Mae shout, *I'm gonna tell everybody 'bout my baby!* She turned to walk away, but I heard two shots. Mae fell to the ground, and in a few seconds Mrs. Carter drove away."

"Did Mother see you when she left?"

Emily wiped her face and nodded.

"What happened then?"

"I left too, drove around awhile before going back to my mother's."

A knock startled them.

"Yes," Stephen said.

"Mr. Stephen," Aaron said, "can I speak with you?"

"Be right there." Stephen whispered, "Emily, does anyone else know this?"

She cried some more and looked away. Stephen grabbed her arm.

Emily said, "Sergeant Smith knows."

"How does he know?"

"He was with me, in my car."

Stephen released her arm, patted it. He stood there looking at the floor. "I will see you downstairs."

"What are you going to do?"

Stephen glanced back, but gave no answer. He stepped into the hallway, closed the door behind him, and walked to where Aaron stood.

Aaron whispered, "Dr. Walls and Sergeant Smith are downstairs."

"They're here?"

"Yes sir. Mr. Stephen, that .38 found on the scene belongs to me. Sol ended up with it when I fought with him."

"Where and when did this happen?"

"At Club Hippodrome around nine. I was there at the bar until the dispatcher called me to come to the murder scene just before midnight . . . Mr. Stephen, there's more. This morning I found two spent .25 caliber cartridges in Mrs. Carter's car. Who was driving your mother's car last night?"

"You know Mother does not drive."

"Well, who drove her car last night?"

Stephen Carter did not answer.

"Mr. Stephen, what are you going to do when you get downstairs?"

"One thing's for sure—neither my mother nor my wife is going to jail."

"Fine, but what about Sol?"

Stephen put his hand to his chin. "Aaron, events like these cause race riots."

"Yes sir, they do."

"What if Solomon Cooper gets eleven months and twenty-nine days for manslaughter?"

"He deserves that for hitting Mae."

"Aaron, I am indebted to you."

The two men shook hands.

Stephen Carter entered the screened porch. "Hello, Dr. Walls." He shook the doctor's hand. The sergeant extended his hand, but Stephen moved away. "Perhaps we can get together tomorrow morning."

Sergeant Smith said, "Mr. Carter, Dr. Walls has completed the autopsy, and his findings cause a bit of a problem that you should know."

"Is that a fact?" Stephen replied.

Smith stepped through the porch door and called out, "Officer Washington . . . Officer Washington. Would you join us out here?"

Aaron entered and closed the door behind him.

Smith continued: "Doctor, why don't you explain your findings?"

"Mr. Carter, the gun we found, the .38 Special, is not the murder weapon. That gun has not been fired in quite some time. In fact, two .25 caliber bullets killed Mae Clark."

"I thought Solomon confessed last evening. Said he shot her with the .38," Stephen said.

Smith said, "Well, yes sir, he did, but he's backpedaling on us now."

"There's another problem," Dr. Walls said. "Officer Washington touched the weapon at the scene, so I knew he would have some fingerprints on the gun; however, I did not think his prints would be on the bullets."

"What are you saying?" Stephen asked.

The coroner said, "If Solomon Cooper killed Mae Clark, he used a different gun. And Officer Washington has handled this .38 revolver on a previous occasion."

The three men looked at Aaron, who said, "I lost that gun in a fight with Solomon Cooper earlier in the evening. He must have picked it up."

Smith said, "Washington, what you doing on duty with a pistol?"

Aaron glared at his superior. "The Colt Detective Special .38 is a standard gun for police use."

Smith edged closer to Aaron.

Stephen said, "Sergeant, it is not illegal for Officer Washington to carry a gun. Be careful that we do not end up becoming a public spectacle when one of our Negro policemen gets hurt because he's not armed. My guests are beginning to arrive. Let's focus on the business at hand. Doctor, have you written your report?"

"No sir, I have not."

"Gentlemen, many moving pieces may make or break my campaign."

The two visitors nodded.

Stephen went on: "For this situation to go away, the .38 must be the murder weapon. And," he looked at Aaron, "Officer Washington never touched the gun prior to his visit to the murder scene."

Dr. Walls said, "Judge Carter helped with my first appointment as Shelby County coroner. The appropriate wording will be in my report. How do you plan to charge Sol Cooper?"

Stephen looked at Aaron, Dr. Walls, and Sergeant Smith. "Solomon Cooper will be charged with manslaughter. I will press for a conviction and sentencing of eleven months and twenty-nine days." He found their eyes. "Why don't you both stay for the party, mingle with our guests?"

Sergeant Smith said, "Don't mind if I do. There might be

someone here for me to speak to. What about you, doctor?"

"Is that fried chicken cooking?"

Someone knocked on the door. The servant opened it and said, "Excuse me, Mr. Stephen, Miss Anna Jean wants you and Aaron to come to Miss Esther's room."

Stephen led the way, and Aaron followed.

In the bedroom, Miss Anna Jean said, "In here, in the bathroom. No matter what I do, every few minutes Miss Esther tries to wash her hands."

Mrs. Carter peered at Stephen and Aaron, her green eyes filled with tears. "I got something on my hands last night." She held them out. "Can't you see it?" She reached for the soap and turned on the water.

Stephen said, "Anna Jean, can you keep her in her room today? I'll get our doctor to bring over a sedative."

"Yes sir," Anna Jean said.

Aaron and Stephen stepped into the bedroom.

"I guess you now know who drove Mother's car last night."

Aaron nodded.

"Looks like Mae's killer paid . . . Pardon me, Aaron, my guests are waiting."

Miss Anna Jean joined Aaron in the bedroom several moments later. "She's very sick."

"I been saying that for years."

"She needs my help."

"Mama, I can't stay."

"Go on home, Aaron."

"Mama, I mean I'm leaving town. I cannot live like this. She killed Mae, my Mae. And I can't do anything about it!"

"Aaron, stay. If you leave now, you can never do anything about it."

Miss Esther called, "Anna Jean!"

Miss Anna Jean hugged Aaron and whispered in his ear, "You'll be surprised at what we can do. I'll get on the phone. Stephen Carter ain't gonna win no election now or ever. Son, go home. Just you wait."

Aaron kissed her cheek and walked away.

CHAIN OF CUSTODY

BY LEE MARTIN

Orange Mound

I'm sleeping when the phone rings, and it's Laura, and she's whispering, and it's after midnight, and part of me wants to go back to sleep, and another part of me wishes she'd come and crawl into my bed.

"Hey, Sexy Socks," I say. "Want some dirty talk?"

I call her Sexy Socks, because the few times we've done the baby-oh-baby she's kept her knee-highs on: lime green with purple and red butterflies, black with white polka dots and white lace at the top, black and red argyle—in that order, first to last.

"Cappy," she says to me, still in that whisper, but more urgent now. "Cappy, listen to me," she says. "You have to come get me. Now."

Folks call me Cappy because of the Stars and Bars skull cap I always wear. Few know that I'm bald underneath, Laura being one. For the record, we're not a couple—friends and on-again, off-again lovers I guess you'd say—and yet, times like this, we count on each other. For any number of reasons, we've never been able to fully sync up our lives and make that final I-do-I-do-I-really-do. Sometimes she seems too dangerous to me. She's a nurse at the Shelby County Jail, and she's been known to pocket a few Vicodin and Percocet and Oxy-Contin and smuggle them out to share at parties. Sometimes my own bad sense gets in the way. I've just put a ten-year marriage in the rearview, and I'm not ready for the ever-after. Still, Laura's the one I rely on to keep me wanting to wake up every morning. Sometimes all it takes is the sound of her voice, or a glimpse of her walking down the street, or, better yet, her hand closed around mine, to convince me that I want to take care of her, and I want her to take care of me. "All right, be a snooze," she'd said to me earlier this evening when I'd refused to go to the party with her. "I'm not about to tell you what you missed. Remember that, mister."

That's where she is now, a house in Orange Mound, in the bathroom, whispering into her cell phone, pleading with me to come get her because there's this guy and he's had his eye on her and she's afraid and she can't just walk out because she's too high to drive and too scared to hoof it.

"Please, Cappy."

I can hear someone pounding on the bathroom door and a man's voice saying, "Nurse Laura, I think it's time for my meds."

"Hurry, Cappy," she says. "Please hurry."

"I'll be there," I tell her. "Just keep your socks on."

I know the house, a shotgun on Saratoga just a block north of Park. Concrete-slab porch out front, dried-up rhododendron vines hanging from the wrought-iron supports. Brick chimney rising up from the center of the peaked roof. Security bars on the front windows. Unpainted clapboards, weathered gray. Old Dr Pepper thermometer tacked up next to the front door. It's this house where a dude they call Hercules lives. A party house on the weekends, and I'll lay money this Hercules is the one who's got Laura spooked.

He's a dick, plain and simple. A lunk who doesn't have time for any work, because he's too busy with his barbells and his muscles.

I met him at a party my friend Richie was throwing at the cottage he rented a few blocks east of me on Spottswood. No one knew who he was, this dude in a tank top and cargo shorts even though it was January. Dude was cut. Biceps and delts and pecs and quads and calf muscles. Dude just wandered in and made himself at home.

"I just started lifting," I told him.

He took a step back and looked me up and down. I knew he was sizing up my lanky frame, taking note of my lack of bulk.

"Yeah?" he said. "And how's that working out for you, my brother?"

"Good," I said. "Just dandy. I'm taking it slow. Wouldn't want to turn into a musclehead, you know. Guys like that . . . ?" I let the question hang there a few beats. "Well, they tend to lose all sense of perspective. Wouldn't know shit if they stepped in it. I'm sure you get what I'm saying. I can tell you're a thinker."

For just a moment, he thought I was sincere. I could tell from the smug grin he gave me, like—wink, wink—he and I were simpatico. Then the grin faded and his brow furrowed and his eyes narrowed, and I made tracks, disappearing into the crowd, out the front door and on to the safety of my apartment. I didn't need to be there when the full realization hit him, when he knew I'd called him a bonehead.

Since then I've avoided him, but now, as I point my truck west on Spottswood and head down into Orange Mound, I imagine we're about to get intimate.

Richie's on the porch when I get there, looking all down in the mouth. "Fucker broke my sunglasses," he says. He holds out his hand, and I see his retro Wayfarers, the ones he said gave him his juju, snapped in two at the bridge, half on his left palm and half on his right. "Fucker," he says again. He throws the pieces of the glasses out into the grass. "Let's get him, Cappy." He unzips his white hoodie, the one with red letters that say, *I'm Kind of a Big Deal in Memphis*, and pats the shoulder holster he always wears, the one for the Glock 17 pistol he packs. "I mean it. Let's get him good."

"Cool that shit," I say. Through the front windows, I can see candles burning inside the house and the shadows of people moving about. "I'm here to get Laura."

I open the front door and step inside, and just like that, I forget about Richie. I've known him since we were kids in Midtown. Short dude, short fuse. I don't know how many times I've saved him from trouble, but right now I'm thinking about Laura and how she told me to hurry.

The place is packed with folks either cranked up on meth or chillin' on pills or weed. The air is skunky with the smoke, and I have to wade into it and the crowd of tweekers doing their herky-jerky dance to Ministry's *The Land of Rape and Honey*. The "Stigmata" track is playing with its repetition of *"You've run out of lies,"* and I think, hell yeah, let's do this.

At a table near the fireplace, a blond woman with a coonskin hat on her head is putting a pill on her tongue. She winks at me.

"You know Laura?" I ask.

"Bathroom," she says. Then she nods her head to the right, and that's when I see Hercules pounding on a closed door. He's wearing a black tank top, and with each knock I see his delts quiver and flex.

"Open up the door, bitch," he says, and, as I make my move toward him, I fear that this is about to get out of hand in a big way.

"Whoa, hold up there, my brother," I say. I put my hand on his shoulder, and I feel the muscle quiver. "No need for that kind of talk."

With a simple shrug of his shoulders, like he's slipping into a snug suit jacket, he knocks my hand away. He turns to look at me. It takes him awhile, but then something clicks into place, and he says, "You're the smart-ass from Richie's party."

"Bingo," I say. Then I try to slip past him. "Now if you'll excuse me."

But he grabs me by my arm and whips me around. "You know what they say, my brother. Everyone likes a little ass, but nobody likes a smart-ass."

From inside the bathroom, Laura says, "Cappy, is that you?"

"It's me," I say. I hear the bathroom door unlock, and I smell Laura's perfume, Chanel No. 5 Sensual Elixir. I remember the name, because I bought her a bottle for Christmas. "I'm here to give the lady a ride home," I say to Hercules, and I try to remove my arm from his grip.

That's when all hell breaks loose.

Hercules says, "She's not going anywhere."

He shoves me away, and I bump into the woman in the coonskin cap who's wandered over to see what the fuss is all about. By the time I get my balance, he's got Laura shoved back against the wall, and he's leaning in close, his knee between her legs. She's wearing a yellow cabana top, the kind with tails like a man's oxford, only tied at her bellybutton— that and a pair of black leggings, tight on her thighs and butt, clinging to her crotch.

"Let me go," she says. "I mean it."

And that's when Richie noses around me, and I see him reach inside his hoodie, and then he's holding the Glock to the back of Hercules's head and telling him to back off, motherfucker, and I think, Lordy, lordy, lordy. How did my life come to this?

Hercules takes a step back, and Laura sees her chance. She kicks him in the balls, and he doubles over and sinks to his knees.

"Cappy, let's go," she says, grabbing my hand.

Richie says, "Wait for me."

But we don't. We bust ass for the front door and my truck that's waiting outside. Someone reaches out and grabs the tails of my skull cap, and the next thing I know it's gone. I don't even turn around. I keep going, following the tug of Laura's hand.

As I head north on Grand Street, I hear a shot. I hit the brake, intending to turn around and go back, but Laura says, "For God's sake, Cappy. Drive."

And I do.

She doesn't live far from me. I'm in the Spottswood Apartments just west of Highland and not far from the U of M campus where I work maintenance. She's in a bungalow a few blocks west of me on Prescott near the C.W. Davis Park. We met in that park one night last summer when neither of us could sleep. I was fretting over my marriage gone bust, and Laura said she always had trouble sleeping. "Don't ask me why," she said, just as I was about to. She was sitting on top of a picnic table, still in her nurse's scrubs—her top had sock monkeys on it. I told her I'd always wanted one as a kid, but I'd always been deprived of the pleasure. "Didn't anyone love you?" she said. I shrugged my shoulders. "Tragedy of my life," I said. She asked me my name, and I told her. "Cappy," she said, "everyone should have what they want." A few nights later, I walked down to the park, and there she was, sitting on the picnic table, a sock monkey in her lap. "It's about time you came back," she said. Then she reached the monkey out to me. "Take it," she told me. "It's yours."

I'm thinking about that as she opens the door to get out of my truck—how she wanted me to have what I'd always wanted even if it was a little too late to get the kick out of it the way I would have when I was a kid. I'm thinking about her big and tender heart, and how sometimes I like to imagine that I'm the only one who knows it. These days, my life is made from tales like this.

Laura turns around and leans back into the truck. She looks at me for a good while. The air has a snap in it this close to Christmas. Blue lights hang from the eaves of her bungalow—she's left them on. For some reason, blue Christmas lights always make me sadder than sad. She says to me, "Richie's always been a hothead. You shouldn't have left him there."

"I tried to turn around," I say. "You were the one who told me to keep going."

She gets that little smile on her lips, the one that always makes me melt, the playful grin that dares me to call bullshit on her, the one she knows I can't resist.

"Did I?" she says.

I reach out and grab her by the arm. "You know damn well you did."

She winces and tries to pull her arm free, but I hold on. "Don't be such a gorilla," she says.

"You owe me," I say.

"Oh hell," she says, "we owe each other. Guess we'll have to just keep paying on the tab."

I let her go then.

"Jesus, what a night," she says. "Don't worry about Richie. I'm sure he'll be fine."

But Richie's not fine. I go into work the next day, and he's not there. He's a maintenance guy like me, and let me tell you it's not a bad job, working on campus, watching the co-eds come and go. "Not bad at all," Richie always says. "Money in the bank."

"Richie sick?" I ask the supervisor, and he tells me he doesn't know. He hasn't heard squat from him.

"That's not like Richie," I say, and the supervisor just shrugs and hands me a work order for a leaking toilet in a men's room at the University Center.

After work, I swing by Richie's, and right away I know something's up. His Jeep Wrangler isn't in the driveway, but his front door is standing wide open.

I park along the street behind a black Ford Explorer and then make my way up the walk. I don't know what to think when I reach the front steps and can hear voices coming from the back of the house. I knock on the door frame. "Hey, Richie," I call out. "Is that you, man? It's me, Cappy."

The voices go quiet, and I try to decide what to do. Finally, I step into the house. It's a cloudy day, late afternoon, and the light is fading fast.

"Richie?" I say again, and then I switch on the living room overhead.

That's when I see it, a bloody handprint on the wall, just inside the front door.

I back away from it. The place is cold, and the chain from the ceiling fan is ticking against the housing, rattled by the wind. All around me are Richie's things—a Carhartt jacket tossed on his recliner; a pair of brown cowboy boots, the toes scuffed, the heels worn down, on the floor beside the chair; a red toolbox in the corner; some shop rags on the kitchen counter; his Gibson bass still plugged into the amp; the pictures of flowers that he takes at the Memphis Botanic Garden

in their frames on the walls, one of them a shot of purple azaleas just to the right of the bloodstain, its frame crooked—but
Richie is still nowhere to be seen.

Before I can decide what to do, a man appears from the
back of the house. He moves with purpose up the hall toward
me, a tall man in a navy-blue suit, a head of thick gray hair,
and a trim gray mustache. A man who's used to being in control; I can tell by the way he holds himself as he strides toward
me, and the way he speaks when he finally does.

"Cappy? That's what folks call you, right? You work with
Richard Bondurant, yes?"

"I know Richie," I say.

Then I see a second man coming down the hall, a bulldog
of a man, short and squat, in a long leather coat that squeaks
when he walks. I can see his white shirt collar digging into
the folds of skin, and his red necktie knotted perfectly at his
Adam's apple. Most of all, though, I see what he's carrying
with him—my Stars and Bars skull cap, the one I left behind
when push came to shove at Hercules's place.

"Phillip Trezevant Morgan?" he says, using my real name,
my full name, which confirms what I've already assumed.
These men are police detectives, and they know more about
me than I'd rather they did. He holds out my skull cap. "My
guess is you're looking for this."

And that's how I end up downtown at 201 Poplar, a place you
don't want to be—trust me on that—especially if the folks
who have questions for you are homicide dicks. The tall one
calls me Cappy again.

"Cappy," he says, "we need to know a few things."

He offers me coffee in a paper cup, and I take it, trying to
be friendly because after all I'm not guilty of anything. If these

dicks want to have a little chat, I'll go along. I've agreed to this. I've even driven myself downtown, the dicks following me.

The tall one pours himself a cup of joe and sits down across from me at the table. He brushes a finger over his mustache. The one who reminds me of a bulldog still has on his leather jacket. I can smell him as he passes behind me—leather and tobacco smoke and the menthol scent of too much Aqua Velva aftershave. His jacket creaks as he settles into a swivel desk chair to my right. He leans back in it, a file folder in his hands.

"Mr. Morgan," he says, and I cringe because all of this reminds me of sitting in my ex-wife's attorney's office listening to him call me *mister* with a hiss to the *s* as if I didn't deserve the title. "Mr. Morgan," the bulldog dick says, "we know you were involved in an altercation last night in Orange Mound. House on Saratoga Street. A party that got out of hand. A shot fired from a Glock 17."

"A little disagreement," I say.

"It was more than that, Cappy," the tall dick says. "Was that the last time you saw Richie?"

I sip my coffee. Then I say, "Is he in trouble?"

"Could be. Cappy, do you know a man named Everett Simpson?"

"Negative," I say.

That's when the bulldog dick leans forward. He lays the file folder on the table and fingers it open. The first thing I see is a photograph of a man facedown on the floor, a bullet hole behind his ear, blood all over his black tank top and his bare shoulder, and over at the edge of the photo, also on the floor, is my Stars and Bars skull cap.

"Everett Simpson," the bulldog dick says. "I believe you know him as Hercules."

"Cappy." The tall dick leans forward in his chair, closing the distance between us. "Do you know where we can find Richie Bondurant?"

"Couldn't say."

"Any idea how your skull cap ended up in this picture?"

"Someone yanked it off my head as I was leaving that house on Saratoga. I left it behind."

"Must have been in a hurry."

"I was. In a hurry to walk away from trouble."

The bulldog dick says, "Some guys just can't walk fast enough for that. Trouble always catches up with them."

"You should get an attorney," the tall dick says. "Trust me, Cappy. Things are about to get tight for you."

"Why's that?"

"We've got a hunch you know who killed Everett Simpson."

"I don't need an attorney," I say. "I'm clean. Whatever went on at that house on Saratoga after I left, I don't have a clue."

The bulldog dick snorts. "'Course you don't. But what went on at Bondurant's house later that night? That's what we want to know. That's where we found the body—in one of the bedrooms."

I agree to let them interrogate me without having an attorney present. I don't have anything to hide. They already have the facts about Richie and that Glock and how he held it on Hercules while Laura and I made our getaway. People like the girl in the coonskin cap have given them the skinny, and I have nothing at all to tell them outside of the fact that I took Laura to her house and then I went home. I went to work the next morning, and when I was done for the day, I drove to Richie's and that's where I met up with the two of them.

"That's all I know," I tell them. "Every bit of it."

The tall dick asks me if I'll agree to let them take my fingerprints and a sample of my blood. "If you're really clean," he says, "the prints and the blood will eliminate you as a suspect."

"Sure," I say. "Absolutely. Take what you need."

A technician takes my prints, and a nurse draws my blood. This is what Laura would do if she were here, and I think how ironic that would be, the woman at the heart of the dustup with Hercules, entering a vial of my blood into the chain of custody, passed from the nurse to the tall dick and from him to an evidence clerk. Laura has told me the drill. The chain of custody is just what it says, a carefully documented trail of who handles the evidence and where it goes, a means of being certain that no one can plant any fraudulent evidence, a system where everyone takes great care to assure that everything is on the up and up.

I roll down my sleeve and button my cuff. I've given the dicks what they want, and they have no call to keep me there any longer.

"We might have more questions," tall dick says, and I say I'm sure they know how to find me.

I drive straight to Laura's.

"You should have let me go back," I say, brushing past her when she opens the door. "I could have stopped it. I could have taken care of him."

"Calm down, Cappy," she says. "What's the story?"

I tell her everything. There in her house with candles burning that smell like peppermint, there with the silver garland on the fireplace mantel and the Christmas tree decorated with red bows and twinkle lights, there where I've sat so many times thinking this is what it should feel like to be home. I tell her about the bloody handprint, the dicks and their questions, and how I had to tell them about being with her the night of the party before they handed over my skull cap and told me I could go; I was no longer a person of interest. I tell her that Hercules is dead and the police are looking for Richie.

For a long time Laura doesn't say a thing. She paces back and forth in front of the fireplace. Then she comes to the sofa where I'm sitting. A big round candle is burning on the coffee table. She bites her lip. "I know where he is."

"Richie? How can you know?"

She bends over and blows out the candle. I sit there in the glow from the lights on the Christmas tree.

"That handprint?" she says. "It's mine."

Now it's her turn to talk, and as she does, I'm feeling what I did when I finally found out my wife's secrets—the sex tapes, the gambling debts. I feel myself shrinking, getting smaller and smaller until I'm sure I'll disappear. I'm thinking, as I did then, that everyone's life is a lie. All the people you walk around with, the ones you thought you could count on to be who you need them to be. When push comes to shove, you're on your own; you have to look out for yourself. When I left Laura at her house the night of the party, I had no idea that she was soon to have a visitor—two, to be exact: Hercules and Richie.

"Hercules was apologetic," she tells me, "but Richie was still pissed off."

They were at Laura's, because Richie figured he'd find me there. He'd made Hercules drive him over, the Glock held on him all the way, and held on him still as they stood there in Laura's house.

"That's just like Cappy," Richie had said. "He starts trouble, and then when I save his ass he disappears." He poked Hercules in the small of the back with his Glock. "Now look at what I got on my hands. What the hell am I supposed to do with him?"

Laura told him that maybe he could just let Hercules go. "At least you haven't shot him," she said.

"I tried to," Richie said. "He was lucky I missed. Now if I let him go, he might do the same to me."

"That's the truth," Hercules said, and then there they were, the three of them. "Your move, brother," he said to Richie. "Aren't you about tired of holding that gun?"

He was, Laura tells me. "I could see that right off. He'd got himself in a fix . . . Well, really, Cappy, you were the one who'd made things tight for him . . . and now he didn't know what to do."

That's when she told him, "Richie, why don't we just take you home?" She asked Hercules if that would be all right with him. If he wouldn't mind, that is, taking Richie to his place, and if he didn't mind if she rode along and then the two of them could come back to her house and . . . Well, let's just say Laura gave Hercules reason to believe that he'd be seeing her in her sexy socks and nothing else in right short order.

"But you were afraid of him," I say to her. "You begged me to come and get you. You wanted me to take care of you."

"Sorry, Cappy," she says. "I thought you knew I wasn't anyone to count on."

I want to believe it's not true, and I don't want to hear the rest of her story, but I know I'll have to listen because Hercules is dead, and Richie's nowhere to be found, and thanks to my Stars and Bars skull cap, those dicks aren't completely done with me. They had no reason to arrest me, but they certainly indicated that they might come calling again before this is all played out. Now I have to find out what sort of trouble Laura might be in and how she came to leave that bloody handprint on Richie's wall.

Then, before continuing, she takes my hand, and I feel the

old twinge of love I doubt I'll ever lose for her.

"Come on," she says. "I'll take you to Richie."

"You know where he is?"

She tells me he's downtown across from the train station at a joint called Earnestine and Hazel's. He's on the down low, waiting for Laura to bring him the cash he'll need to buy a ticket for the *City of New Orleans*, which will take him north to Chicago.

"You drive, Cappy." She picks up her leather coat and her purse. "I'm too nervous."

Just as she opens the door, the two dicks step up onto her porch. The tall one flashes his badge.

"Lauralee Devereaux?" he says.

Her knees buckle, and I grab her so she won't go down. I've never forgotten the way her lifeless body felt as she sagged against me—like air or water or second chances that never work out.

"Well, look who we have here," the bulldog dick says. "About to go somewhere, are we?"

I don't know, as I stand there holding Laura, the whole story of Hercules and how he ended up shot to death. That story waits to be written in the *Commercial Appeal*—the story of how Laura and Hercules drove Richie home, and how once they were there Hercules said he had to use the bathroom. Richie balked at that, but Laura insisted. "Oh, for God's sake, Richie. You still have a gun, don't you? What could go wrong?"

Plenty, as it turned out. I was sleeping when this all went down. I had no part in it. I didn't know that Richie had picked up my skull cap from the floor of the house on Saratoga and stuffed it into his jacket pocket, knowing I'd want him to do that. I hadn't deserved that kindness, not after the way I'd run out on him.

And I didn't know that when Hercules came out of the bathroom at Richie's place, Laura was holding the Glock. "Richie had already pulled back the slide to load a round into the firing chamber. He was showing me how to squeeze the trigger."

That's when Hercules rushed Richie. He lowered his shoulder and drove Richie into the wall. "Shoot him," Richie said to Laura. "Shoot him. Now."

Hercules jerked his head toward Laura and saw her holding the Glock. Richie took that chance to make it to his bedroom. Hercules said to Laura, "You won't shoot me, will you, baby? Not a sweet piece like you."

Then he headed toward Richie's bedroom. Laura followed, and when she got there, she saw Richie swing a baseball bat and catch Hercules flush on the side of his head. That's when my skull cap came out of Richie's pocket. That's when Hercules went down.

I had dreamt about Laura that night. I remember it very distinctly. We were in bed and she was taking off her socks, but there was always another pair underneath. She took off one pair, two pair, three pair, four, and as she did, she recited these lines from Dr. Seuss:

And here's a new trick, Mr. Knox . . .
Socks on chicks and chicks on fox.
Fox on clocks on bricks and blocks.
Bricks and blocks on Knox on box.

I woke up crying. I tried to tell myself not to be mad at Laura. It was just a dream, and really, even if it was real, how would she have known what I'd chosen to never tell her— that the thing that finally broke my wife and me, the thing that drove us both to do crazy things with no regard for the hurt we were causing, was the death of our little girl, whose favorite Dr. Seuss had been *Fox in Socks*. Laura had no way of knowing that I'd read that book to my daughter over and over while she was at St. Jude's, nothing to be done about the neuroblastoma in her brain.

That had happened in the real world, the one I counted on Laura to help me forget. And in the real world, while I slept and dreamt and woke up trembling, Laura knelt on the floor beside Hercules, put the Glock to his skull, right behind his ear, and, just like Richie had taught her, she squeezed the trigger.

"There was so much blood," she told the reporter from the *Commercial Appeal*.

Now, wherever I go, and whatever happens to me, I know I'll be thinking about how it's wrong to put so much stock in one person. No one can save us. And I'll be thinking about Richie that night at Earnestine and Hazel's. Maybe he was at the bar enjoying a soul burger, or maybe he was shooting pool, or listening to the juke box that folks swear is haunted and plays tunes to fit the conversations going on at nearby tables, or maybe he was at the bar upstairs where the brothel used to be. Maybe he was thinking he was almost gone. Just a few minutes more, and Laura would be there with the money. He'd ride the train north, and a whole new life would begin.

Then he heard someone call his name. A man's voice— Richie told me all of this later when I visited him at Riverbend over in Nashville. He heard this voice. *Richie*, it said—and he turned around and saw the cops.

He thought it was me. He thought I'd come to help him, just like he always knew I would, but by that time Laura was being questioned downtown. And me? I was all alone.

PART III

MEMPHIS MISFITS

PART III

THERE IS NO REST

BY Arthur Flowers

Riverside Park

1st Movement

cast your vision, young hoodoo, as far as you can see
determine the challenges the tribe will face
prepare the tribal soul to meet them

I am Flowers of the Delta Clan Flowers and the Line of O. Killens. Ima Hoodoo Lord of the Delta and power is what I do. Attend me, Lord Legba. It is I, Rickydoc Trickmaster, would tell the tale of a people, a prophet, a way.

In the name of the Conqueror let this work be done.

I am known by many names. In the Delta I am known by the horses I choose. The Delta has always been fertile ground and it is altogether fitting that in Memphis a conjuror awaits on the bank of Oshuns oldest water. As yet he defies me. I regret what must be done. It is not easy. To be the Horse of the Conqueror.

First you must be broken.

Old boy dont break easy. Bearded dread and built to take punishment, a redeye bluegum twohead man what live in a frugal manner in a little house perched on stilts in a riverside park by the Mississippi.

Oldschool park, more woods than park, I man often seen walking through the underbrush and the cramped little streets of the colored community that sprawl along the river there.

Riverside its called and inordinately proud of its local conjure-man. Feel like he give them a flavor not too many neighbor-hoods can claim.

Live out there in the woods like a wildman, the Queen Mother tell visitors from neighborhoods with fewer blessings. Classic neighborhood busybody what live at the mouth of the park in a little gingerbread house next to the Riverside Baptist Church; warm months you see her on her front porch, watch-ing over the neighborhood and that bridge connect the park to the city, the one cross the expressway leading downtown.

I see him most every day, she say. Since he come home from the war, she say. No baby no, Vietnam, she say. Grew up over on Fay Street, Corinna Conquers firstborn. Come back whole to the eye but he move out there into that park and he been there ever since. The more gullible folk round here tell you he been there since the Civil War, but you know how that is, some folk believe what they want to believe. You want to know the truth, you come see me. Truly, she say, nodding just so. Look, baby, see, that light there between the trees, thats where the High Hoodoo stay. In a house on stilts. So he can see.

2nd Movement
listen, o ye firstborn, to the geas of rickydoc, and I will give you a mission greater than your adversity, I will give you a destiny

Somebody killing hoodoos. All over Memphis, hoodoos com-ing up dead.

Margarite run her finger around the edge of her glass and lick at the salt. Two of them in a week, she say.

Lt. Douthet she called by everybody else. Memphis Police Dept. Soon to be captain. Ive had a schoolboy crush on her since we were about ten, I guess. Known her since I can remember, our fathers had been in practice together. Some forty, fifty years later, one wife, two husbands, many loves, we still claim besties, more or less.

Been doing this margarita run for a couple of decades now, just one, chips, salsa, conversation. Our respective doctors probably wouldnt approve but some things are sacred, dont you think, specially when it include murder most foul. So we sitting there in Mollys and Im bracing myself. Its gon be awkward. May not know everything, like some folk claim, but I know this gon be awkward.

Jubilation T. Conquer. Thats me. Most folk call me Jubal, some call me Jubilation. Some folk call me Dr. Conquer, some flat out call me the Conqueror. Then there some call me the High Hoodoo, the High Hoodoo of Memphis, but those in the know, know that aint so. The High Hoodoo a hidden hoodoo, live over there in the park somewhere, like some kind of urban legend. What I am is the Finder of Lost Things. Closest thing Memphis has to a hoodoo detective. You name it, its lost, I will find it. Ive helped the police find things before. Money, papers, bodies, felons, reputations, things like that.

Three, I tell her. Old Man Rivers wasnt as well known, but for those in the know, he was one of the best.

I brace myself. She doesnt like it when I know more about her crime sprees than she does. But what does she expect. Somebody come to my town and start killing off hoodoos, Ima take it personal.

She give me the look. One of many she has perfected over the years. When did you plan to tell me, she ask.

When I had something for you, I tell her. Honestly, I say, honestly. I only put it together yesterday. Yesterday Im thinking there is a pattern here. Next thing I know you call.

Old Man Rivers had been poisoned Monday. His own blend of Cudjoes Freedom, named after Loyal Cudjoe, who was told back in 1842 that he would be freed upon his masters death. Tuesday Mama Joy shot. Nine times in the heart. Nine. Hoodoo Prime. Nine. Wednesday, Papa Nod, hit and run. A hearse. A fucking hearse. Somebody playing games.

Old Man Rivers I took personal. Homeless hoodoo, just as harmless as he could be. Played his little out-of-tune guitar for the tourist types on Beale. Never made much money doing it that I could see, but I guess it was enough. Beale Streeters had adopted him, natives and tourists, cops and hoodlums, players and civilians, everybody dug Old Man Rivers, fed him, clothe him, old boy living off the fat of the land. Every time I see him he call himself giving me advice, some of which was actually useful. Cant imagine anybody want to do him harm. Others either, for that matter.

Margarite brought out a file and threw it on the table. I went thru it. Margarite prefer I not officially be on the case. She prefer I not come to the office unless necessary. They like my batting average but they dont think much of my procedures. I knew she knew when she ask for a table. Otherwise we would have sat at the bar. But the bar is not private. Everybody there would have had an uninformed opinion to offer.

The file is sparse. Details, bodies, witnesses. Not a lot to go on and nothing about Old Man Rivers. Still early but I know they have more than this. I will get Shine to access their case files. MPD not as digital as they should be, which make it difficult sometime to track them, difficult but not impossible.

For the moment I will work with what they give me. I note the names and addresses of the witnesses, such as they are, more like commentators than witnesses. I spiritvision the crime scene shots to see if maybe I see something the police techs hadnt, but those dead bodies fucking with my head. My friends, my colleagues. I take a couple of photos with my cell phone. She act like she dont see.

I can tell without looking she still irritated. What else is new. Pretty much any time of day she irritated. I take what notes I need and hand the files back to her. Told her Im on it. Most often she have to push me, get me to focus. This time no problem. This time its personal.

Anything else I need to know, I ask her.

You tell me, she snap, you supposed to be the bigtime hoodooman in this town.

I dont respond in kind. She stressed, Im stressed, everybody stressed. She leave money for her drink and say she got to go but then she hesitate. You should be careful, she say. I know where this is going but its like her way of apologizing, I let it play out.

Its all highs, she say, no bushwizards, no wannabes, all high hoodoos. Not that many of you, she say, sooner or later, whoever killing them will get around to you.

I nod cool like Oscar Brown say do, like that dont faze me, you know. But soon as she leave I pull out my cell phone with the quickness. Papa Joe wasnt home, I leave a message for him to call me, defcon2. Dont want to leave it on his phone, best I talk to him personal. Papa Joe one of those folk live out there cross from Voodoo Village.

Even I dont know whats going on out there in that compound behind that gate, what with all those folk art sculptures, all those crosses, Xs, and masonic such and such. My mama knew ole boy Walsh Harris, say he was a regular fellow once upon a time, work for the post office, she say, but once they got up there in that compound they shut out the world and withdrew from the human condition. That how my mama called it, withdrew from the human condition, I think about that sometime. Im not quite sure what she meant. Wish I could still ask her.

What I do know its the folk around them that pull guard duty, that call down spirits start whistling at you if you drive up in there wrong, whistling you not welcome here. They not the kind of folk you want to rile up unnecessarily. Best I catch Papa Joe when I catch him.

Wanganegresse pick up but she in the midst of canvasing for Obamas reelection. Told her call me as soon as you can, somebody killing hoodoos. I name the dead.

She pick up the significations right away. Ask me if I had called the others. Then she call a Gathering of the Hand. Tomorrow, she say, the Hole in the Wall. I agree. She say she will call me back soon as she thru gathering souls for Obama.

I caught up with the Dancer and she say she will be there. Say she will tell Ma Grace. I tell her, no, bring Ma with you. Otherwise Ma Grace, she might be there, she might not. Ma Grace closest thing I know to a hoodoo queen, but she prickly. Very prickly.

Last time I spoke to her she jack me up. Said I tell too many secrets. Say the bushwizards, they just want to do the hoodoo they have read about. Problem is, by the time somebody has written it down, weve moved on. Not our job, she say, to keep them schooled.

Unfortunately, I think it is. Cant have them running around doing slaverytime hoodoo and calling it power. But Ma Grace you got to deal with her real gingerlike. Better the Dancer than me. I call Papa Joe back and tell his machine whats what.

Blind Mary I dont have a number for. Blind Mary off the grid. Thats the way she roll. She say she the grid. I go to her spot on Beale, little hole-in-the-wall hoodoo shop across from Handy Park. She claim that statue of Baba Handy holding his horn got power like nothing she know and thats why she set up there, she say. Make her readings more powerful to know Baba Handy watching over her, she say. Help her see, she say.

But her place not open, no surprise, its just midday and Beale lying in wait for sundown, when the neon rise. I like new Beale, not as much as old Beale, but it will do. The old Beale Ave was a big playground when I was growing up. By night it was a redlight district, haunted by the blues. By day it was the heart of professional Black Memphis, my father had his office there, my godfather, Ike Watson, did too. It was Ike took me, eleven, twelve, something like that, to Tri State Bank to open my first bank account. I sit there with Brer Handy and consider my next move.

I check my watch, kinda late to be running down witnesses. Im tired, like Im weary in my bones, Im going home. Last house on Riverside, or first, depending on your perspective, right up on Parkway. I sit on the porch for a moment, contemplating the ways of the universe and stroking a purring Serenity while watching Riverside Park go dark. Martin Luther King Park its officially called, but folk in the neighborhood call it Rickydocs Roost, haunt of the High Hoodoo.

Just another playground when I was growing up, more woods than park, blackfolk werent allowed then, the golf course, the clubhouse, the archery range, the rotunda on the river thats still there if you know where to look.

Might be blackfolk werent allowed but how you gon police the woods from kids grew up alongside it. Whitefolk had the fixed-up areas, the rest belonged to us, and when I see it I see it the way it was, before the subdivisions and the expressway cut it up. Oshuns Porch. Our gateway to the river. Entering it had been like crossing over into another dimension. I dont know about multiverses but I do know dimensions.

I notice a broken bottle on my frontyard bottletree. When I first put it up, the neighborhood kids would chunk rocks at it. Now they leave it alone. Over time they have come to understand. Now their children understand. Must be four, five bottletrees on this block alone. Storm wind only thing break bottles now, when Oya feel, for some reason, she need to pull my coat.

It was my father built the first bottletree I recall. First bottletree in Memphis far as I know. Folk remember him as the eminent Dr. Conquer, but he had started out as a country doctor making housecalls on farms in Arkansas, produce payments in the back of that Valiant station wagon.

I recall when he was dying and young doctors on the hospital staff come to his room, he damn near comatose, they tell him the tests say this, this, and this, doc, what should we do next you think, and I remember all these folk from across the bridge in their country finery, sprinkling him with holywater, chanting and such, talking about how he was a full-service doctor.

Apparently referring to his willingness to use folk remedy when called for. I guess. Cant imagine him going no deeper than that. South Memphis joke: *Half the babies born in South Memphis still belong to Doctor Conquer, because they havent been paid for.*

Call myself walking in his footsteps. He took care of their bodies, I take care of their souls.

Took me with him the evening he planted bottletrees all four corners, and if he believed they keep evil at bay, so do I. Most folk hear hoodoo they thinking slaverytime hoodoo, folk magic hoodoo, spells, hells, and blackcat bones hoodoo.

About one hundred years out-of-date hoodoo. Cutting edge of hoodoo long since moved into high magic: making real into the world that which was not. *Awaken the sleeper, protect the weak, guide the strong.*

As you probably know, bottletrees are Congo theology, keep evil spirits off your property, out of your life. They get distracted by the sun glinting off that colored glass, get caught up in those bottles. Wind just so and you hear them ask to be let free into the world.

Oldschool yes, but some oldschool worth keeping. Im replacing the broken bottle when I notice another one broken. What the fuck. Then I notice the wind has gone still on me, the earth bracing itself, another storm out of the Gulf, big one. Probably cost me another bottle but I dont mind Oya taking her due. Bottles replaced and still some light, Im antsy, I decide to walk to Blind Marys. She live on the other side of Riverside Drive. I anchor one side, she anchor the other. I decide walkabout clear my head.

First thing I see, no wash on Frankie Lees line. Sundried mean she good. Grief mean the drier, mean Johnnyboy on the prowl, mean she dont feel like being bothered. This is not a good sign.

On the corner of Person, where the bridge cross the expressway downtown and connect the park with the city, I see the elders of Memphis gathering on the porch of the Queen Mother and this reassure me somewhat. The well-regulated neighborhood is not one thats free of stress, but one that is . . . well . . . regulated. I wave in passing but Queen Mother Miriam bestow a blessing upon me and I wonder why she think thats necessary.

Generally walkabout compose me, but this evening Im unsettled. Things that generally ease me—folk sitting on their porches, nodding good evening, the warm light of shaded windows—today they dont do me.

I pass Outer Parkway and its like a ghosttown and I remember it pre-integration, a vibrant commercial strip. Generally Im in a magical state of mind, but today I see the hood for what it really is. No mythic space, no folkloric holyground. Just a tired little innercity neighborhood, modest little houses and barebones yards, little streetcorner businesses and ghost-town streets upon which I sense a gathering of restless haints and I believe maybe thats what the Queen Mother was trying to tell me. The boys of Fort Pillow are stirring.

That generally mean war of some sort. But I dont feel like war. I try to turn away but the premonition is fed by the arrival of Ida B. and the once familiar sensation of the Conqueror coming down on me. I feel power nestling, but all around me I got folk struggling to make it, hitting straight licks with their crooked little sticks, this brutal grind of stunted potential we call black life in America. What right have I to disrupt such fragile little lives.

It was Zora Neale claim the Conqueror was a slaverytime hoodooman helped blackfolk escape by tricking ol Massa. It was Zora Neale say when the slaves was free, the spirit of the Conqueror withdraw into the conquer root, prepared to return whenever blackfolk in need. Thats what Zora Neale say.

Ask her yourself if you dont believe me.

In my youth I was a sorcerer. By God I was a man of power. Plan then was to forge blackfolk into a conquering horde and fling them into battle. Everybody in the world was just pieces on the Board.

One day my mentor, Babajohn Killens, the great griot master of Brooklyn, pull me aside and he say, Young Jubilation, you a brilliant force. But with a little compassion you could be profound.

All I heard was brilliant. That was before cocaine and heartbreak disabuse me of any notion of power. Before reality buke, buse, and scorn me. Drove me back to the Delta with my tail tucked firmly between my legs. Now Im just a finder of lost things and the only thing certain is that depending on me is not a good strategy. For anybody. You, them, anybody fool enough to believe in me.

Who am I to think I could found a Way.

By the time I get to Blind Marys, Im alert, my spiritvision is on, Im battleformationed. I notice immediately that her door is not fully closed. That dont strike me correct. Not Blind Mary. Her little shotgun house look skull empty.

On the porch I call out to her, but she dont answer. I push the door in. Just as cautious as I can be. She sitting there in her sitting chair, TV on, Michael Duncan in a jail cell being magical. Look like she watching but she stone-cold dead. Reason still coiled in her lap. Water moccasin, viper, something, I dont know my snakes, but I do recognize when the damn thing lift up and look me in the eye.

Vibrant in life, in snakebit death Blind Mary a washed-out still life. I back away without disturbing the snake. Wasnt like I was no Marie Laveau. I call the police, and an ambulance, just in case, but I know dead when I see dead. I sit on the front porch to wait. Far end, eye on the door, just in case.

Blind Mary and I werent close. We were colleagues, traded little rituals of respect whenever we crossed paths, but I dont know her like I know, for instance, Wanganegresse or Papa Joe. That dont mean I dont like her. Im a hermit by nature and profession. I dont get close to nobody.

But Blind Mary I liked. Blind Mary I respected. She was

seventy-four years old and still getting around, still sharp, still doing her hoodoo thing. She had been the salt of the hoodoo earth and whoever killed her was going to have to answer to me.

I am the Conqueror.

You need me, you call me. I will come.

A GAME OF LOVE

BY SUZANNE BERUBE RORHUS

East Memphis

"Another glorious day in paradise," Cookie Shay said, descending the main staircase and entering the foyer. She wore her tennis whites, as she did most mornings. Sometimes she even played.

Justin scrutinized her appearance. Her flawless makeup and carefully styled hair were at odds with her sporty attire. "Are you heading to the club?" he asked.

She sighed. "I'm carrying a tennis racquet, Justin," she said. "Of course I'm going to the club. Where else could I go dressed like this?"

To the cheating side of town, he mused, hearing the Eagles song in his head. Aloud, he said, "And which of your young fellows will be your doubles partner today?"

She favored him with a smile that almost reached her eyes. "Well, bless your heart, Justin! Are you feeling all fragile-like?"

He didn't answer. A man had a right to feel fragile if he thought his wife was looking to step out on him.

Cookie kissed his cheek. He gave a discreet sniff as her floral perfume wafted over him.

"Sugar, you know I only have eyes for you. By the way, don't forget we're having dinner with the Jackmans tonight."

"Why can't we just stay home? I hate having to make small talk at dinner."

She blew him a kiss as she crossed to the front door, nodding perfunctorily at the uniformed maid who handed her a coat. Her cherry-red Audi convertible waited in the portico in front of the home, its motor idling. "Six o'clock, Justin. Try not to stay late at the office."

After the door shut behind his treasure, Justin continued into the kitchen where his breakfast and newspaper were waiting. He knew his wife had married for love—the love of money. They'd struck a bargain that suited them both—his wealth purchased her beauty. They'd been happy enough for years.

He'd been so proud of his young, athletic wife, smiling tolerantly when his friends ribbed him about robbing the cradle for his obligatory second marriage. She was only twenty years younger than he; it wasn't as if he'd married a child.

Last year, though, he'd become aware of a certain distance on her part. In public, she still laughed at his jokes, held onto his arm, and deferred to his wishes. But in private, she now expressed an independence that he found both worrisome and annoying.

She'd begun to change last February, during the annual US National Indoor Tennis Championships, held at the Racquet Club of Memphis. Cookie had volunteered at the tennis tournament for as long as he'd known her.

"You want the cherry preserves this morning, Mr. Justin?" the maid asked. He grunted. He always wanted the cherry preserves. Why did they have to have this conversation each morning? Despite the troubled economy, it was difficult to find a decent maid willing to work full-time without living in. Justin insisted the staff went home each night so they could have their privacy. He wanted Cookie to himself whenever possible.

Cookie's volunteer position for this year's tournament involved seeing to the needs of the players. "Player liaison" was a critical position in the tournament hierarchy. Cookie was thrilled to be entrusted with the responsibility and crowed about her significant "promotion," as if that word could be applied to a volunteer job. The US Indoor attracted the top talent in the tennis world each year as well as a fine roster of up-and-coming players.

Up-and-coming players with youthful, hard, athletic bodies, legions of fans, and a sexy self-confidence with which Justin (and his burgeoning potbelly) couldn't compete. Many of them also sported foreign accents that increased their appeal with their fans. And with Cookie. Justin could tell. He knew his wife better than she thought he did.

One player from Spain had been Cookie's pet project last year. Enrique and Cookie were inseparable during the week-long tournament. Cookie hosted a party in his honor at their home after he won a place in the semifinal competition. She'd paraded Enrique in front of their friends while Justin had seethed. He'd been pleased when Enrique lost his semifinal match by a large margin, due in no small part, he was sure, to the hangover the young man must have suffered in Cookie's care.

He dunked his cherry-laden toast point into his coffee. This year's tournament, scheduled to start next week, would be different. Justin wouldn't leave Cookie's side. He'd already alerted his staff at the bond division of First Tennessee Bank of his intention to watch the entire tournament with his season tickets rather than only attending the evening matches. The staff would have to placate his clients while he protected his most valuable investment, Cookie.

* * *

Cookie spent the week prior to the tournament at the Racquet Club, tied up in meetings that kept her out long after Justin returned home each evening. If he'd wanted a working wife who was too busy to cater to him, he'd have kept his first marriage, Justin mused. Still, he forced himself to refrain from upbraiding her. The US Indoor only came once a year, mercifully, and Justin could allow Cookie her little indulgences.

"How's this year's crop of players?" he asked her Saturday over a rare lunch at home. Cookie preferred to make reservations rather than food, so the meal consisted of leftovers from last night's visit to Folk's Folly Prime Steak House.

"Lovely!" she enthused. "It's been so exciting watching them qualify. I can't wait for the first round to start Monday, can you?"

"Mm," he said. "Can't wait. Any players in particular seem like they'll do well?" He watched her face carefully, looking for signs of deceit. If she had her eye on any tennis boy-toy, he wanted to know as soon as possible. He'd let the situation get away from him last year. He wouldn't make that mistake again.

"Well, there's a Norwegian I think will do well. I watched him today." Her gaze dropped to her plate, appearing to search for something within the spinach soufflé.

So the Norwegian would be this year's threat. "What's his name, darling?"

"Trygve" she answered. "Isn't that the cutest name you've ever heard?" She pronounced it again, slowly, "Trigg-va."

"Cute all right. How's he ranked?"

"He's not even ranked in the top tiers," she said. "That's what's so excellent. He's going to be a total surprise. He's won a few tournaments in Norway, but nothing outside that country. Still, he won his qualifying match easily today. We should host him, don't you think? He's staying at the Doubletree next to the club, but I imagine he'd be so much more comfortable with us."

Justin thought about this. He was a proponent of the maxim to keep one's enemies close, but to host his wife's crush in his own home again? What would their friends say? That he'd gotten what he deserved for marrying someone so much younger?

"I think it best we leave him where he is," he said. "As the player liaison, surely you can't be perceived as having favorites?"

"Maybe you're right. Let's just plan a party for him after the tournament is over, okay? I know he's going to do well."

"Absolutely," he agreed. "We'll just keep it our little secret until the end, okay?"

Impulsively, she gave him a hug across the table. "You're so good to me," she said.

He gazed into her eyes. "Don't you forget it, baby."

After lunch, they walked across the property, stopping at the horse barn. Nathanial, the stable master, greeted them with his usual somber expression.

"Did the stallion settle in?" Justin asked, clapping a hand on the older man's shoulder.

"Full of energy, but coming along nicely."

"Fancy a ride?" Cookie asked, the twinkle in her eye reminding Justin of the mischievous young woman he'd married. "We won't have much time all this coming week."

Justin agreed and allowed Nathanial to saddle up the stallion and Cookie's roan. They rode to the far reaches of their estate, allowing the horses to ford the stream that separated the pastures. Cookie's horsemanship was as flawless and graceful as her tennis playing. The twilight reflected on her face, emphasizing her beauty. It was chilly for Memphis, with temperatures in the forties, but it was, after all, February.

Spring would arrive in a few short weeks. Justin could wait. He'd always been a patient man.

On the far side of the stream, Cookie and Justin rode to a small cave. The cave itself was an anomaly; the high water table of West Tennessee didn't allow for basements, much less caves. Justin suspected that the "cave" was really a burial mound built by the Chickasaw centuries before. He'd explored such mounds at Chucalissa, the Indian village south of downtown. He had no intention, of course, of allowing archaeologists to invade his property.

He dismounted the stallion and squatted at the entrance to the cave, careful to keep the knees of his trousers out of the dirt. He reached inside and pulled out a half-full bottle of chardonnay.

"Me first!" Cookie said, leaning down from her saddle to reach for the bottle.

With an indulgent smile, he handed it up to her. She uncorked it and took a swig then passed it to him.

The week unwound in its slow, familiar course. Monday morning, Justin descended to his company's gold box on the east side of the court and took his seat. The box was deserted, as he'd expected. None of his fellow partners in the bond division had scheduled any guests today. The big action in the tournament wouldn't occur until later in the week.

Once settled, he consulted his program. Cookie's Norwegian was scheduled for the final qualifying round beginning at eleven a.m. Theoretically, of course, the young man could fail to qualify for the tournament, especially since he was virtually unknown. Justin doubted that would happen, however. Cookie had an instinct for success. If she said the boy had a chance to win it all, she was probably right.

"Justin!"

He glanced up from his program and stood, offering his hand to the sheriff. "Buddy! Good to see you! June," he said to the sheriff's wife, kissing her on both cheeks. "Y'all are here early. Do you watch the qualifying matches every year?"

"Why, we sure do," June said, folding her jacket and placing it on the seat next to her. She and her husband sat in the row in front of Justin. "You're the slacker who only comes for the big matches. And poor Cookie's here practically around the clock."

"Well, someone has to earn a living," Justin said. "And how do you have time to attend all the matches, sheriff? Does crime take a break during the US Indoor?"

Buddy laughed. "Not quite. June usually brings a friend to the daytime matches. I'm just killing time before an appointment later."

Cookie tightened her grip on her clipboard as she dispatched the last volunteer to her duties. Honestly, it was such a nuisance to manage a volunteer staff. The legion of housewives who comprised her hospitality team cancelled commitments at the last minute, chatted when they should be focusing on their jobs, and flirted outrageously with players half their ages.

She glanced at her watch. If she hurried, she could catch Trygve's final qualifying match. She was confident he'd win, but she'd like to be there to provide a bit of emotional support. After all, the guy was only twenty-one, and here he was alone in the USA, competing against some of the top players in the sport.

She intended to ignore the fact that Trygve was slightly younger than she was. No matter. She knew she looked good for her age—slim, athletic, and with the best skin spa treatments could buy. The boy was clearly smitten, and he'd be leaving the country in a week. A perfect friend.

Of course, there was the little matter of Justin to deal with. His devoting an entire week to watch the tournament was unusual and therefore alarming. He couldn't suspect her of having had an affair with Enrique last year. After all, they'd entertained him in their home. She was sure Justin wouldn't have agreed to that if he'd been suspicious.

Dear Justin. He was a good man but not very exciting. When she went out with him and his friends, she felt like a teenager who'd rather sit at the kids' table than listen to the adults drone on about their business affairs.

"Cookie! I am glad to see you."

She turned at Trygve's voice with its sexy accent, a cross between Arnold Schwarzenegger and the Swedish chef from *The Muppet Show*.

Trygve crossed the players' lounge in two strides and grasped her hands. "A kiss for luck?" he said. "I must win this match, or I go home tonight."

Reflexively, she scanned the room to ensure they were alone. Satisfied, she tiptoed to plant a gentle kiss on Trygve's stubble-covered cheek. "Don't worry, you've got this."

He buried his hand in her straight, raven-black hair and tugged her closer, then bent to plant a kiss firmly on her lips. "You will be watching, yes?" His second kiss parted her lips and invaded her mouth.

"Not here, Trygve," she said. "There are too many people with access to this room. My husband can't find out about us." Despite her words, she was unable to resist cupping his angular jaw, then sliding her hand down the sinews of his neck.

"Your husband is idiot to let you leave his side. If you were my wife, I'd have you next to me all the hours of the day and night." He pulled her closer, nestling her against his broad chest.

What a suffocating thought! Cookie shivered. It was bad enough having Justin haunting the tournament this year. At least her connection to Trygve had a time limit. This time next week, he'd be back home in Ålesund, just a fond memory to tide her over until next year's tournament.

"You'd better get ready, and I have work to finish before I can watch the match." She nudged the muscular arms encircling her waist, and Trygve released her. "I'll see you after the match. Good luck!"

He stole another kiss before she made it to the door.

She met him again in the players' lounge after he won his qualifying match in straight sets. Several competitors, early for their own matches, relaxed in the lounge, watching the stadium action on the closed-circuit televisions.

Cookie was putting the finishing touches on the lunch buffet when Trygve swept into the lounge, bristling with excitement. He caught her in a bear hug. "Did you see me?" he demanded.

"Yes, I did, Mr. Nilsson," she said, wriggling free. "We all did. Congratulations!"

He glanced around, seeming disappointed not to be alone with her. "Yes, well. Now I suppose I am qualified. I do not play again until the second match tomorrow. What shall I do with my free time?" The upturned corner of his mouth contained hope and an invitation.

"Mr. Nilsson, if you'll follow me, I will show you the Racquet Club's weight room as well as the spa, in case you wish to book yourself a massage." She led him from the curious glances of the other players.

186 // Memphis Noir

"Trygve, you have to be more discreet," she admonished him once they were in the hall. "You're going to get me in trouble with my husband *and* with the officials." She'd hate to lose her volunteer position at the tournament, but losing her marriage wasn't even an option. Justin wasn't too demanding, as far as rich older husbands went.

"I don't care. I want to celebrate with you. And when I win the whole tournament, I want you by my side when I accept the trophy."

"We'll worry about that later. For now, why don't you go back to the hotel and swim or something? I'll take a meal break around three, and I'll meet you in your room then, okay?" She graced him with a smile promising future favors.

Justin plopped into his seat for Tuesday's first-round matches. June sat in front of him, this time accompanied by another lady. Justin greeted them, and June made the introductions.

"Justin, I'd like you to meet my bridge club partner, Ms. Camilla Barnes. Camilla, this is Justin Shay. He's a bond trader for First Tennessee and has just the loveliest wife."

He took Camilla's hand. Obviously a stay-at-home wife. He could tell a woman's employment status by the strength of her handshake. Businesswomen gave a decent pressure, but the ladies-who-lunch crowd tended more toward a limp hand. Justin never knew if he was supposed to shake it or kiss it. Camilla, with her Talbots dress, coiffed silver hair, and delicate grip, was a lifetime luncher.

They settled in for the first match, an unexpectedly exciting contest between two young American players. Justin tensed when the opponents for the second match were announced.

Trygve.

"Oh, Camilla, you'll like this next fellow," June said to her friend. "Just you wait."

The Norwegian won his first set 6-2. Before the next set began, June took the opportunity to turn and speak to Justin.

"Isn't he marvelous?"

"He moves so quickly for such a massive man," Camilla interjected, "and my goodness, he's got the wingspan of a condor! He can reach just about anything his poor opponent hits at him."

"Yes, he's a marvel," Justin said.

"And I just love his ponytail," June said. "He looks like a Viking, if Vikings wore tennis shorts and carried rackets instead of battle axes."

"Ooh, look, June! He's fixing to change his shirt! Pay attention!"

When Justin left the stadium at the dinner break, he saw that he'd missed a call from Nathanial, his stable master. He returned the call.

"What's up?" he asked. "Is the stallion acting up?"

"No sir, I just called to see if you were on your way out east."

"You know I'm at the tennis tournament with Cookie all week. Why would I be heading home before the evening match even starts?"

"Well, I went to the Belmont to pick up something for my supper," Nathanial said. "And I saw Miss Cookie seated at the bar, holding court with a young man. I assumed you'd be joining her shortly, sir."

Translation: your wife is cheating, and I want to tell you so that you don't lose face. Justin gripped the cell phone tighter. Message understood.

"Oh, she's doing her liaison work," he said breezily. "I expect she'll be back here soon."

* * *

The Belmont Grill was more family restaurant than dive bar, but it was the seamiest place East Memphis had to offer. Still, it at least had a bit of atmosphere. The building was ramshackle-looking without being decrepit, and the lights were kept low. Strings of Christmas lights wove across the ceiling.

Cookie signaled the bartender to bring her another lemon drop martini. Trygve rubbed her knee. "You sure you want another drink? We could leave and make our own party."

"Come on, isn't this fun? I don't want to spend the whole week locked in your hotel room." Like staying with Justin, night after night, trapped in the golden birdcage they called home.

"That sounds good to me," Trygve said, pulling her closer. His ice-blue eyes seemed to pierce her soul, or at least some of her naughtier bits.

She giggled and pulled away. "Well, aren't you sweet? Maybe we'd better go. There are too many people here anyway." She drained her fresh martini while Trygve paid the tab.

She allowed him to rest his arm on her shoulder as they made their way to the exit. The door banged open, and Justin stormed in. He stopped, apparently surprised to encounter them at the door.

"What are you doing here with *him?*" he demanded. "You're supposed to be at the tournament. Your big 'promotion,' remember?"

"Justin, lower your voice! Let's not make a scene!"

But a scene appeared to be precisely what Justin wanted, because he made a big one. By the time Cookie convinced the bartender to cancel his 911 call, hustled the two men out the door, and separated them, she was exhausted. Trygve and Justin had been eager to fight, a ridiculous thought considering the younger man's greater strength.

After a short and silent ride home, Cookie exited Justin's car, not even waiting for him to open the door for her. Before she could storm off to the sanctuary of the guest bedroom, he grabbed her arm and spun her around.

"I won't be made a cuckold," he said.

"Who even talks like that?" she shot back. "Welcome to the modern era. You don't own me, you know."

"Bought and paid for," he said. "Don't you forget it."

She tried a more conciliatory tack: "Look, Justin, I'm sorry you're upset. You have to understand, nothing happened with Trygve and me. We're just friends. Give him a chance, and I'm sure you'll like him too." She touched his chest. "Come on, let's head up to bed."

She was able to lead him to their bedroom. By the time Justin fell asleep, she may even have convinced him of her loyalty.

Justin found his seat Thursday night before the first of the quarterfinal matches began. Buddy leaned back and tapped Justin on the knee, startling him. Justin pasted on a hearty smile and greeted the sheriff and his wife.

"I heard what happened at the Belmont," Buddy said softly. June affected interest in her program. "You come to me if you need to talk, you hear? Don't let this situation get out of control."

He'd been warned, Justin knew. He said nothing.

"He's a cocky S.O.B., I'll give you that," Buddy continued. "You see that interview with him in the *Commercial Appeal?*"

Justin shook his head. Please, God, let the newspaper not have covered Trygve's extracurricular activities.

"That Norwegian boy claimed his name means 'Brave Victory' or some such horseshit and that he was going to win this whole tournament. Doesn't lack for confidence, does he?"

"You sure you want to ride?" Cookie asked. "What if you break your arm? You've got to play tomorrow." She already regretted abandoning her duties. If Justin discovered she wasn't at the tournament, he'd kick her out for sure.

"I won't get hurt. I'm a real American cowboy."

"Okay, if you say so. But you'll have to ride the stallion." She hoped the horse had settled in enough for an inexperienced rider. "You know what, why don't we just head back and watch the tournament? You have a big day tomorrow."

"I am stallion. I am going to have a big day tonight."

Cookie gave up arguing with him and set to work saddling the horse. Nathanial's job, normally, but tonight was his night off. She'd lead the stallion on foot. Considering how the Norwegian clung to the saddle horn, he wasn't ready to ride on his own.

When they returned, she groomed the stallion and stored the tack while Trygve explored the barn. He called to her from the hayloft: "Cookie, come up here!"

She climbed the ladder to the loft and laughed when she poked her head through the opening. Trygve lay sprawled, buck naked, on a horse blanket.

"You hoping for a roll in the hay?" she asked.

"Roll? Yes, come here, and we will roll." He held out his hands invitingly and Cookie joined him, though she knew the hay would be unbearably dusty and itchy. Trygve had great enthusiasm and energy for everything he did, whether it was playing tennis or making love.

Afterward, he propped himself up and brushed her hair back. "You are beautiful, and you are mine. Leave tonight, and come with me."

She turned to him, eyes wide. "Trygve, I can't. You know that. I have a very comfortable life here. I can't just throw it all away."

"You can because you love me."

"Look," she said, searching for the words to explain. "This is like a summer romance."

"It is winter."

"Granted, but my point is this is just a holiday romance. Haven't you had fun while you're here? Just think of all this," here she gestured to include their naked bodies, "as part of our famous Southern hospitality."

He scowled. "I am a toy for you? I want you to come to my home."

"You knew I was married," she said. She sat up and gathered her clothes, pressing them to her chest.

"You do not love him." He said this as if it mattered.

"I love the life we have together, Trygve. I have no intention of leaving my husband to join forces with a tennis hopeful. What kind of security is that?"

"When I win, I will earn big prizes."

"And if you get injured, what's your backup plan?" She slid into her panties and slacks. They were covered in hay, but there was nothing she could do about that now.

He looked genuinely puzzled. "I do not need a backup plan. Tennis will not be over for me."

She fastened her bra behind her. "You are so immature, Trygve."

He sprang to his feet, naked, and grabbed her shoulders. "Do not call me this. You make love to me, but it is only a game to you?" He shook her. "I will tell your husband about us, and you will lose everything."

He shoved her, knocking her off her feet. Trygve loomed, a wild look in his eyes, and Cookie realized how little she knew of this man-child.

She scrambled up and seized a pitchfork from the floor.

Trygve laughed. "Come! Are you going to hit me? You love me."

She circled him. "Leave. I don't want to see you again."

He rushed her, forcing her to step back. "You will leave with me. We can stay at my hotel. I will win the tournament for us." He grabbed for her hand.

Cookie drove him back. The torrent of sounds that streamed from his mouth were presumably Norwegian expletives.

He tried to grab the pitchfork's handle, but Cookie aimed it at his bare chest. Trygve narrowed his eyes. "Bitch!"

She lowered the pitchfork to a more sensitive target, and Trygve took another step back. Cookie didn't notice the open trapdoor until Trygve's right foot landed on empty air.

The stallion in the barn below shrieked, and Cookie heard the tattoo of its hooves. When she looked down, she saw Trygve's crumpled body. She glanced at her shaking hands and dropped the pitchfork.

She needed a plan, fast.

This was all Justin's fault. If he weren't such a control freak, she wouldn't have to sneak around. If he were someone she could love, she wouldn't want to sneak around. If he went to jail, she could do as she pleased.

That was a plan.

Cookie glanced at her watch. The evening's match should have ended by now. Justin would be home soon. He wouldn't waste time, as he called it, socializing.

Okay, she had to focus. She began noting what needed to be done. One: finish dressing. Two: grab Justin's work jacket from the house and put it in the barn. Three: hustle to the tournament and help close up for the night, making sure to greet as many people as she could. Four: establish a story explaining how Justin and Trygve ended up in the barn. Five: explain Trygve's nudity.

"Cookie? Are you in here?" Justin's voice called from the barn door.

She swore and grabbed her shirt and pulled it over her head. Swearing again, she pulled it back off and turned it right-side out and put it on again.

"Oh, honey," she called from the hayloft, "wait for me downstairs. It's been horrible!" Her tears took little effort to manufacture.

By the time she scrambled down the ladder, dusty and disheveled, Justin had discovered Trygve's body. His very dead and very naked body. He'd also secured the stallion into its stall.

Justin turned to Cookie. She found his silence unnerving.

She spun him a tale, a tale of her plying her liaison duties by showing Trygve a real American stable. Of encouraging him in his tennis career. Of getting him an hour or two away from the high-stress tournament atmosphere.

In her version, Trygve said he'd discovered an old trunk in the hayloft. "I just wanted to know what was in it," she said, in tears, "but when I got up here, he raped me." She lifted her sleeve to show Justin the marks where Trygve had gripped her.

"Help me! We'll drape his body over one of the horses and take him up to the cave. No one will ever know. And then we'll burn the barn."

Justin's calm frightened her more than anything. "That's

a brilliant plan, Cookie, but listen up. Here's how it's going to be. I'm going to stand by your side. We can make this work. We can't be forced to testify against each other."

He circled Cookie as he spoke, examining her as if she were a particularly troublesome bond issue.

"I don't like the rape story. I won't have our friends looking at you like that. They'll assume you lured him here. Believe it or not, your reputation isn't as unassailable as you might think."

Cookie opened her mouth to protest then thought better of it.

"You're going to quit the tournament after this year, understood? No more 'liaisoning.' No more mixed doubles."

"I don't need your help, you know," Cookie responded. "It's not like I killed him. That sorry hunk of horseflesh you insisted on buying killed him, not me."

"Try to use your head for once," Justin said in that oh-so-patient voice Cookie hated. "I spent the evening watching the tournament with the sheriff and his wife. I bet your whereabouts are less established, am I right?" He didn't wait for an answer. "So we're going to say that I saw you periodically at the tournament and that we even ate a hot dog together during one of the breaks. That way, my alibi covers you too. This one," he said, nudging Trygve's arm with his shoe, "broke into our barn because he's been stalking you. We'll put his clothes down here, like he was waiting for you naked."

He rubbed his hands in satisfaction. "We left the tournament together, came home, found him here when we decided to go for a ride. Got it?"

She nodded.

"By the way, my lawyer will have a postnuptial agreement ready for your signature tomorrow."

Cookie allowed herself to be sent into the house to change. Her golden birdcage, now a tarnished trap, seemed even smaller than before.

MOTHER

BY EHI IKE

Germantown

It's been a few years now, but I'm older. I have spent more time trying to understand it: our culture.

As a girl born into wealth, I've met some interesting people—people who have worked for my father, schoolmates from other wealthy families, cousins, aunts, and uncles. None of them know how to be sane in our environment. None of them understand consideration. They deceive for their own benefit, even my father. I love him, but he's a part of this depleting way of living that I vow to never be a part of. Then there are people like my teachers, who allow themselves to ignore our snide attitudes, shallow souls, and materialistic way of living and help us, hoping to find a heart. Little do they know, most of our hearts were gone the moment we called our nannies *Mama* and grew up to treat them like slaves instead of people.

Lastly, there's Helen.

She doesn't fit into any of the categories; she may have been the most interesting person I ever met. But I never knew her, considering she was my mother and all. My father developed his mailing company, found Helen, and married her, but we never spoke of her side of the family. I was never allowed to ask. So believe me when I say, it is nearly impossible to write about this woman. I was never even told her maiden name.

I know it sounds quite odd to have never understood the

woman who "raised" me, but what needs to be understood is that she never actually did that. The best way to explain is to introduce my childhood.

I was born November 2, in Baptist Memorial Hospital off Humphreys. I've always been a rather independent child—from my parents, that is. My father nearly slept in his suit after long days at work, and Helen was hardly ever around.

As I got older, I attended the most prestigious private schools Memphis had to offer. An award-winning movie was even based on a family that attended my school. They apparently brought in some poor boy from North Memphis, and he later became this famous football player, but I never knew them. I'm fully aware of the blessed—no, that's not the word—spoiled life I lived, and the even more spoiled kids around me. Even after that movie was released, envious parents spat hateful words about that family. They were the talk of the school and soon became the talk of the city, but my parents would have never done what they had. Stories like that don't happen in Germantown.

My whole childhood I had nannies take care of me. Helen never had to be a mother. She never had to change my diaper, cook for me, or take me to school. Housekeepers and a driver took care of that.

The first nanny I can remember was Betty. She was always caring; she's old now, definitely beyond retirement, yet she continues to make these fabulous breakfasts. My favorite was her blueberry pancakes and veggie omelets. I don't understand how I wasn't obese those days. She always helped everyone out, like doing laundry. She would pick up my father's suits and Helen's dresses from the cleaners. She even cleaned the bedrooms, including mine, but she disciplined me too. She never allowed me to leave the house unless my room was tidy and my homework was completed. She was almost the perfect nanny, perfect mother really, but Betty had her own problems. She never married or had children, and now it was too late for her. Looking back, I understand that no one wants to be that old and alone. At times I felt the cooking, cleaning, and taking care of me—all of it kept her going. It gave her purpose, and Betty was the closest thing to a mother I ever had, even when I'd find her with my father's bottle of Gran Patrón. My father soon caught on, but he appreciated Betty. By this point, she was family, and he could never fire her, so he hired Stacy.

Stacy was much younger than Betty and always helped me with clothes I wanted to wear for school and with boys I had crushes on. She came into my life when I was about thirteen, and I have appreciated her ever since. The only problem with Stacy was she would rarely arrive on time, and if she did, she would fall asleep, sometimes while making my lunch on the weekends. There were many times I saw her sleeping on the living room couch, her head smothered into the cushions as I got ready, but by the afternoon Stacy was perfect. She would help with my homework, and if I went on dates, she would always find the best outfit for me. Sometimes she would even allow me to borrow her clothes. So I had Betty in the morning to fix me breakfasts and Stacy in the afternoon to help with boys. There wasn't much else I could ask for, except for Bill, of course.

My driver was always in my life, and I always called him Bill, never knowing if that really was his name or not. I wasn't certain if he enjoyed his job, but he was always kind, driving me into East Memphis for school and occasionally stopping to take me and my friends to restaurants, when I told my father we were "studying." Bill constantly worked, and though he was considerate, he hardly ever smiled. There was something admirable about his work ethic, but saddening as well.

I can't deny that Betty, Stacy, and Bill played a huge role in my development. Not to say that my father was a bad man, he was just a busy one. He spent most of his time in an office, but he always made an effort to be home for my birthdays, loosening his tie from his cold pale neck as he walked into the kitchen, kissing my forehead and saying, "Happy birthday, love." He attended many of my plays and horse shows too, which was more than I could say for many of my friends' parents . . . and Helen.

It's not that I never saw my mother. She just never saw me. When I was younger, I tried getting her attention. I was a strange kid, putting on shows for my parents of songs I had written or dances I had created. I would do this in the family room with Betty watching with her eyes big in false awe, but Helen would never watch. Her eyes would be moving and all, but mostly as she turned the pages of her *Vogue* magazine, occasionally looking up. That magazine gave her more than I ever could. So, as I got older, I decided I didn't need her attention. I stopped trying, and soon after my father apparently did too.

One day, Bill took us to Houston's off Poplar. It was my father's favorite family restaurant. He announced that he and Helen were filing for divorce and that he would be moving into a condo downtown. I have to admit, it was a surprise. I may not have been happy with my mother, but nothing ever indicated he wasn't.

"So I will be moving in with you, Dad?"

My father was expressionless, as Helen raised her left eyebrow. "You'll be staying with me, of course," she said. "The condo is too small for you and your father."

Now, my mother could have won the mother-of-the-year

award during the first week my father was out of the house. She had Betty and Stacy leave early every day. She drove me to school and had Bill take a break for a few days. I even saw my mother smile, and it looked like a genuine smile—not the one she placed on her face that seemed filled with contempt for the divorce, but one she spread wide with her cocoa-colored cheekbones up to her round brown eyes, just to show she could. But after a week, something changed.

I had just finished my AP US History homework, and it was around six p.m. By this time, dinner was normally ready, but I found my mother sitting at the long glass table out on the patio with a glass of sweet tea. She had been out there all day, and she still hadn't moved and her tea was untouched.

I gently opened the patio door.

"Hey, are we going to make anything for dinner?"

She didn't speak. She didn't turn her head. She just stared at her finger that was getting used to being bare.

"Mother," I said. It felt unnatural calling her that, but I felt she needed to hear it.

"Not now, honey."

I was surprised to hear my mother say that. Her words came out so desperately. I didn't understand how divorce would affect her, but she had been trying to appear strong—not for me, but for herself. My mother needed time. That was all. So I walked back inside and ordered pizza with Stacy.

"She's just grieving," Betty would say the next day, as if she knew something about grief. Maybe she did, but I always pictured her as a lonely soul. Never having anyone to grieve over.

"Yeah, maybe."

I let my mom take a few days off from being a mother, and she spent most of that time on the patio. The following week, I figured it was time. I went out to ask her a homework question.

"Not now, honey," she said.

She got up and walked back inside the house. Had I done this to her? Was I such a burden? I sat in her chair on the patio. I wanted to know how it felt to sit there for hours. I felt nothing but distance from people, from society. Maybe that's what she needed—to sit out there and escape—but she couldn't escape forever.

Helen would sit anywhere now: in the kitchen, in the living room, and in her favorite spot, the patio. As long as that spot was not near me, she seemed fine. But I would still speak to her.

"I need you to sign this form for my school trip to Italy."

"Not now, honey."

"I'm sleeping over at Ashley's tonight. We're going to a concert at FedExForum. What should I wear?"

"Not now, honey."

"Oh hey, Helen. I'm heading out to go snort some coke with a few friends."

"Not now, honey."

I don't know why I hadn't given up on her yet. It wasn't hard to do when I was a child, so I didn't know what made it difficult now. Regardless, I needed that form signed for my class trip. When I walked into the living room, Helen was sitting on the panda-print armchair my father purchased years ago. God knows why.

"Helen, I need you to sign this. Just two words."

She continued to read her magazine.

"Helen, I told you this weeks ago."

"Not now, honey." She said it in the same melodramatic tone every time. So I did what any seventeen-year-old girl would do: I ripped that idiotic magazine out of her hands. She didn't flinch. She just placed her tiny hands in her lap and looked down. I'm not even certain she heard me rip the magazine apart.

"Nothing?"

She didn't move.

I pulled my blue lighter from my pocket and lit the shreds of magazine. It burned quickly, so I dropped it on the white rug and watched the fur burn with it. Helen would not even acknowledge my existence. It was like I was a ghost. And why? My dad?

"Dad's not going to come back. Not with you like this," I said.

Helen got up. I thought, *Wow, I finally got something out of her.* I wouldn't have cared if it was a slap in the face. But no. Instead, she walked past me, almost stepping onto the burning rug, not really looking at anything. It was almost as if she was the ghost.

Betty came in. She was beginning to get tired of my mother's *not nows* as well. "Here, I'll sign it," Betty said with a sharp tone.

"She may have never been a mother to you in the past, but now would be the appropriate time to start." She patted the rug with a rag she had used to clean the kitchen windows.

Weeks passed, and there was no change in Helen. I didn't know what it meant or what to do, but I couldn't live in that house anymore. Knowing she was there disturbed me. I told my father, and he decided it was time to get a house of our own. We moved into a home off Brierview. Betty and Stacy didn't mind. Nothing bothered Bill.

"We're moving in two weeks," I said to Helen one day. "Dad told me he's going to put this house up for sale. You will need to leave."

She remained silent, drinking her tea in the kitchen. I couldn't wait until she left. She was finally going to step outside the house, whether she was ready or not.

"Thank God we're not in that place anymore," Stacy said. "I don't have to watch your mother sit quietly for hours. So unsettling."

I didn't want to think of Helen either, until my father told me that the new owners were ready to move in and needed my mother out. For some reason, he thought I could help.

"Your mother admires you. You might give her some . . . inspiration."

I didn't know how I could inspire her or if my father even believed his own words, but I went back to the house. I looked at Helen. Her head seemed smaller, and her hair was thinner with barely any curls left as she sat in the corner of the living room floor. Chairs did not suit her anymore. The new owners were there too, and they were furious, yelling at her and waiting for me to work some sort of magic to get my mother out of *their* house.

"Helen. You have to leave." I tried being gentle. I didn't know what was wrong, but it seemed far more than my father abandoning her.

Her little head slowly tilted up, still staring at nothing. I noticed the wrinkles around her eyes, but her eyes looked so hopeless. I didn't know someone could appear so old and so young at the same time.

"Mom. Is that what you want to hear? I can call you that if you like." I got no response.

"If she doesn't leave soon, I'm going to call the police." The wife was frustrated, but I could see genuine compassion on the husband's face. At this point, I just needed to see

Helen make a new facial expression. I didn't want her in this catatonic state.

"It's time to go. You can stay with us for a few days." I grabbed her arm, but it quickly slipped through my grip. It felt like a soft gesture, but I knew it took all of her strength to pull away from my grasp.

"I'm sorry, but the police will be here soon," the husband told me.

I turned to Helen to see if she understood; she didn't flinch. "Please don't do this."

"Not now, honey." Her voice was raspy like she hadn't had anything to drink in days.

The police came, and I watched them be kind to Helen and ask her to leave as the wife yelled to throw her in jail. I watched the husband rub his wife's shoulders to calm her, but she immediately jerked away. I watched the police cuff Helen's hands. It wasn't until she got up that I noticed how thin she was. I thought if they had touched her with even the slightest bit more force, she would have shattered. She finally left the house as I had hoped, but not like this.

Helen was placed in a hospital a week later. My father and I were able to see her after her first few days. She was in the cafeteria along with a nurse. Her mouth was so dry that crust had formed around her lips.

"She needs to eat. Why haven't you been feeding her?" my father asked. We could see the outline of every bone in her body.

"She has been refusing for the past two days. We were going to ask your consent to hook her up to a feeding tube later this evening," the nurse responded calmly, as if he was blind to the lack of fat on her body.

"Can you not see? Start her on the feeding tube now!" I

was beginning to get angry. The nurse stared at me, then at my father to see his response. He tucked his chin down, stressing his eyebrows.

"Do it."

"Okay."

"No . . . no." Helen's voice was emotionless. She fought as a male nurse came to escort her out of the cafeteria. But as soon as they reached the door, Helen gasped. Her body no longer struggled. Her eyes glazed over, and my heart sank. The nurses immediately took her away, while my father ran to her screaming and I stood there unable to breathe.

I watched as she allowed herself to die. I wanted to cry, but I couldn't; no matter how many times I tried, my body wouldn't allow it.

We had a funeral for Helen a few days later. We searched for family members to come, but couldn't find any. I didn't understand how my father had married her without knowing anything about her, but whenever I asked, he ignored me.

It was only my father, Betty, Stacy, Bill, and me at the funeral, while a priest spoke fondly of her, saying she had a beautiful soul and a smile as bright as the sun—but he didn't know her. How could he speak of her when she had never stepped foot inside his church? He mentioned how her spirit would be missed. But how could I miss something I never knew?

BATTLE
BY STEPHEN CLEMENTS
Hollywood

Amos leaned his elbows on the rusted sign in the median of North Parkway. He steadied himself, so he could twist the cap off the malt liquor he picked up from the corner store. Selling his mama's things and smoking a rock gave him cotton mouth.

He took no note of the irony that he was coming off his high while leaning on a decrepit *Memphis City Beautiful* sign. Indeed, Memphis was once beautiful, one of the cleanest cities in America. That was a long time ago.

Turning the cap one last time to break the seal, Amos looked over his shoulder when the howl of police sirens roared to life. Two vehicles flew by, lights flashing, and kept going. Whatever got their attention was somebody else's problem. Amos pressed the bottle to his lips and got back to the business of forgetting himself.

Amos Johnson grew up watching drug addicts wander the streets of his neighborhood, and he chuckled at the crazy stuff they would say while trying to con him out of a quarter. His mama told him to never give them a damn cent, because all they were going to do was waste it on more drugs. Years ago, one of his friends cajoled two bums into fighting over a five-dollar bill, and Amos had laughed. He did not remember that last week when he beat up another hobo for a dollar.

His father died when Amos was young, but mama said he was an upstanding Christian man. Mrs. Gladys worked hard to provide and keep Amos away from the wrong crowd, running the streets all night, joining up with gangs. For the most part it worked, and he stayed away from the worst parts of trouble young men get into, except for one epic night when Amos snuck a peek at the wonders of *Perfect 10*, tasted some Fuzzy Navel, and smoked his first hit of weed.

In school, his motto was *Cs get degrees*, but he liked to read and write stories, which got him teased for "acting like whitey." He was a short brother, which meant he got made fun of and beat up a lot. He was awkward, which meant he had no luck with the ladies.

But his life changed in senior year, when the Marine recruiter with a funny mustache set Amos's imagination ablaze with the tales of sex and danger he could have, just like in the books he read, if only he signed up at the MEPS station downtown. He was so excited, Amos begged his mama to let him go. Mrs. Gladys thought it would do him good to serve his country and get out of the ghetto that had already devoured many of his classmates, so off he went, intent on marching to battle under the red, white, and blue.

"Hey, Battle. How you living?" asked Bachs as he slapped a handshake onto Amos, who was standing near the squad car. Officer Bachs was a blond giant of a man who dwarfed Amos in every respect: height, stature, and respectability.

"You know, same day, different shit," said Amos, his voice cracking. Coherent speech was not a common trait of crackheads, and Amos was no exception, but around Bachs he made an effort. Amos never could say why his demeanor changed when his "battle buddy" from Iraq showed up; maybe it was that Bachs had known Amos when he was a real person, before he became this chewed-up image of a man. Bachs still served as an infantryman in the reserves and saw some action in the war, but with the rough upbringing he'd had, war hadn't phased him.

Amos had found only trouble waiting for him in the military. He served as a human resources clerk, but in the military, HR duty meant it was safer for everybody else to stick him behind a desk, where the only thing Amos could screw up was paperwork. Being a desk jockey did *not* make him feel like one of the few and the proud.

Before his unit based in Camp Pendleton deployed to Iraq, he met a girl named Tanisha, who happened to be from the projects next to where Amos grew up. She'd moved to the military base with her husband, but they'd divorced because he was violent. Amos wasn't violent; Tanisha said he was sweet. She said he just needed an older woman to take care of him, and Amos agreed.

Amos remembered his platoon leader giving his men a lecture one Friday, something about being careful with the women around the base who looked at Marines as a paycheck-in-waiting. Those words bounced off Amos, and just a week before deployment he got the good news Tanisha was pregnant with his baby. He was excited to be having a son (Tanisha said she could tell the sex, just as she did with her first two), to have a woman who loved him, and he planned to save up his combat pay for a wedding worthy of his future wife. While Tanisha insisted on getting married before he deployed (so they could get extra money from the military), Amos paid her no mind, because he wanted to do the wedding right: his mama would be there, it would take place in a pretty church, and there would even be a chocolate fountain at the reception.

Just two months into his eight-month tour, Amos took a break from the stifling heat and made a trip to the USO tent. He couldn't wait to check his in-box: he hoped the next e-mail from his fiancée was something sweet or sexy. He logged on and saw a new message from her and instantly clicked it.

There was a picture attached! Amos watched it slowly download. Care packages in the mail were awesome, but the thing that kept service members motivated were pictures of hot, appreciative women from back home. The picture loaded little by little, and he soon saw Tanisha's eyes flashing all sexy-like. *Aw yeah.*

Then he noticed the two dicks pointed at her mouth. *Cudda bn u,* read the caption.

From a furious string of e-mails and phone calls to folks on his company's rear detachment, Amos heard that his fiancée had been screwing every guy she could find. Their joint bank account (where all his checks went) was cleared out. There were pictures of her grinding on dudes all over MySpace.

The only woman he had ever loved (and had sex with) had left him, and he could not do a thing about it. He was in the middle of the desert: there was no quick drive for a *Baby, come back* plea. There was no making her look him in the eye to say she didn't love him. He didn't want to kill himself, but he wouldn't be mad if an incoming mortar got lucky.

Even though alcohol was forbidden for deployed Marines, Amos found it, at least until his platoon sergeant found him. When he got back to the States, he earned a DUI, lost his rank, then popped hot on a drug test. Amos used to chuckle when he processed the paperwork to kick out a Marine who showed positive for marijuana, but he didn't laugh when he saw his own packet. Most guys who tested positive made excuses, but not Amos. When he popped hot, he didn't try to hide it.

210 // MEMPHIS NOIR

His commander, his sergeants, his mama, and his friends dumped on him. Bachs was the only one who stuck by him.

"You hungry? I brought some sandwiches," Bachs said, handing over two plastic bags.

Amos took the sandwiches. "Thanks, Battle. Mama kicked me out again."

Bachs's eyebrows rose. "I thought she kicked you out a long time ago."

Amos shrugged as his bony fingers worked through one of the sandwich bags. "Well, I had left some stuff there and went back, but she told me to get to steppin'. Now I ain't got nothin' to sell. Nothin' to sell, nothin' to eat."

"You want me to drop you by the Union Mission?"

Amos shook his head. "Naw, man. They don't like me down there. Keep tellin' me to get right with Jesus and stuff. I ain't got time for that."

Bachs nodded. He wished his friend would take a step in any direction except the wrong one, but Amos never listened. After a moment, Bachs pulled out a small slip of cash and palmed it over. "Now, you're not going to spend this all on bur-uh, right? Remember, food is a good thing. Water too," Bachs said, trying to pass off chastising Amos as a joke.

Almost violently snatching the crumpled dollar bills out of Bachs's hand, Amos stopped himself from being outright rude. He never treated Bachs like this, and he wasn't about to start. "Thanks, man. You take care now."

Before Amos could leave, Bachs asked, "Hey, Battle, got a question for you. You heard anything about a girl gone missing?"

"You know where I live, right?"

"Nah, I mean have you seen *this* girl?" Bachs asked, flashing a picture of a teenage black girl. She was not particularly attractive, with straightened, pseudo-blond hair and a pudgy face. "Her mom called her in as missing two days ago. They live in your area. Crime usually starts close to home, you know."

"Cracka, you know all black folks look alike," Amos said, smiling.

"Right. But you will tell me if you see her, right?"

"A'ight," Amos said as he turned away. He never liked it when Bachs asked him to snitch on people who broke the law. Amos never knew when those same people would be his only fix.

Amos bought a pack of Twizzlers with part of the money this time. He blew the rest on crack and a forty to wash it down. Promise kept.

He walked out of the abandoned house that his dealer's gang had taken up in, a fresh bag of rock in his hand. He walked to the side of the house where the streetlight didn't shine, even though he could have smoked up right there. This was the Backyard Posse's block, and they kept it tight. Since Amos gave them all his money, he was a'ight by them. He was still a crackhead, though, to be made fun of, slapped around, humiliated.

Amos hooted as he fumbled with his glass pipe, the tiny metal screen already crunched into place, and his lighter, which he hoped had enough fluid to light his world up one more time. He almost dropped the rock as he put it into the pipe, but he got it. The lighter sparked, the fire danced.

The smoke streamed into his mouth, and his lungs went numb as that familiar feeling crept in. It felt like his entire body buzzed, as if every nerve vibrated with every shock and tingle of experience imaginable. The rock let off the smell of burning aspirin and baking soda. One minute later, his stomach turned sick, and he began vomiting uncontrollably for far longer than the fun part of the ride.

After the high wore off, Amos found himself on all fours, searching in the grass of the unkempt lawn. Crackheads know when they are out, but just maybe he'd dropped some when he was on another planet. Lucky for Amos, he'd brought a forty to even out the comedown.

When he heard a loud scream coming from the front of the house, Amos backed against the wall, his left hand protectively cradling the forty. It was a girl's scream. Inching toward the front of the house, he peered around the corner through one bloodshot eye to see two thugs from the Backyard Posse dragging a girl into the crackhouse. She almost broke free, but one punched her in the back of the head, rendering her silent. Amos watched as they tossed the limp girl through the door.

He sat trembling, clutching close to his heart the only vice he had left to blot out his conscience.

With the hum of the police radio crackling and then going quiet for a moment, Officer Bachs's partner sniped, "Man, you must take building contacts seriously to hang out with that reject. I mean, I know we have to deal with scum, but that guy? He smells worse than shit!"

The chatter on the radio kicked back on, but Bachs paid it no mind. "Yeah, but Amos gets around. And he was a battle buddy, you know?"

"Oh, come on! Even his mom said he's just a crack pipe looking for a rock."

"No, I guess you don't know. We went through training together, to Iraq together. Looked after each other," Bachs said, knowing that the time when his friend could look out for anybody, even himself, was past. "You know?"

In those desperate moments of coughing agony that wracked his body when the crash came, Amos always remembered the worst he ever felt in his life. When he found out that no-good woman ran around on him, it hurt him so bad that all he wanted was revenge.

Amos got back stateside only two years into a five-year contract, so he got himself kicked out. She was banging some piece-of-shit Navy boy back in Memphis, and he decided to kill them both.

After getting dropped outside the base gate and told to not come back, he set out to find the whore. He hitched a ride back home and found her mama's house, where he planted his feet on the porch of her unit at the housing project.

"Hey, Tanisha! Yo' man is back. Git yo' skank ass out here!" Amos yelled under the midday sun.

Silence. A couple kids around the project yard stopped playing and stared.

"Tanisha, I know you home, 'ho! Git yo' ass out—"

The door creaked open.

A'ight, he thought to himself, *go time.*

The woman peering at him was not Tanisha. It was her mama, giving him a drop-dead look perfected over years of experience. "What you want, Amos?"

He had no time for this. "I'm here for yo' daughter, my fiancée. We gots to talk."

Her mother's silent gaze did not move, but her large, round eyes began to glisten.

Anger rose in Amos. "I'm not messing with you, woman. Call Tanisha, and tell her to get her ass out here. I got words for her." He readied himself, minding the gun in his pocket. He was ready for that Navy piece-of-shit lover of hers too.

"Amos, go home. She ain't here. She dead, boy. My baby girl is dead. She ain't gonna be botherin' you no mo'. God bless you, Amos," she said, closing the door.

He stood there, stunned. The little kids in the courtyard told him she got ate by pneumonia. They went to the funeral last month. She looked real pretty in her dress.

He was mad. He was jealous. He loved that bitch. He was gonna jack her up for how she hurt him. He was gonna make her cry and say she was sorry. When she did, he would forgive her. He would take her back.

But now he never could. Amos sat on top of her tombstone, rubbing his hands up and down his withered arms. His lips convulsed as he wanted to cry out the words he never got to speak when it mattered, and now could not.

A very human scream broke the night. It was the girl's scream, not far away, but too far for help to come. He used to know what courage was. He used to be a man. He had been trained to kick in doors and take on bad guys. The girl screamed again.

When he woke up and wiped off the morning dew, Amos staggered away from the graveyard behind the church. He stole and sold a little girl's tricycle, carelessly left sitting in a backyard. It took all day to sell it, but now four dollars richer, it was time for a smoke.

He opened the door to the crackhouse and saw three members of the Backyard Posse sitting on busted-up recliners. The leader, a brother named Jamal, sat next to the unconscious body of the girl, lying facedown on the ragged carpet. She was naked, maybe breathing.

They were all high, so Amos got the drop on them, rolling up on Jamal with his handful of dollars. "Hey, man. Got enough for one more."

Jamal scrambled in alarm. "Man, fuck you, bitch. Damn, don't be sneaking up on people like that." He dug around in his hoodie for the goods all the same.

One of the others spoke up: "Hey, snitch nigga. We know you dropped a dime on Trey to the 5-0."

The only thing that could distract Amos from getting a rock was being called a snitch by people who kill snitches. "What do you mean, man? I don't snitch. You know me . . ."

They glared at him. "Bitch, you ain't worth killin'. But we got you. And we got yo' bitch friend, that cop. Next time we see him, we gonna kill him and fuck his dead white ass."

Another barked, "We gonna hit it so hard, his white ass gonna holla!"

As they all laughed, Amos only managed a quiet, "You trippin'."

Jamal piped up, "Naw, nigga, it goin' down tonight. We know when he be 'round here, we know where he go, how to get his ass. We gonna fuck him up."

Amos said nothing, because he still had no rock. Whatever jive they be talking, he needed that rock. Jamal handed it over and smacked Amos in the face when he bent to grab it. Another jumped up to kick him in the ass all the way to the door. He took his beating like a bitch, and they shoved him outside.

Amos didn't know what to do: those guys had murders on their rap sheets. That girl looked bad. The way they talked about Bachs was different from when they just talked shit before. They sounded for real this time.

He grabbed his pipe and started fumbling for a rock. He

pulled out his lighter, maybe good for one more light. He shook so much that the lighter fell out of his hand into the high grass. Clutching the rock to his chest, he dove toward the ground, desperately trying to find his fire. His hand combed the grass, clawed the dirt, only stopping when he felt the sting of a broken needle bite deep.

He pulled his hand back and saw his blood ooze out under the streetlight. For a moment, it reminded him of all that blood Jesus shed for him, like his mama used to talk about.

In that moment, his head cleared. He looked at himself, realizing he wasn't a man anymore: he was just a dirty soul trying to drown in sin. His mama used to love him. Jesus used to love him. Bachs still called him Battle.

Those guys want to kill his Battle. Fuck those guys.

"Hey man, it's my birfday. Lemme share my rock with somebody, wish me a happy birfday." Amos was standing in the half-open doorway to the crackhouse.

"Get yo' stank ass out of here," Jamal said. "You ain't got no cash, we ain't got no time. Now get out, before I shoot you."

One of the thugs felt a twinge of pity. "I gots you," he said, and headed out back.

Amos went to walk through the house to the overgrown backyard, but Jamal yelled, "I said I'd shoot yo' ass! You go 'round, bitch!"

Amos took the hint and headed outside. When he got to the backyard, he saw a silhouette in the dark. "Got a light?"

The thug reached into his hoodie, and Amos sprang like a serpent, grabbing his throat and smashing his head into the busted concrete on the ground. The thug let out a groan, and Amos took the pistol from the guy's pocket, along with his cell phone. And the lighter. Can't forget the lighter. And screw Jamal: Amos went through the back door.

He tactically stalked into the unlit kitchen with the confiscated Cobra and followed the light coming from inside the den. When his first target came into view, he put one round into that thug's chest. When Jamal sprang up, Amos raised the pistol and pulled the trigger, but he got nothing for it. Cobras were crap and jammed like a champ.

Jamal popped a couple caps into Amos, staining his threadbare undershirt with blood. When Amos went down, Jamal started punching.

Amos took it. He was not strong enough to fight back on a good day, much less now. Acting from pure instinct, Amos broke his crack pipe and stabbed that nigga in the throat. Jamal gargled in panic, struggling toward the front door, but it would do him no good. He would bleed out before the ambulance ever got there.

Amos drifted into silence, toward unconsciousness.

Then he heard something that brought him back: it was the girl. With his bloodshot eyes, he saw her screaming, terrified by the carnage. Slowly focusing, he motioned for her to pull him up. She struggled to help, and eventually he was upright again.

Steadying himself on her shoulder, Amos said, "It's okay: I'm a Marine. I protect people. I won't hurt you."

They hobbled out the front door into the street, and Amos pulled out his cell phone.

"911 Emergency, how can we help you?"

Amos coughed. "Hey, I found that missing girl." He handed the phone over, saying, "Tell them where you are, and don't hang up. Ask for Officer Bachs. You'll be a'ight."

Confused, the girl took the phone, but when her rescuer

started limping away, she shouted, "Wait! Where are you going?"

"I got something to settle," he called back, and kept moving.

Officer Bachs sat her down in the car, covering her shoulders with a blanket. There were flashing lights in front of the crackhouse.

"Wait! You got to find him—the guy that saved me! He's going to die!"

"What guy?" Bachs asked.

"The guy . . . He's been shot, the guy who called."

Bachs told his partner he had to check on a potential perp and set off on foot, flashlight on. The blood was easy to follow.

It led behind a church, the one Bachs knew Mrs. Gladys went to every Sunday. Noting that the front door was closed, he moved to check around back. The small cemetery would provide an easy hiding place, so Bachs made straight for it when he saw the back door was locked.

Making his way through the headstones, Bachs's flashlight fell on Amos, lying on a grave. He was shivering, his clothes soaked in blood.

"Amos! What the hell? Hold on, you're going to be okay," Bachs said as he called for assistance over his radio. "We're going to get you help. Hold on."

"Naw, man," Amos mouthed, "I got you."

"What?"

Amos smiled, blood staining his teeth, but the joy reached his fading eyes. "I got you, Battle. I got you . . ."

PART IV

ABANDONED MEMPHIS

STINKEYE

BY CARY HOLLADAY

Medical District

Late to an exam on the inner ear, Sheila Allen, a med student, leaned over and kissed the man she'd spent the night with. He was a guitarist named Mark who hoped to revive the Antenna Club. His sheets and walls were purple.

His eyes opened, purple too, and Sheila's heart squeezed: he would never love her; he was too good-looking. He said, "I kept hearing a baby last night. Did you?"

"No, I didn't hear any babies." She recalled meeting him at a tattoo parlor, going out for drinks—she stuck with hard cider but still got drunk—and having sex in this room, which smelled of grapefruit. A memory pinged in her brain, of a shadowy shuffling from closet to door, but it was dark. "There was nobody else here, was there?"

"You'll have to ask around," he said, like it was a joke. "Does your ink hurt?"

Their new tattoos. It was her first, a tiny heart like a cinnamon candy on her knee.

"A little. It's supposed to, right?" She hated how uncertain she sounded. "Let's see yours."

He held up a hand and flexed it. A new purple guitar decorated his wrist. She made an admiring sound.

Through a yawn, he said, "The Antenna Club. I'll bring it all back—dronebilly, synth pop, country punk, garage punk."

"You'll do it. I know you will," she said. Then: "I have to go. I have a test."

He chuckled. "What kind of test? Where do you go to school?"

She'd told him last night, of course. It was always that way—she paid attention to everything a guy said, but what she said was forgotten.

So she told him again, adding, "Don't get up." She smoothed his ragged black hair away from his temple and kissed his cheek. It hurt that he didn't ask her to stay. By the time she reached the door, his slow, even breathing indicated he was asleep again.

Thank goodness his apartment was close to the med school. She ran down the steps—how silent the building was, an oughta-be-condemned set of flats—and cut through Forrest Park. High wet grass brushed her bare legs. Her mind was full of hammers and anvils, the mechanisms of the inner ear; oh, she should have studied harder. The park grass was cold; she felt grimy in last night's skirt and sweater. She tried to put her mind on the inner ear, but all she could think about were the bands Mark talked about—Calculated X, The Modifiers, The Hellcats, Impala, The Grifters, Big Ass Truck. How come the names of bands were easier than the inner ear? Should she call Mark and try to see him again? Yes, she would, and together they would revive the famed lounge on Madison Avenue, reclaim it from graffiti and neglect. More names pounded through her head: Metro Waste, Pezz, Slit Wrist, Raid. Pre-Internet bands, their glamour the dark glitter of pawnshop gold. Oh, she had to pass the test. She needed to look at the inner-ear diagrams again.

When she reached the equestrian statue of Nathan Bedford Forrest, she set down her pack, pulled out a book, and heard a baby.

Its cries tink-tinked into her head, above the sounds of traffic. *Tink-tink, whahhh.* She looked down into the grass and found a tiny baby, naked in the dew. She picked him up. He opened his mouth and revealed a full set of dark, pointed teeth.

She gasped. He was weak but alive as she took him to class with her, because she couldn't think what else to do. He squirmed in her arms, a wriggly weight, but by the time she burst into the room and held him out toward the other students and the teacher, Dr. Prince, he was limp and blue.

Sheila must have screamed, because later her throat was sore. Must have cried, because there were dried salt streaks on her cheeks. EMTs arrived, instantly it seemed, and took him away. Police came and escorted Sheila into an empty room and asked questions, and she kept saying, "The baby, where's the baby?"

"Is he yours, ma'am?" the police asked.

"I told you, I found him by the statue," she said.

Ten minutes of interrogation, and they almost made her believe she'd given birth herself.

"Show us where you found him," they said, and she led them outside. It was raining, a spring shower, and a morning that should have been lovely was all messed up. She guided them into the park—someone held an umbrella over her head—and pointed at the grass. She hadn't noticed before how much concrete surrounded the statue, and she couldn't remember exactly where the baby had been. Rain fell heavily, sweetly.

"There," she said, "or maybe there." Her backpack was gone. A bee buzzed into her face, and she swatted it away. "Where is he now?"

"He's deceased," a policeman said.

The hammers and anvils of Sheila's ears shut down. She

sank to her knees, hitting her leg against the concrete plat-form. The men in uniform said things, but she didn't pay at-tention. She wasn't herself any longer, wasn't a med student on her way to a final. She shed that girl, shucked her off.

"You're bleeding," a policeman said, because she'd cut her leg.

She looked into his face—green eyes—and beyond him to Nathan Bedford Forrest's high bronze head in the rain. She took a handkerchief the officer handed her, not a Kleenex, an actual cloth—her mind registered that—and held it against the cut. Her blood shocked her, running down into her san-dal. *Turn back the clock. He was right here.*

"Ma'am," the policeman said.

"You want your handkerchief back," she said. "I'm sorry, it's ruined."

"Is there somewhere you'd like to go?" he asked.

"Somewhere . . . ? Like the movies?" she asked, baffled.

"Home, I mean. I'll drive you." He was done talking about the baby.

"Says he had teeth."

"Yeah, kinda crazy. Sheila something. She's in my Neuro-science."

"Girl with real short hair? Like a Roman emperor?"

"Wears little green bottle-cap glasses. Definitely crazy."

"But there really was a baby, right?"

"Yeah, but now they don't know where it is. Christ, did you hear? Somebody stole it and tried to kill the M.E."

"Chaos, man. Be careful out there."

"We're all marked for death."

"Don't say that."

"Isn't that why you wanna be a doctor?"

"No, I want to help people. I . . ."

"Teeth, man. A baby with teeth."

"Where's these bees coming from? Get away, bee."

"Who was Nathan Bedford Forrest, anyhow?"

"Some Confederate general. A calvary officer."

"It's *cavalry*. And he was a military genius. Before the war, he made a fortune as a slave trader. After the war, he was mayor of Memphis."

"How d'you know all that?"

"I read. This is a grave, dude. Him and his wife are buried here."

"It was probably a crack baby. Some homeless person had it and left it."

"This girl at my high school gave birth at the prom. In the restroom. In the toilet."

"Like, 'scuse me, save me a spot on the dance floor?"

"Said didn't know she was pregnant."

"How could you not know?"

"Old story. Every school has like a dozen girls having babies at the prom."

"So a guy beat up the M.E. who was doing the autopsy on the baby; wrapped him in barbwire and stuck a bomb on his chest."

"He must've made somebody mad. He testified against a cop-killer who got sent to death row. He gets death threats all the time, is what I heard. And he's this quiet little guy. There's been bombs outside his office, Molotov cocktails. It's dangerous work. I so look up to him."

"I'd fight back. Did he fight back?"

"Just don't get in a car with anybody, if they want to kill you. If you get in their car, it's over."

"But who was it?"

"It was dark. He never saw. But he used to be a Marine, a combat surgeon. You can't get tougher than that. They over-powered him."

"It's a little too close, man."

"Don't tell my mom. She's already scared something horrible'll happen to me. She brings me a new mattress every six months cuz she's afraid I'll get bedbugs."

"Speaking of mattresses, I think my roommate's girlfriend might be a whore. She makes these comments."

"What kind of comments does a whore make?"

"It's just a feeling I get when I'm around her."

"They want to dig this guy up. Kick him out of his own grave."

"Want to go horse riding some time? Out at Shelby Farms?"

"Nah, horses get weird shit. Botflies and worms, and they bite. One bit my cousin."

"My cousin's had a period for like a month. She won't go to the doctor."

"Whenever somebody says something about a relative? I've started to think it's them. Have you had a period for a whole month?"

"Juvenile and rude, dude."

God made me a deal. Said, Bedford, you lie here five hundred years awake, and after that, we'll see. What say ye, Bedford? He didn't say, Repent of your sins, but I think that's what He meant. Hell yeah, I said. Ain't so bad. I think about what I done in the army. And with women, and as mayor, and don't regret none of it. My wife went to heaven with nary a backward look, so it's just her cold carrion alongside me. I can hear people talking outside the tomb, the Sons of Confederate Veterans having their rallies, and bootleggers selling hooch. They use different words now, but I recognize the talk. There's tunnels, and ain't ants in 'em neither. Secret passageways between hospitals, and some of what I hear is right bothersome. The screams, the prying loose of a soul sped on its way. And earthquakes, they scare the hell out of me. It's ten times worse in the ground than up top. Them tremors put me to feeling all over myself. Head? Cock? Accounted for. Another tooth shook out of my jaw. I say, Lord, you got the best of me. He says, Bedford, ain't no arguing with Me.

I never was the patient type.

It all finds me, every bad thing in town, every sin and hatefulness is known to me without no work on my part. It comes to me easy, the way I used to draw breath. I keep track of the days, and all the people I knew are dead and gone. My mind's a gazette of abominations. Man poured boiling water on his woman and beat her with a pot. Man stabbed his girl, stuck her in a trash barrel, and tried to sink it in the river, only it floated, and before she died, she got her hand out. They found her with her arm out and the barrel riding high in the water. A gal hit a man with her automobile, him stuck in the windshield, sliced near in two by glass, and she drove home. He was all night dying in her garage. She waited him out.

Used to think yellow fever was the scariest thing. I'd rather think about my raids on the Federals, and the railroads I owned before they went bust. At least Big Muddy ain't changed. The flatboats is gone, and the steamboats, mostly, but deep down, the channel cats still grow to mighty size, and from the bridge, the hapless and despairing still throw theirselves in, and oftimes ain't missed.

I can see out the eyes of my statue. Don't ask me how. Over yonder is a Scottish Rite Temple. To the left, the medical school. All around me, my own park, my last stand. Someday I'll take my metal horse for a ride. There's a nest of bees in the mane. Hear them buzz? God's joke, my honey in the rock. I heard and saw that *baby. Heard the girl cry out. A body gets stiff in the musty crypt, and earth's a hard embrace. Five hundred years of lonesome, but that ain't forever. When I walk again, the river will have riz up over this land, and Memphis won't be no more.*

The M.E. read the police report and examined the body, weighing, probing, palpating: umbilical inexpertly cut, another case of *all this poverty*. Legions of children were abandoned and damaged and sick, thrown away, changelings bred of violence, but this one was a treasure, its price beyond rubies: teeth fully erupted, the edges rough and pointed, the surfaces dark on both the lingual and facial sides.

"Call you Sharky," he said.

Oh, the morgue's cupboards were full of specimens, jars of barely recognizable flesh, like pieces of the devil himself—two-headed fetus, embryo with a hoof for a foot. This infant was an anomaly, found alive by a woman of questionable stability, died while EMTs tried to insert an IV for fluids. The body was stiff, reluctant to yield its secrets. *Who are you?* Full-term infant. Race: white. Weight: six pounds, one ounce. Length: twenty inches.

He was aware of an unfamiliar feeling. Happiness. This baby would make headlines and carry his name around the world. Before he completed the examination, he would celebrate with a snack. He set down the baby, stripped off his gloves, and made his way out of the morgue to a vending machine in the long, shiny corridor.

Someone was at the machine. He laughed with joy, recognizing Jackie, the black-haired, wide-hipped beauty he loved. What an extraordinary day—the baby, and now Jackie alone with him in the hallway. She was a helicopter nurse. Her hospital was blocks away. There was no reason for her to be in this building—unless she hoped to run into him.

He was married, but he had loved Jackie obsessively for six months. They had never exchanged more than *Hi*. He knew her the way he knew all the medical people, working among the living, the dying, the dead. As he approached, she glanced over her shoulder, her marvelous brown eyes surrounded by blue shadow. Close up, she dazzled him: a chipped incisor, a streak of gray in her hair. She pressed buttons on the vending machine, but nothing came out.

"It's not enough," she said.

"How much do you need?" He fed money into the slot, put his shoulder against the machine, tilted it, and was rewarded by a thump and a thud. He lifted the plastic flap to reveal not one, but two candy bars.

"Your lucky day," he said.

"I guess," she said.

"Are you going to thank me?"

"Okay. Thanks." To reach in, she had to bow beneath him. He was close enough to smell her powder-fresh antiperspirant. Her scrubs were printed with cartoon airplanes.

"You could share." Feeling debonair—his racing mind registered the word—he held out a palm.

She stuffed both candy bars in her pocket.

"You must be hungry," he said. She blinked. He observed a broken vein in one eye. "Do you have to fly out tonight?"

"We can be called anytime."

He tried another tack: "Have you heard about the baby with teeth?"

"That can't be true."

"It is. Come to the morgue and see."

"No," she said.

"Have a look, and then we'll go out to dinner, anywhere you want."

She gulped. "No, I have a boyfriend. In fact, he's security for this building."

Maybe she meant if the boyfriend weren't nearby, she'd be available. "Is he the reason you're in this neck of the woods? Or am I?"

"Look, I don't even know you. I mean, I know who you are, but . . ."

"I love you, Jackie. I'm married, but we can . . ."

Her lips twisted into a rosebud. He recognized an invitation, but as he bent down to kiss her, she leaped away, fixed him with a glare, and said, "Leave me alone." She hurried down the hall, her lovely, heavy calves with thin ankles pounding the floor, and disappeared through a set of double doors.

Stunned, he stared at the doors while the conversation replayed in his mind. He came on too strong. Made a play for her. Were those phrases even used anymore? He had to let her know his feelings. She was lonely too, he was sure of it. *It's not enough,* she said, and she didn't mean money for candy.

The encounter happened so fast, yet he would think about it for the rest of his life.

His bladder twinged. He headed back to the morgue, to his private lavatory, ever a refuge. As he peed, he imagined Jackie a suicide, dying horribly in the blades of a chopper, too shy to admit she loved him back. It was Jackie he should be married to, not the wife he wedded long ago, the wife fascinated by cat mummies, having read an article about them—one article, and cat mummies were all she talked about. He couldn't picture her face, only Jackie's. That was a substantive conversation they just had, wasn't it? There was some satisfaction in that.

Your lucky day.

I guess.

He shivered. The morgue was arctic.

But no mistaking that look she gave him, the stinkeye. *Leave me alone.*

He flushed, zipped, and moved to the sink. Oh, the world would stand still if it saw what he had seen: coyotes roaming downtown streets at night. Last week, at dawn, he observed a woman rip out another woman's tongue. Such things he had longed to tell Jackie, but his life was to remain as it was, with clammy bodies his companions. *It's not enough.* Maybe she would think of him as she made her way to the hospital roof and stepped out into the wind, high above the city: *Your lucky day.*

He turned off the faucet and dried his hands. Tomorrow he would deal with reporters. Word of the baby was out there. He would grant interviews, impassively facing cameras. His thoughts were a scale, with doomed love on one side and hopes for renown on the other. He searched for the happiness he felt earlier, but it was gone.

What was that sound? He froze. He knew every beep and click of the building and its machinery, and it wasn't that. It was more the sound of an ice maker in a refrigerator, spliced with the sniff of a stuffy nose. The lights went off.

"Hey," he said. "Who's there? What's going on?"

Sheila hung around the statue, hoping the baby's mother would show up. The grass was weedy, peppery, and dandeliony. She sneezed. Her phone alerted her to a message from Dr. Prince that she could make up the exam, but she didn't respond. She remembered how the others' heads swiveled when she burst into the classroom with the baby. She should never have surrendered him. How did you feed a baby? Did they suck on the bottle or did you squeeze it? The teeth, though. She could have handed him a hamburger and said, *Have at it, kiddo.*

He had to have a father too, but Sheila imagined only a mother would return to search. He must be on a dissecting table. Like a freak toad, he would end up in a jar, cloudy and pickled. He was her chance to have somebody all her own *to love*, and she blew it.

Why didn't she at least take his picture?

In the twenty-eight hours that had elapsed since she found him, terrible news had reached her ears: word of a nighttime assault on the medical examiner who was performing the autopsy. A thug jumped him, threw acid in his face, dragged him out of the morgue, bound him with barbwire, and lashed a bomb to his chest. A security cop discovered him. He was at the hospital, injured but alive and under guard, and the mad bomber was on the loose.

The worst of it was, the baby was gone. By the time they got the barbwire out of the M.E.'s mouth, and he convinced somebody to go back to the morgue, the baby'd been stolen. Downtown was alive with the news, as if katydids in the trees were broadcasting.

Unless the baby was located, nobody would believe he was real, let alone that she found him. She had spent her life not being taken seriously. It was infuriating. Mark's sleepy purple eyes came to mind. She would call him up and give him a piece of her mind. She was not a woman to be bedded and forgotten. She yanked her phone from her pocket and realized she never got his number. All right, she'd go in person. Crossing Dunlap Street, she decided anger wouldn't work. She'd act vulnerable; men liked to feel they were rescuing a woman.

A car squealed to a halt, and she jumped back, shaken.

Forget Mark. She returned to the statue.

Who had the baby, and what would they do with him? When she was a child, her father let her go to a freak show at the Mid-South Fair. *World's Tiniest Woman*, and there was a little-bitty person crouched in a plastic tub, crocheting. Sheila felt ashamed of herself, reproached by the Tiniest Woman's dignity, the way she ignored the crowds tromping in from the midway. Sheila's mother claimed there used to be more freaks. These days, they got aborted. Sheila imagined how the baby would look on a sonogram, his teeth black. Was his mother creeped out? Was that why she ditched him?

Maybe the paramedics lied about him being dead. He was alive, in a cage, and they would experiment on him for the rest of his life.

As she circled the statue, muggy, swampy air rose around her. Bees flocked to her bottle of Dr Pepper. Shit, one got in. She poured out the drink in dribbles, but the bee worked its way farther in, swimming in cola. This was all she had eaten or drunk today. Deprivation helped you concentrate. She learned that in an MCAT prep course it was good to be a little hungry and cold when you took a test. She was ravenous, and it was no use, since the test was yesterday. In her apartment, there was only passion fruit juice and some wild onions she picked in the yard. They were in vogue. Ramps, they were called, and fancy restaurants apparently served them, but they made her hands smell bad.

She choked back a sob.

The clouds resembled balls of lint, and the sun emerged in a hot, wet shine.

She upended the bottle so the Dr Pepper ran out, but the bee clung to the inside, and here was another bee. God, lots of them. Pain seared the thin skin on the back of her hand. Two, three, four stings, up and down her arm. She tossed the bottle away. A swarm surrounded her and attacked her face and neck. She screamed and ran to the edge of the park.

Panting, safe, she sheltered beneath a tree. Fragrant smoke reached her nose, the scent of Tops Bar-B-Q, but she wasn't hungry anymore. The stings hurt, and she was seized by dizziness and parching thirst.

Anaphylactic shock. She reached into her pocket for her phone, but it was gone. She must have dropped it when she ran. She needed Benadryl. Was it better to wait for this to pass, or to stagger out for help? This was how you slipped through the cracks. You collapsed in full view of Madison Avenue.

She smelled exhaust. A car stalled, and men jumped out to push it. Head throbbing, she wove back toward the only place to lie down, the stone bench farthest from the statue— no bees in sight—where she sank down and stretched out.

Would she never get out of this park?

She was twenty-three. The last time she had sex was spring break in her hometown of Ripley, with a bartender who had invented a delicious drink involving gin, tomatoes, and basil. He called her "Doctor," making fun.

If she dropped out of school, would anybody notice?

"It's so unfair," she said. Her backbone hurt, every vertebra grinding against the bench. The new tattoo burned as if her knee were being branded. Her face felt hot, yet her teeth chattered. Sun glowed through her closed lids. The men pushing the stalled car were shouting in Spanish. Their hearts must be straining like hers was.

The policeman's green eyes came to mind. She wished she'd talked with him when he drove her home. Maybe meeting him was what this whole business was about. She was supposed to marry him, and med school and the baby were irrelevant, except for leading up to him. What was his name, anyway? Did he say? He'd be wild for her, and she'd wear his holster when they had sex, and—

A shadow fell upon her.

And somebody laughed.

"He was in a cross position. Like this. The guy wanted to crucify him."

"How come he had so few cuts and bruises? And the burns were nowhere near his eyes. If somebody throws acid at you, wouldn't they aim for the eyes?"

"What d'you mean?"

"I helped cut the wire off him. It's weird it wasn't worse."

"The bomb squad said that thing could've blown the place to kingdom come. You saying he faked it?"

"Don't get mad at *me*."

Why he did it, I can't tell you. Had his reasons. I learned that in the war. What looks crazy, could be the logicalest thing a man can do. Might be loneliness drove him to it, his Romeo heart. It'll cost the taxpayers a mint. That's the wrong of it. The courts was always slow, and time this thing gets to trial, years'll pass. Hung jury, and he'll go free.

What punishment I'd give him that'd be fair? It'd have to hurt his pride. Not a whipping nor a fine. Put him out of town quiet-like, no send-off and no fuss.

Was it worth it? I'd like to know. He wrapped it careful around his face, like a mask, and hooked his mouth over it—lemme show you—so's to claim he couldn't yell. That barbwire a crown of thorns upon his head, and a bomb he made hisself, ticking down the seconds of his life. Did he feel excited, waiting for a savior to come along? That's all of us, ain't it, with knots we tied around our arms. Others have expired in this here park, same bench where that girl is laying. The baby's dead, all right, passed among white hands, black and yellow hands, bound for a New Orleans hoodoo parlor where he'll be dried and powdered. The great-great-great-granddaughter of a slave girl I sold, she'll dole him out for love potions bit by bit, his magic strong enough to stop a paddlewheel.

Sheila, ain't a thing you can do. Your clock's been ticking since the day you were born. What you started here, you won't see the end of—FBI men with light catching on their spectacles, another scandal, another long dry summer, while the city council connives to dig me up, and the Sons of Confederate Veterans gird theirselves in battle gear and wish they was born long ago. Each of us our own assailant, hankering for glory.

Sheila honey, goodbye. The men pushing that car will have to rest. They'll stroll over, find you, and send for help. They'll try to give the breath of life. A stranger's breath it'll be for you, one last kiss as you cross over.

A SHUT-AND-OPEN CASE

BY JOHN BENSKO

Midtown

As they broke through the plastered brick wall in the Midtown Memphis mansion they'd been hired to renovate, Jerry McTarne was swinging the sledge-hammer when Hector Lopez shouted, "*Para, para!*" stop, stop, and Jerry glanced over to see Hector staring wide-eyed into the hole they'd opened. More than what Hector said, his expression of fear made Jerry stop with the hammer suspended and gaze through the dust. Beyond was a hidden room, just as the new owner had suspected. Luther Self, their boss, had assured the owner that the difference between the room's inside and outside dimensions was merely an unusually large space left for the chimney. "You ain't gonna find no treasure in there," he drawled, with a toothpick hanging from the corner of his mouth. The owner, Antoine Fargé, who in spite of his name and vaguely foreign accent seemed to Jerry no more French than, well, Jerry himself, persisted.

"I must see into everything," he said, waving a French-cuffed arm and flashing his diamond ring. "Every shadow of this house." Only he didn't say *see* and *this*, he said *zee* and *deez*.

Jerry peered through the cloud of dust and made out what he could only describe as implements. *Implements*, as if they were farm machinery left in a barn to rust and gather pigeon droppings.

"*Dios mío*," said Hector, crossing himself three times, then kissing his fingers and crossing himself again. "*Es la guarida del diablo*."

Jerry had to hand it to Hector. Describing what they saw as the den of the devil made about as much sense as anything. His next thought, one he regretted later, was: *Delphi has to see this*.

Tall, lanky, and redheaded, Jerry McTarne appeared out of place among the Mexicans he worked alongside, but he got on so well with them that he overcame his self-consciousness. Born in Mexico, he'd lived there until he was six, when his mother, Delphi, an Age of Aquarius hippie who went by the one name only, turned up a hand of tarot that caused her instantly to pack her hand-woven Peruvian wool backpack and leave 'Schroom, her boyfriend of seven years, whose fathership of Jerry she was vague about anyway. She hitchhiked with her son from Ajijic back to Memphis, the city of her forefathers, where the cards said her destiny would unfold.

At that age, Jerry spoke better Spanish than English. He remembered too vividly the series of creeps who picked them up once they crossed the border into Texas. This and other *adventures,* Delphi's word, that she took him on made Jerry surprised he survived into adulthood. Yet he loved her. His attachment to her and her odd ways he couldn't fathom, much less explain. Maybe there was comfort in despair.

Yes, Delphi would have to see *this*. Whatever *this* was, *éste*, in Mexico, that word used sometimes for things or people who were unfathomable yet close. And the word almost like *es tú*, it's you. *Éste*, which he sometimes used silently toward his mother.

Working construction was not a profession Jerry would

have chosen. Under Delphi's influence, he smoked too much weed, dropped out of high school, and fell into it. As a teenager, he was thin and, with his red hair, a target of jokes at school. The jibes grew worse when Delphi came to the high school one time for Cultural Awareness Day. A flyer about it had accidentally slipped out of his notebook on the dining room table where he did his homework, and she'd latched onto it. "They have to learn about Accidentalism," she'd said with a gleam in her eye. It was the religion she'd founded. She had ten followers.

Faced with the devil's den, Hector put down his sledgehammer, and without another word turned and left Jerry alone to ponder. Jerry shoved a few loose bricks aside and stepped into the long, narrow room. At one end was the chimney, a deep fireplace like an oven with a steel door opening at waist level, and a long bench covered with tin in front of that, as if someone could lay stuff there and feed it into the fire. To the side by the far wall was another long bench at waist height made of wood. It had metal clamps at both ends and could be separated in the middle with a screw device to spread the two ends apart. Dark stains covered the wood. From blood? There were other things, an old hook with a wooden handle like the kind used on bales of hay. A heavier hook, chain, and pulley dangling from a rafter, as if sides of beef were hung from it. Considering the oven, and Memphis, Jerry wondered if the room were some unusual place for cooking barbecue. He heard a gasp and turned toward the opening in the brick he'd stepped through. Hector and Feo and Chucho were huddled close, staring into the room. Feo and Chucho slowly backed away.

"*No he visto nada,*" Chucho said. I haven't seen anything.

And Feo: "*Yo tampoco.*" Me neither.

Jerry spotted something on the floor, a matchbook. He picked it up and wiped the dust off. An advertisement read, *The Delta Club*, and under that, *Where the River Sings*. He'd heard his mother talk about it. His great-grandfather had worked there as a bouncer before he'd left his family and vanished without a word. Jerry put the matchbook in his pocket and stepped out of the hole in the wall.

"*Qué vamos a hacer?*" Hector asked. What are we going to do?

Jerry looked at his watch. It was five p.m. on a Friday. Luther had gone home already, leaving him the keys to lock up. Antoine Fargé was out of town and wouldn't be back for several days.

"*Nada,*" Jerry said. But he already knew what he was going to do, and it wasn't nothing.

Delphi's irritation at having to stop while Jerry unlocked the door of the mansion verged on menacing. She tried to project an aura of being laid back, which fooled most people, but Jerry knew the real her. Inside she was seething. Always. His hand fumbled with the key, couldn't get it into the keyhole, dropped it. "Maybe this wasn't such a good idea," he said. It was midnight Sunday. Delphi had insisted on the time.

"The cards say it's the only time we'll be protected." She had a tight expression on her lips. This week she had hennaed her hair. Last week it was green. Accidentalism required such things of its priestess. It took Jerry a long time to learn the religion. Dyeing one's hair, for instance, was no accident, and yet it was the type of thing essential to Accidentalism. Delphi explained that the whole philosophy of Accidentalism was that it, like everything else in the universe, was the opposite of what it was. Even though Jerry didn't understand how, if something was the opposite of what it was, it ever could have been the thing it was to begin with, he could not argue with the fact that the religion, being inexplicable, suited his mother well.

When he'd told her about the room and showed her the matchbook, she'd snatched it from his hand.

"Where did you say this house was?" She put the matchbook up close to her face, as if not only to give it a close look but to smell it, even taste it. She often did that, to feel the spiritual presences. She rubbed it against her cheek with a slow, smooth gesture that seemed to Jerry almost sensual, as if she were trying to seduce it. When he told her the mansion was on Peabody Avenue, she said, "Yes." Then, "Yes, yes, yes."

"What's yes?" Jerry had just opened a beer. With no idea what his mother's response to the room and the matchbook would be, he knew only that it would be entertaining. She was like a sporting event between two closely ranked teams that hated each other.

"The rumors," she said.

"What rumors?"

"About Boss Crump's henchman."

"What about him?" Jerry, like anyone who'd lived in Memphis, knew of the legendary political boss who controlled the city for nearly a half-century, but what he knew were shadows and myths.

"Never you mind. Just take me there. I'll be able to feel it. If Pawpaw's there, I'll know."

Jerry learned long ago not to press his mother too hard with questions. The answers only became more bizarre. *Pawpaw, there?*

Fumbling with the lock of the mansion's front door under

the patchoulied scent of his mother, Jerry wished he'd never taken her the matchbook or told her of the room. He was glad they were partly concealed by the neglected shrubbery that nearly hid the house from the street. Breaking into an empty house in the witching hour wasn't his idea of a brilliant move.

"Wait," his mother said. She pushed his hand away from the lock. "Give me the key."

He handed it to her, and she drew out a velvet bag from a pocket in her dress. She waved it over the key. "Okay, now try it."

The key went right in.

"The forces of evil were blocking us from the truth," she said.

He wanted to tell her that the only forces in play were her making him nervous as hell, but he knew that arguing with her was fighting the wind. As if to make the point, when the door opened, a warm breeze wafted from within. It smelled of food, a faint smoky aroma sweet yet vinegary. His heart froze. Had the Frenchman returned early from his trip? Was he up cooking at this hour?

But Delphi was barging past him, pointing the beam of the large flashlight she'd brought around the room. It was a house from the 1910s with the heavy cornices varnished dark and a curving staircase going from the entry hall to the second floor. "Where is it?" she said. Then, "No, don't tell me. I want Pawpaw's spirit to lead me." She handed him the flashlight and lifted her palms to the air.

"What's Pawpaw got to do with this?"

"Neveryoumind," she said, quickly and in a hush as if not to interrupt whatever was speaking to her.

Then, as if one of her spirits had brought it, a long-ago drunken night in a bar named the Lamplighter came back to

Jerry. It was a place where old-timers hung out, and one regular, who was blind and always sat at the far end of the bar,
was telling Jerry a wild story about Boss Crump. How men
who worked for him made people disappear. "It's rumored,"
he had said, and the old lush paused to loom close to Jerry's
head, fumble against the side of it with his palm, and cup his
hand around Jerry's ear to whisper, "they burned the bodies in
a special-built fireplace in one of 'em's house." With the word
house, a mist of warm spittle met Jerry's ear. Even as drunk as
he was, Jerry remembered. And the old guy pulling back and
staring at him with his cataract-clouded eyes, as if he could
see right through Jerry.

Jerry and Delphi walked in darkness through the house to the
room. Jerry did not look back at his mother, but a few times
he heard her whispering. He knew she was not speaking to
him. When they reached the room, which was windowless,
he closed the door behind them and turned on the flashlight.
"There's what you wanted to see," he said, swinging the beam
to the opened hole in the plastered brick wall.

"I know," she said. "I felt him drawing me here."

"Him?"

"Pawpaw."

"Oh, right. You want to tell me about that now?"

"We have to go in. Show me."

He helped her through the hole in the wall with a sense
that perhaps he would never come out the same. That he and
his mother stepping into that room would be stepping into
other selves. As for his mother, maybe it would be an improvement. But for himself? He didn't want to be another Jerry. Or
did he?

He was pondering the question when she said, "It's just

like in my dream. Give me that." She snatched the flashlight from his hand and swung it toward the tin-covered table in front of the chimney. Then she climbed on the table, lay on her back, and folded her arms across her chest. "Slide me in," she said in an urgent voice.

"Come on now. You can't be serious." As soon as the words left his mouth, he knew how ridiculous they were in relation to his mother. Everything she did was absurd. Yet she was serious about every last velvet-bagged crystal of it.

Her head was pointed toward the opening, and he didn't quite know how to manage it, but he decided to grab her by the ankles and push. She stiffened, and he shoved her in. With the tin surface on the table it was surprisingly easy.

When she was in there, her hand stretched out with the flashlight. "Here," she said, "I want it to be dark so I can imagine the flames."

He was about to ask her how the dark could help her to imagine flames when he heard a creak that chilled his heart. It seemed to come from the whole house, as if it had found its voice after long years of disuse. In his mind, the sound reverberated into the high squeal of an animal stabbed in the throat. Cold air rushed past his mother from the chimney and into the room. His hand went limp, and he dropped the flashlight. For a moment they were in utter darkness.

The light in the main room came on, and a voice said, "Who eez that in there?"

"Oh shit," Jerry said under his breath. Before he could answer, Antoine Fargé was climbing through the hole.

"Ju," he said. "Vat are ju doing here? And who is theez?" Fargé pointed to the moccasined feet protruding from the oven.

"That's my mother," Jerry said.

"Ju are working at meednight and jur mothair eez helping?"

"She wanted to see what we'd found."

"Jes," he said. He looked around as if he'd only then noticed the hidden room they were in. "It eez just as I thought." He walked over to the chain hanging from the ceiling and slapped it so it clanged against the pulley. "A raigulair chaimbair of horrors."

Jerry, who wasn't aware that there was any regularity to chambers of horrors, suddenly felt even more skeptical. The combination of his mother and some fake Frenchman was too much, as if the dam holding back long years of absurdity had burst.

"Who are you?" he said.

"Who air any of us?" Fargé replied. He pointed again to the feet protruding from the chimney. "Ju said she vas jur mothair, but who eez that? And who air you?"

"He's in here!" Jerry's mother exclaimed, as if she hadn't heard anything of Fargé's arrival.

"What eez she talking about?"

"Pawpaw," Jerry answered.

"Ze tree?"

"I wish."

"You can pull me out now!" his mother shouted. Jerry grabbed her ankles and pulled her from the oven onto the tin-covered table. She sat up and involved herself in dusting herself off. Antoine Fargé watched as if witnessing a ghost.

When she looked up and saw him, she didn't seem surprised at all. "Ah, you," she said. "I was expecting you."

"What?" Jerry said. "You know him?"

"Not yet," she said. "He was foretold. In the matchbook you gave me."

Fargé, even in the dim light, turned pale enough to add

light to the room. Jerry wondered if he needed help to sit down somewhere.

"My mother reads the future," Jerry said. Then, as if to explain, "It's a hobby."

"It's a gift," his mother said brusquely.

"I must have ju," Fargé said.

"What?" Jerry said. The Frenchman was staring at Delphi with a wild expression on his face.

"Right here, right now. In deez place." He fell toward her and clutched her around the waist. It was as if he were trying to keep himself from falling, but with a mad, romantic insistence that required he save himself from plunging to the floor by groping Delphi.

Jerry pulled the Frenchman loose from his mother and punched him in the face.

"Jerry!" she screamed. "Don't. He's our only hope."

Jerry shoved Fargé away from his mother, and the Frenchman's back hit the wall where some old electric lines ran down to an antique breaker switch. When Fargé hit it, the breaker closed, causing his body to jerk with electricity and fall to the floor. Immediately, a hissing came from the fireplace. A loud whoosh, and flames shot from the oven. Perhaps from old grease on the bricks, the whole structure bristled into flames that reached the ceiling and turned the room searing hot. Fargé was on the floor, passed out or dead, Jerry didn't know. Delphi was screaming. Jerry yelled at her to get out of the room, and he rushed to Fargé to see if he could rouse him or somehow pull him across the floor. The wood in the far wall was smoking. Any second, it too would burst into flames.

When he reached Fargé and turned him faceup, the man's eyes were open. He looked at Jerry and said, "A vizion. I hev zeen a vizion."

"I'm seeing one too," Jerry said. "Only it's real. We need to get out of here." He pulled Fargé's arm, but the Frenchman jerked away.

"Zair," he said. "Ze box." He pointed to an old metal box under the table that Jerry's mother had been lying on only moments before. "I must have eet." He lunged free of Jerry and grabbed it, but lost his balance and fell against the table, hitting his head and dropping again to the floor.

Jerry grabbed him and dragged him from the room. When they were out, the Frenchman came to and shouted, "Ze box! I must have ze box!"

"What box?" Delphi asked. "There's a box? Is anything in it?"

"Forget it," Jerry said. "We need to get out of here and call the fire department."

Smoke poured out of the hole in the wall. An ominous crackling and popping came from the room as if it were about to explode. Jerry was dragging the Frenchman to the door when his mother rushed back through the hole. He yelled at her to stop and dropped the Frenchman, but she was already in there. He ran to the opening, and all he could see was the glow of bright orange in the smoke as fire filled the room. The heat was incredible, and he put his arm in front of his mouth so he could breathe through the sleeve of his shirt. Jerry was about to jump in, when his mother dove out, crashed into him, and sent them onto the floor. Her hair was on fire, and he ripped off his shirt and smothered the flames.

"I have it," she said. "I have it. I have it." Her hair was half gone, and her face was black from the smoke. But she was holding the tin box.

From the front yard, Jerry watched the flames eat through the roof as he called 911 on his cell phone. Neither Fargé nor his mother seemed to care about the house. They sat cross-legged in the grass, the box between them, pulling out one thing after another. When Jerry finished the call, he went over.

"We might be too close," he said. "No telling what's going to happen when the fire gets through the roof. With the gas lines and everything, the place could explode."

"And zees," the Frenchman said to his mother, handing her a ribbon-tied stack of photographs and ignoring Jerry. "Vat do ju make of zees?" Between them on the grass was an old revolver, some police badges, a pair of handcuffs, and assorted papers, some of which looked like legal documents with official seals. Jerry picked one up. It was an oath of some kind, stating that one Darquemus, member of the Loyal Order of H, solemnly swore not to reveal any deeds, exploits, identities, locations, signs, or other secrets of the Order, under pain of death. At the top of the page was the name *Loyal Order of H*, surrounded by flames. Darquemus's signature at the bottom was in a brown ink that reminded Jerry of dried blood. Drops of it ran across the paper, as if a wounded hand still dripping with blood had signed the document.

Just then his mother cried out: "Pawpaw! It's him!" She handed a photo to Fargé. "I told you, Jerry," she said. "You've never seen a picture of him, but you'll recognize the family resemblance right away." Her soot-smeared face with its burned hair smiled up at him.

"I'm sure I will," he said.

Fargé studied the picture as if carefully reading something in it, then handed it up to Jerry. "It eez ze one," he said.

The picture showed a man with dark hair slicked back, wearing a pinstriped suit in the broad-lapel style of the early fifties. He was heavyset and looked to Jerry more than anything like a thug. This was the beloved Pawpaw? "What do you mean, *the one?*" he said to Fargé.

"Ze one who bring me to deez place."

"It's all been foreseen, Jerry," his mother said. "Mister Fargé and everything."

"Call me Antoine." He lifted her hand and kissed it. Then he did not let it go but leaned over and kissed Delphi on the lips.

Jerry didn't know what to feel. The house was now an inferno. The sirens he'd been hearing grew louder than the fire, and two fire trucks were suddenly there at the curb. Still, this odd person did not stop kissing the scorched face of his mother. Firemen rushed past them dragging hoses.

Jerry watched as the hoses came to life and the firemen doused the structure. It was clearly too late to do anything except try to stop the blaze from spreading to other houses. When he glanced back, to his horror, his mother was on top of Fargé. She'd straddled his prone body, and even though her dress covered his midsection, Jerry could tell Fargé's pants were down.

"For God's sake," he yelled, "what are you doing?"

His mother looked up at him, and from the wild look in her eyes he knew she wasn't really there. "It's the dead, Jerry," she said. "They've taken us over, and I can't help myself."

The firemen, holding their spraying hoses against the fire, turned to watch.

"Have you no shame?" he said. Beside his mother and Fargé was the tin box, and in it Jerry saw a gleam. A scene from his childhood came back—he and his mother leaving their house in Mexico and 'Shroom by the door, crying. He wasn't coming with them, and Jerry didn't understand. 'Shroom knelt and hugged him and kissed him and said, "Take care, old sport." That was what he often called Jerry, *old sport*, as if he were older than 'Shroom himself. "And just remember, you can always take something good away from everything."

He snatched up the box and ran. He would run, back to Mexico maybe, to wherever. Away, he thought, away from *this*.

When he reached his truck, which was parked a few hundred feet down the street, he flung open the door and threw the box across to the passenger's seat. He climbed in, closed the door, and stared at the flaming pieces of the house floating out over the neighborhood. By now, people had come to watch, and he wondered if his mother and Fargé were still there getting it on, in front of the crowd. It would be just like her to go on, and then afterward to get up and start proselytizing. Yes, Accidentalism, folks, see where it will get you?

Jerry sighed. He realized he would not run away. He was her flesh and blood. He looked over at the box on the seat beside him. He opened it. The thing he had seen shining was a dagger. Its handle was made of gold encrusted with diamonds. He held it up and turned it in the light from the fire. The red gleam in the diamonds caused a fascination to arise in him. He pointed it toward his heart and stuck its tip against his skin. He wrapped both hands around the handle. It would be so easy. Only a second. He would be free. Then he saw that in the bottom of the box was a large photo. He put the knife down and took it out.

In the flickering light he had difficulty seeing well, but it was taken in the hidden chamber. The chimney was in the background, and six men stood around the table that led to the oven. They wore robes and masks. The masks were the faces of pigs with horns. One of the men held a dagger, the same dagger, Jerry realized. And on the table that the men surrounded? Was it human, or hog? It was impossible to know what was stretched there, ready for sacrifice.

NIGHTFLIGHT

BY SHEREE RENÉE THOMAS

Vollintine Evergreen

Three o'clock in the morning, Old Mama Yaya walks at this hour unobserved, past tumbled-down apartment buildings, empty lots, and shuttered storefronts. She limps slowly in the streetlight, but there is another light. She looks up to her left, grimacing as if the gang graffiti has suddenly come to life, her gaze arcing toward the candle burning in the second-floor window. "Close your eyes, child," she mutters. "At this hour, even haints sleep." Adjusting her cart, she continues down the sidewalk, rattling as she goes.

The child sits at her makeshift desk made of cinder blocks and her daddy's old albums. Led Zeppelin, Muddy Waters, and Parliament Funk stare back at her. The child likes the album art, although she does not understand it. What does it mean to "get funked up"? She wants the "P-Funk" too. She loves Minnie Riperton's Afro, so lush and wild as a black sun. These are her friends, the music and the beautiful math behind the music. She imagines it as a kind of sacred geometry, a language that speaks to her when words are too difficult to say. It gives her the same feeling as when her daddy lifted her up into the sky by her elbows, as beautiful as seeing a moonrise over stunted willow trees. In her daddy's hands she feels neither too fat nor too black. Skyborn, she is no ordinary, plain girl. She is a magician.

* * *

When the sun stopped shining in Memphis, Nelse decided that she was better suited to theory than to operations. After all, theory was not a product, and Nelse was a ponderer. Her grandmother, who raised her after her father got shot in a failed home invasion, had called her a natural-born Figurer. All math was *figurin'* to her grandmother, and all math came easily to Nelse. She was inexplicably moved by it, the possibilities shifting like a multicolor Möbius strip, like the rainbow ribbons in her hair when her daddy's arms lifted her as a child, skyrocketing her into that other space. There she could sit with the cinder blocks that now looked like two ancient columns, sit with the paper Big Mama collected from the office building's trash cans: "Cuz most people wasteful, and the rest ain't got no good sense."

Theory allowed her to work mostly alone, and alone was how Nelse preferred life. There was less margin for error. When Big Mama would come home from the third shift at the factory, she would cry out in her tin-can voice, "Girl, don't tell me you been sittin' up figurin' all night, wasting your eyesight." She would gather Nelse up in her arms, stare deep into her eyes as if trying to guess her future, then she would scold her once more, saying, "If you don't sleep more, you'll stunt your growth and have only one titty." Nelse would pat her flat chest and giggle at this, then finally drift off to sleep, the beautiful equations and figures filling her head.

Big Mama was always saying funny things, but the words that meant the most to Nelse were, "Get yo' lesson, child, if you don't get nothin' else." And get is what Nelse did. Lying on her bed, the sky outside her window as dark as in the morning as it was in the night, she wiped away the final remains of the odd, recurring dream and wondered why the sky used to turn perfect red at the end of the day. She wondered why the soap bubbles in her childhood magic wand formed in nearly perfect spheres, and why the human voice filled with emotion could urge a dying plant to grow or impact the cellular life of water. She wondered why a spinning top didn't fall over but instead slowly gyrated, its speed inversely proportional to the initial turn, why outer space goes on forever. And when the city did not burn up, when the sun went out, she wondered how life continued to go on, the way sap rose in the remaining trees, rose against gravity, the way the people rose, hoping to see that shine again, glimmering along the muddy river, hoping against probability, against fate.

The sky now was as muddy as the river. The first day the city woke and the sun had not, people stood out on their porches, circled the pavement around their lawns, and stared, just stared at the sky, as if willing the sun back. The young folk danced down the streets with flashlights, flirting and laughing loudly as if the sun had gone out for their pleasure. The sick and shut-in sat hunched at windows, clutching curtains, shaking their heads at these end days. Then the cell phones rang out until every line was busy. The media was in an uproar, and the newly minted mayor had to be rushed to the Med after having a minor stroke. The children, those in public school and in private, were unashamedly happy. They leapt in their yards, jumped like grasshoppers until frightened mothers and fathers shooed them back into the houses. When the airwaves cleared, the mayor, mildly recovered, finally made a speech. Memphians were to get duct tape and garbage bags and seal all their windows and doors. This could be the result of a terrorist act, directed at the good citizens of Memphis. Who would do this, why, and what for were the questions that needed figuring. No one had answers.

Not the Shelby County Center for Emergency Preparedness, nor the governor and the congressmen; even the president and the CDC could not explain why the sun had gone out only in Memphis. Some said it was because the city had given up its charter, others said it was a Chickasaw curse for building on the bluffs and bones of the city's first inhabitants. And then there were some who blamed every crooked thing on Voodoo Village. Whole families went by car, truck, and foot across the arched bridge, zooming across I-40 like hell had opened up behind them. Barbecue pits, student loans, and thirty-year mortgages, even some marriages, Elvis, and Graceland, were left behind without a backward glance.

No one commented on how the darkness lifted and the sunlight shone at exactly halfway across the M-shaped Hernando de Soto Bridge. If nothing else, that oddity alone was enough to prove to some that the city had been specially marked as cursed. "The Lord done spoken!" the preachers cried, and gathered their flocks with them to safety. SUVs and church buses honked and stalled on the crowded bridge, the people turning their backs on the hulking Pyramid that glowered mutely behind them. Many remained hovering in the fields, camped out in the West Memphis bottomlands in their cars and tents. They didn't worry about waiting lists for trailers, FEMA had not bothered shipping any. Still others headed on down to the dog track and casinos, carrying their last dollars and their emergency preparedness bags with them. And those who once thought they lived in Germantown and Cordova and Collierville soon learned the true geographical reach of East Memphis. It was sunless in their neck of the woods too. Yet the good citizens in North Mississippi sat smugly in their homes, daylight shining through their curtained windows, shaking their heads at the spectacle that had finally overcome the city.

* * *

Nelse lies in her bed in what would have been late afternoon, twilight, just before the old evening, when the first lightning bugs would come out. Her head aches, migraines, vestiges of the crazy dream. The same she'd had since she was a little girl. Had someone already figured out why a focusing mirror must be parabolic in shape? Why a flat or spherical mirror won't work? There was a logical reason, a kind of quiet grace, she knew, but none for why the sky in Memphis remained forever dark, nor why she stayed when so many others had fled, praying and crossing themselves, never looking back.

Closing her eyes, she imagines various shapes; her mind traces the trajectory of light rays, ancient messengers of stars long dead before the journey. Silvered glass curving, nothing like the shadowy glass in her grandmother's chifforobe.

Big Mama, are you with the stars, up in the heavens shaking your head, trying to help me figure this out? Yellow and gold light rays careened at angles to the perpendiculars, reflected at equal angles, slow-danced like she used to by herself with her father's quiet-storm albums, her mind heading back into space. Polished glass flexed and curled, like the dark lashes of her closed eyes. She wiped a tear away, imagining glass gently sweeping through space as helicopters droned above. Glass holds memory, mirrors distort reality. There had been no mirrors in her grandmother's house.

The world buckled to its knees when the sun stopped shining in Memphis. Just as it had when Nelse took her first algebra class. The lesson began with word problems, and while the teacher went on and on about state tests, Nelse had felt herself warming inside, like when she'd lean her head against the window and let the sun warm her skin. At first they thought it was a power outage, a fluke by Memphis Light, Gas & Water, but when the signals uncrossed, MLG&W had promptly released a statement that basically translated as, *We ain't got nothing to do with the sun!* Nelse remembered when a straight-line wind had come flying off the Mississippi River, cutting down hundreds of the city's oldest oak, pecan, and poplar trees, all the way from the banks to the city's limits at State-line, how they lay piled up across the city like corpses. But this was nothing like that. The only trauma was that which was building inside of people. They spent the first day trying to figure out if they'd finally lost their natural minds, but NPR and the National Guard soon told them they had not gone stone-cold crazy. Memphians were fine. The sky was not.

"How the hell can particles in the air do this?" Marva, Nelse's next-door neighbor, wanted to know. Nelse usually only saw her when Marva darted across her yard in the mornings to steal her water ("My dahlias take better to the sweet water in yo' pump").

Truth was, Marva didn't want her own water bill to be sky high. Today she didn't even try to hide her hustle. Marva had stood in the middle of the devil's strip, clutching the flowers to her chest. "What's gon' happen to my garden?"

That first night-day, Nelse opened her bedroom window, and the wind fluttered the lace curtains as if a handkerchief waved by invisible hands. It had to be a mistake, a grave error, as if someone had taken a great cosmic clock and sprung much too far ahead into the future. It had to be a power outage in the night or the work of Nelse's diabolical pills—which dulled the migraines, felled her nightly like an ax to a tree, and turned her into a sleepwalking clock-changer—or a dark cloud sent by terrorists, terrorists who hated the South and its barbecued pulled pork. Perhaps they really *had* lost their minds.

"What is the mayor going to do about this?" Marva wanted to know. She sat now on Nelse's lumpy sofa, too frightened to look outside again. Every light in the house was on, a parody of morning, as if it were the eve of a new year. All they needed was some black-eyed peas.

Nelse sat bravely by the window. "They say it happened after Tanzania, all those years ago," she said. "The ash was so thick that for three whole days it was utter darkness."

"But nothing's happened. We aren't in a war. Well," Marva said, giving Nelse an exaggerated side eye, "those foreign ones don't count if nothing's happened *here*."

"The weatherman said it isn't dangerous. The sun just isn't out."

"Are you going to the lab?"

"I don't think so. Were you going to the gym today?"

"I don't know."

Nelse stared out at the gloom, shivering. She could only imagine the commotion downtown at Buckman Labs, or in the hood, whose footprint was getting larger with every wave of white and hanging-by-the-skin-of-their-teeth black middle-class flight. All down the street, on the other end of the city, the young people wandered beneath the still-unlit streetlights, some with flashlights or lanterns, laughing. No old people out on the street at all, not in this kind of confusion, not with the sidewalks as loud as the Memphis in May festival and the flash of police lights like *Cops* everywhere. The Chargers speeding up and down the expressway, menacing and panicked, sirens blaring. In the house across the street, Nelse could just make out a couple sitting down to a candlelit breakfast. And below, in front of the neighborhood eyesore, a mango-colored house in the cove, stood a Haitian woman and her daughter, hand in hand, nearly indistinguishable in head wraps, talking quietly, looking straight up at the black sky. It was ten in the morning and as dark as the inside of an eyelid.

And Nelse hated it.

"We'll be all right," Nelse said, trying to sound like she believed it. "Not time to worry yet." But she looked over at Marva rubbing an ink spot out of the sofa's upholstery, and though it was not time to worry yet, Marva began to cry. Finally the woman announced they must call family and friends. No one should be alone. Nelse, who had no friends beyond her work at the lab, pretended not to hear as Marva desperately called one adult child after the other, until there was no one left to call. And so Nelse found herself doing the unthinkable. She agreed to invite Marva's friends over for lunch and make what they could from the pantry. For some unspoken reason they dared not go outside, though the city had finally put the streetlights on. Nelse imagined that the throngs of young people downtown had lessened with the dimming novelty of it all. Perhaps they'd gone inside to make love, busily conceiving the population boom they could look forward to, if and when the darkness finally lifted. *No-Show Sun Spawns Blackout Babies*, the *Memphis Flyer* might announce.

Marva made Caesar salad and pasta by dropping eggs into the crater of a flour volcano. She did this in silence, flour puffing into the air as if she had burst the seeds of a milkweed. Nelse thawed and roasted a chicken with cilantro, lemon pepper, honey, and herbs.

As she worked her stomach groaned, not from hunger but from fear. The idea of strangers rambling through her kitchen, rifling through her silverware, put her teeth on edge. And most importantly, she had no idea what she should wear. She had long since stopped worrying about style, or the mysteries of her hair that broke combs and spat out plastic teeth and grease, or her problems knowing when folk say what they mean or when they mean what they don't say.

At noon, she heard a rattle from the living room, Marva drawing the curtains. Nelse understood. They were not chosen, they could not bear witness to the constant night. Then she heard—like an exhalation of relief—the sound of a match. Candles. The scent of vanilla and pears filled the air. Only two neighbors came, those who had heard of Nelse's work in "the sciences": an elderly colleague of Marva's who'd also retired from the college and a kindly, nervous painter Nelse had once met briefly at an artist's reception at the Brooks. They were good, intelligent small-talkers at a party; neither was suitable for the endless night. They had clearly come out of loneliness. Nelse and Marva found themselves smiling and dutifully filling dusty wineglasses and listening for a doorbell that never rang. What was meant as a time of solace had become one of civic duty.

"I hear they are turning to rations," said the colleague, a professor of magical realism with a graying Afro. Nelse wanted to know what kinds of rations. "Gas," he said. "And fresh food and meat. Like in the war." He meant World War I. The helicopters hovered, dropping water bottles and energy bars from the dark sky. Marva had stumbled on some, after raiding Nelse's water hose. "Who knows? Maybe nylons, Marva."

Marva would not have it. "Ridiculous," she said, regretting the company of this pompous man. The curtains blew open to reveal the unearthly blackness. Nelse said she could not remember much about the war, nor anyone who had ever been in it.

The painter spoke up, and what she said chilled them: "I think they've done something."

Nelse quickly said, "Who? Done what?" Marva gave her a look.

The painter winced at her own thoughts, and her brass jewelry clanked on skinny wrists. "They've done something, and they haven't told us."

The professor seasoned his salad with a practiced flick of his wrist. Nelse feigned indifference. The chicken still sat in the kitchen, glistening and uncarved, smelling like burnt sugar.

"You mean a bomb?"

"An experiment or a bomb or I don't know. I'm sure I'm wrong, I'm sure—"

"An experiment?" Marva said.

Just then, they heard a roar. Instinctively, they went to the window, where in her haste to open it, Nelse knocked a little sandstone elephant over the sill and into the afternoon air, which was as red-dark as ever, but they could not hear it breaking above the din: the streetlights had gone out, and now the city was alive with cries. Nelse wanted to kick them all out and listen to her father's albums. Why did the streetlights go out? It's unclear. Perhaps a strain on the system, perhaps a wrong switch thrown at the station. But it was a fright to people.

That was when the blackouts began, the rolling blackouts, meant to conserve electricity. Two hours a day—on Marva and Nelse's block it was at noontime, though it made little difference—with no lamps, no clocks, no Wi-Fi, just flashlights and candles melting to nubs. It was terrifying the first few days, but then it was something you got used to. You knew not to open the refrigerator and waste the cold. You knew not to open the window and waste the heat. You knew not to open your mouth and waste your breath.

"Temporarily," the mayor said, now composed. "Until we can determine the duration." Of the darkness, he meant, of the sunless sky. When he said this over the radio, Nelse glanced at Marva and was startled. As a child, she had noticed how sometimes, in old-fashioned books, full-color illustrations of the action would appear—through some constraint at the bindery—dozens of pages before the moments they were meant to depict. Not déjà vu, not something already seen, but something not-yet-seen, and that was what was before her: a woman in profile, immobile, her hair a wild puff like a demented dandelion; her face old-fashioned, last century's features, resigned; her eyes blazing briefly with the fire of a sunspot; her hand clutching the wineglass in a tight fist; her lips open to speak to someone not in the room. A song in reverse, played much too fast.

"Marva?" she asked. Then it was gone. Her neighbor turned to her and blinked, and Nelse continued, "What on earth does he mean by *duration?*" What she really wanted to ask was why didn't Marva's children ever come? She didn't ask, because she already knew the answer. They all did. They were afraid. They all were. They were all waiting for someone or some answer to come to them, to help them figure this all out. They sat alone in the darkness, reading by candlelight, as Nelse had done as a child, panicked as pigeons, waiting for someone to come, and yet they would not stir an inch. Why, the children had asked, didn't Marva just drive in her Benz and come to them? They were closer to the authorities and could take care of her better from their homes in Harbor Town. Why wouldn't she when she'd always done so before? They were busy with their own children, trying to keep them calm, entertained. No, they weren't afraid, just . . . The adult children finally decided to leave without Marva, when they'd run out of reasons not to come to her. After the riots began, about two weeks later. She'd be all right, they rationalized.

She was staying with a very responsible neighbor. Didn't matter that they didn't know Nelse from Booboo the Clown.

Unused to company, unused to another mind living and breathing and tidying and, goodness gracious, *commenting* on her things in *her* personal space, Nelse doubled the doses of the sleeping pills, began floating through her day in a fog. It made the time huddled in the darkness go faster.

One night-day Marva convinced Nelse to drive out with her to the farmer's market in Klondike. Surely there must be ripe tomatoes still there? It was only the second time they had gone out of the cove since that first day of the darkness, and they were still unsure if they were right to do so—if it was frivolous to be seen in a tiny market with overhead mirrors to discourage the thieves and poor people jostling against wealthier ones, all grasping at the last remnants of normalcy and good health. Marva felt everyone should be in mourning. She had taken to wearing her pearls and best black dress, just in case.

"The mirrors should be covered," she had said to the artist and the professor at that first gathering. "Mirrors are portals to the spirit world. There are enough haints here now, don't you think? Shouldn't there be wailing somewhere? Nelse, put on one of those whining, crying, hiccupping records you call 'classics,' why don't you?" Nelse could hear the exaggerated sniff from the kitchen.

"If you covered the mirrors, we won't have nothing," the Graying Afro had said, anxiously glancing at a reflection of himself. As the darkness hung over the city, unmoved, he had slowly begun to lose the iron grip he held over his tongue. He was a parody of a parody, a kind of Cornel West gone to seed despite his fastidiousness and absolutely pristine pedigree; he seemed to be losing his diction and his battle with the belly, and each day his ability to code switch effortlessly seemed to slip and fade. Despite the gray in his goatee, and the lines now permanently tooled across his forehead, he appeared all the more goatish as his tongue failed him. "Don't matter no way. They still gon' blame You Know Who. I can hear them now, *Black president done burnt up the sun!* Mark my words, we'll be reading about that in the paper come Sunday." The artist shook her head. Light gleamed off her gold-rimmed glasses. Light gleamed everywhere: off cutlery and plates and crystal, sequins and earrings and pearls; it was indescribably beautiful to Nelse. Perhaps like the discovery of some rare bird, the last of its kind.

"I have a blind friend," the Graying Afro said, then suddenly, hopefully, as if he'd only been waiting politely to ask, "Hey, aren't you a scientist, a physicist working with lasers? Why don't you know what's going on?"

For the first time that long night-day, Nelse found herself laughing. "Oh, I just study light theory," she said. "I don't actually do any blockbuster movie–type experiments. I think . . ." As she struggled to describe her work, the group stared at her as if she'd suddenly sprouted wings. For a moment she felt panic. Did she misunderstand? Did she make a mistake? Did the professor mean for her to answer or was he just being polite? Nelse stood, pondering this, feeling once again like an imposter, a faux human being.

"You mean, you don't *do* anything?" the Graying Afro asked, incredulous. "They pay you to just sit around thinking up ideas?" Nelse wasn't sure if he knew he had said *thankin'* instead. The professor's speech was shifting, like Nelse's grasp on social decorum.

They stared back at her expectantly. "Yes," she said finally. "A little like what you did at the college. You didn't actually *do* anything yourself, did you? You thought and discussed what other writers did. You didn't actually *create* anything original, did you? That's not actually doing anything, is it?"

While his mouth opened and shut like a fish without air, Nelse found herself thinking about his friend. She hadn't thought about the blind. Aren't they lucky? she thought, and absently drank from Marva's wineglass. Marva gave her a look. Nelse ignored it. She couldn't possibly know what it could mean. She couldn't possibly explain to them that the star they'd once loved had an iron heart and was dying, had died ages ago.

The professor continued on about his blind friend: "She says she can't help it, but it's satisfying. She says she hates herself for feeling it, but it amuses her that the rest of us think the world is going to end. Because it's the same world for her. Ain't nothing changed," he added and frowned, as if he'd only just heard himself. "Nothing has changed."

"It can't be," Marva said. "She can't tell there's no sun, and the plants . . ." She thought of her dahlias.

"For her, it *is* the same world, dark as it's always been."

Nelse relaxed her grip on the glass and pursed her lips. "That's stupid," she said. "I'm sorry, Marva, but it is."

Marva turned to Nelse. "Child?"

A moment later there were splinters of glass all around them, then great shards, and then what seemed like a thousand dark-robed men running down the street, filling the cove, spilling into their manicured yards, and . . . torches, and lanterns, and certainly things were already set on fire in the street before the awestruck neighbors had the sense to stand up and run to the back of the house. It happened all at once, as if in a dream, and yet took an extraordinarily long time. There was no way to remember it right. First came the shapes, then came the colors, and when they moved, Nelse had to focus all over again to comprehend it, like a kaleidoscope. Without pen or pencil, all Nelse knew was that, when she awoke, wiping sleep from her eyes, she found herself shoved against the wall with Marva and all of them, her napkin in one hand and the wineglass in the other.

They spent the night at Nelse's place on an inflatable bed and the lumpy but irresistible cobalt-blue love seat she'd bought at an estate sale. Marva had sensibly found one of Nelse's throws and tossed it over the wretched thing. Alvin, the Afro-Am prof, slept on the living room couch. Nelse stayed awake, *figurin'* and *figurin'*, clutching her father's albums and running fresh equations through her head. They had always been so beautiful, now they were useless. Six billion years before they would even notice that the sun had burned out, six billion years, eight minutes, and nineteen seconds. Could the six billionth year be now? If so, why only in Memphis? Outside, the darkness seemed to deepen. They could hear the low moan of the rioting streets as if a great monster, Godzilla or Ultraman, were being tamed.

"It feels like World War III," Nelse whispered, tracing the outline of the painter's Minnie Riperton haircut. "I've never felt so dumb before in my whole damn life, not even when I was a child."

"Enough. You too hard on yourself," Marva said, yawning. "You'll figure this out. And if you don't, somebody else will. They have to. They always do."

"Do you know any blues songs?"

"Get some sleep, girl. We'll see how things are tomorrow. If they ain't blocked off all the roads, we can drive out to the river, think about crossing that bridge. Get on out of here. Hell, there's still sun in West Memphis."

"Well, shit, that's *all*," the professor muttered, then laughed in hyena bursts.

This was Nelse's turn to sit in silence. Then, after the numbers stopped turning in her head, "*I had a dream,*" she said quietly, "*which was not at all a dream. The bright sun was extinguished, and the stars . . .* I can't remember how it goes. No," she shook her head, as if to erase the poem, and began to sing, "*Well, all last night, I sat on the levee and moan . . .*"

"Hush, child. It ain't yet time for no Negro spirituals."

"*I had a dream, which was not at all a dream . . .* Oh, what is it?" Why couldn't the words come to her as surely as the math? The numbers were racing faster and faster now.

"Hush," Marva whispered, pulling the throw overhead. "Close your eyes, child. At this hour, even haints sleep."

Nelse turned to look at her, but in that moment the bay window crashed and the room was filled with glass and splintered screams. In the darkness, the women reached for each other. Nelse snatched Marva's hand and dragged her into the pantry.

They spent the night wide awake, afraid to speak.

In what should have been morning, things were no better; debris lay everywhere. The others had gone. Outside, the quiet street looked worse. Rattled, Nelse and Marva prepared to leave too.

"Do you want me to take you to your children? I'm sure we can find them. They couldn't have gone too far. Just over the bridge."

Marva bit her lip, finally gave a grateful smile. "Yes, I would like that. Thank you."

Nelse had just started the car, filled with the last of their food and water, and had barely made it down the street, when Marva grew still.

"Turn back," she said.

"What is it?"

"Turn back. I can't leave . . . without it."

Annoyed, but thinking Marva had forgotten yet another of her endless bottles of medication, Nelse steered the sensible gray sedan back into the cove, parked halfway in the drive, the engine running.

"Do you want me to go look with you?"

"No."

Nelse did not like the flatness in that word. Something in the back of her throat, an itch like the beginning of a cold, disturbed her. This time, Marva's voice was devoid of its music. There was no echo, only that unspoken *Hush, child, please.*

Confused, Nelse waited in the car. And waited. Then waited some more. Finally, when the engine started to rumble, sputter in protest, she decided to go in. She had never been invited into her neighbor's home, never thought anything of it, but what she saw reminded her of that last, recurring dream.

In her dream, it is another night-morning and Yaya has gone to park her cart, lay her head on the steps of the Church of the Holy Name of Jesus. It is three in the morning, but the hours mean nothing here, and the child is not tired, though circles like half-moons border her eyes, ashen her cheeks. From the window the child watches the elder asleep on the stone bed. Yaya is so still, so very still, like a statue. There is so much the child wants to say. If she could, she would call out to her. Instead, she is drawing strength from the numbers, the mathematics pouring into her like breath, drawing strength from the stillness inside her.

Nelse stumbles, pushes through Marva's front door, and steps into the living room. It is dark and still and almost as silent as the dream. Forcing her mind to take control of her feet, Nelse walks up the stairs to the second floor. In the time it takes her to reach the bed, to grasp Marva by her thin shoulders, to hold her damp head, Nelse is certain she has lost her ability until she hears herself speak.

"Marva, wake up. I'm here. Wake up."

On the way to the bridge, Nelse drove silently past burning ranch-style houses, past green *City of Memphis* garbage cans kicked up and down the streets, lying open on their sides like split carcasses. The radio was full of static—whatever had blocked the sun now blocked all the signals. Nelse drove, not quite sure if she would even make it downtown. As she turned on Chelsea, she found herself thinking about a different kind of figurin'. Her mind filled with shifting possibilities that made her stop at Manassas to wipe away fresh tears. And in these dark memories, Nelse would always later place one more figure in the scene, collapse or fast-forward time, just like in her dream, so that Marva made it to the bridge with her, and never looked back. Ridiculous to have thought of then, but there it was. Glowing dimly in her memory, the memory of her friend, the memory of the sun.

TELL HIM WHAT YOU WANT

by Troy L. Wiggins
Uptown

And the night was black, the black of the silence between jilted lovers. It was half past midnight, the time when good folks were keen to lose the string that connected them to their god and let the nasty things inside them roam free.

The only person on the darkened streets was a man, a man carrying a camera, and maybe that camera was his name or his soul, but right then it was just a piece of hard black plastic with some metal bits and glass. A soggy C-note lined his pocket. You couldn't see the nastiness there, but his god could.

"It's all changin'," Fat Red had been saying when Jackie came into his tavern that night to take photos.

The only thing fat about Fat Red was his lips. They looked like purple bruises against his copper skin. His face was scored with a battlefield of pockmarks, and his thick Afro was the color of a fresh penny. The rest of him was thin as a lost breath.

Fat Red's was a weekend ritual for many folks. The tavern's location was a mystery—if you didn't know where it was, or knew somebody who was privy, you wouldn't find it.

And it wasn't much of a place to look at. Inside, it was about as spacious as a medium-sized kitchen. There were five or six metal tables spread in a horseshoe pattern, and each table was ringed with folding chairs. A big speaker sat in a corner near the back, amplifying the blues that oozed from a wood-paneled jukebox. Behind the rickety walnut bar, Fat Red had hooked up an industrial Coca-Cola cooler and packed it with canned beers and soda. Tall bottles of brown liquor with white men's names adorned the wall behind the bar. Fat Red made sure that folks ate as much as they drank, so the air was spiced with the scent of barbecued turkey legs and red sausages cobbled together from cuts of meat so undesirable that they had to be burned black before eating.

"First they shut down Firestone, then they closin' up Hurt Village, and now Lauderdale Courts is somethin' totally different," Bubba Strong said, leaning back in his chair so far that the metal groaned. Bubba was a philosopher king of North Memphis, as only a transient Negro with five kids could be. "They puttin' all the folks out and startin' to call it Uptown."

"The fuck is a uptown?"

Bubba opened his eyes wide and said, "Shiiiiiit, you ain't know? It's what they call a town where all the niggas gotta get *up* outta there."

All the men and women laughed, but the laughter was strained. Fat Red pushed open the front door to expose the deepening night, saying, "I need to let some of this North Memphis *up* outta *here*."

It was only ten thirty, and Jackie had a little bit of Wild Turkey in him. He fished around in his pocket for a loose Newport—he'd got a handful for a dollar from the Arab store up the street—and fixed it in his mouth, holding it tight with his bottom lip.

He set up his tripod and unrolled his backdrop—a long piece of plastic airbrushed with a scene of the city: a faded blue sky stretched over a wide green-brown stripe that was the

Mighty Mississippi. The Hernando de Soto Bridge was a skeleton of shadows across the water, and the Pyramid stood tall, gleaming, as if spreading a cleansing light. The blue glow from a leaning lamp illuminated Jackie's corner, cutting through the red-black darkness to shine on some of the hard faces in Fat Red's.

Liquor flowed and stoked the nastiness. Sir Charles Jones was asking if anybody out there was lonely, and the crowd was replying with their hips and hands and, "Yeah! That's my record!"

Jackie loosened his tie and moved almost unseen through the dark club, only betrayed by the flash of his camera capturing the grinding of black bodies. Many of them greeted him, "H'lo, Jackie" or "Jackie G, my nigga! Make sure you get my good side!" He made his way to the bar, where Fat Red poured fingers of whiskey into glasses stolen from local restaurants—each glass had a different logo. Jackie leaned over the bar as if ordering a drink.

"You gonna have my money after work, right?" Jackie whispered.

Fat Red grimaced like he had bitten down on a sour pickle and said, "Yeah, fool. Come in here bustin' my balls about a hunnit dollars. Yeah, I got it."

Jackie narrowed his eyes at Fat Red, but held his tongue.

Three women were waiting when he got back to his corner. All of them wore dresses so tight you could see what they'd eaten for dinner. He recognized one, Tickey, a neighborhood woman who worked at the train station downtown, but the other two were strangers.

"What up, Jackie?" Tickey said, her two gold incisors making her smile worth a thousand dollars. Her skin was polished ebony, and her dark brown eyes had a pantherish look.

"Tickey, how you doin', baby?" Jackie glanced at her legs and had a notion of asking her out back behind the club, but he let the Newport burn that notion away.

"Me and my friends wanna coupla pictures." She flashed a twenty-dollar bill.

Jackie motioned over to a pot of red, pink, and white roses. Each flower was wrapped in cellophane. "Nice night like this, y'all ladies want some flowers?"

"We ain't ask for no flowers," one of her friends snapped. A snarl crossed the woman's bony face, and Jackie knew that she was nasty through and through.

"Don't pay Tabitha no mind, Jackie," Tickey said smoothly.

"Yeah," the third friend said. She was taller and curvier than the other two, her glossy black hair shot through with strands of bright blue and purple. "She really just mad at her boss, because the bitch won't just go on and pay all her bills. She get a little drank and a big dick, and she be good."

"Well," Jackie said, "plenty of both in the house tonight."

Something clicked to life in Tabitha's eyes even as her friends laughed. Jackie stared into those eyes. There was an apology in the back of his throat, but it tasted like bile and he didn't want that flavor on his tongue.

"Y'all pose in front of the drop," he said. "I'ma take a few, y'all choose which ones y'all want."

The women assumed a group pose in front of the camera, pointing their curves in the direction of anyone who could see. Heat bloomed in Jackie's gut, but his hands stayed still. Four flashes brightened the night. Afterward, the women chose their photos from the display on Jackie's camera, and he hooked it up to his portable printer, which spat the images out on glossy paper.

"Fat Red takes the money," Jackie said when Tickey pushed the twenty dollars his way.

"Thank you, Jackie," Tickey drawled, leading her friends away.

"Hold up," Jackie said, and fished a red rose out of the pot. He went over to Tabitha, put his hand gently in the small of her back, and presented her with the flower. "Don't let your night stay sour, baby."

Tabitha took the flower but didn't smile.

Jackie lit up another cigarette and went back to his spot, waiting for the right moment to capture folks moving their bodies to low-down music that made them shake and holler and spill their drinks. Jackie enjoyed watching. He hated talking and held folks who talked too loud or for too long in contempt. He'd learned long ago: you could find out much by watching people, which is why he became an eye, capturing slivers of folks' lives as they let themselves hang loose.

Over at the bar, Les Jackson had his wife Anne hemmed up, trying to beg up on something that she wasn't coming down off of. Anne rolled her eyes and popped her lips in annoyance.

Jackie captured that annoyance in a flash.

Tickey and her friends were on the dance floor now, bumping hips and fending off the advances of men made doubly aggressive by drinks and the high-speed thrumming in their loins. Tabitha moved her shoulders in a slow rhythm but cradled that rose like it was her dear child.

Jackie drank that tenderness in, captured it.

Eleven thirty rolled in, up, and out. Fat Red closed the front door and opened up the back one, greeted some folks coming in that way, and told his heavy-chested wife Vera to fry up some catfish. Bone Lyles walked in wearing a linen suit as bleached dry as his name, ordered a tall whiskey and a plate of fish. The air inside Fat Red's blackened a bit.

"Whatcha know good, Bone?" a voice called out.

"Chasin' up after this money," Bone hollered, "but the bitch won't slow down."

"I know that's right!"

Jackie watched with a scowl as Bone slid his white-suited ass up to Nikka Coleman and put his arms around her, his hands black against her yellow skin. Nikka Coleman talked with those hazel eyes of hers, and she had a way of saying things that made you think she was in love with you, and only you, and there was no other man in the world but you getting any of her loving. Bone was eating that honey up.

Jackie knew when there was something that needed capturing. His whole body twitched, and he glanced around. Willie Coleman materialized, watched Bone running his thick fingers up and down his wife's arm. The set of Willie's lip told Jackie that the man's bed had been too cold lately.

Bone was a quick wit. Nikka laid her mouth open, and Bone fell on her lips like a predator. Jackie readied his eye.

Willie Coleman was six and a half feet tall, with hands like cast-iron skillets and the disposition of a straight razor in the hands of a poor man down to his last nickel. He rose up, and the room got quiet except Bone snacking on Nikka's lips— only now it was Nikka having a taste of Bone.

Willie stood over Nikka and Bone for two or three seconds. Jackie watched anger bubble to the surface and twist Willie's lips. The big man snatched his wife away and slapped Bone twice across the face so hard that the music stopped.

"The fuck you hit me for, man?" Bone cried, shooting to his feet. Willie slapped him again.

"Stop it, Cole!" Nikka screamed, but there was no love for Bone in that cry. "Let him alone! I done told you that I don't want yo' ass no more!"

"You comin' back home with me," Willie rumbled, "whether you like it or not."

The nasty thing in the room fled from the shadow of the blues and whirled around the three of them, Coleman standing tall with his wife hanging off his arm, Bone on the floor shaking his head slow.

Rumors had carried around the hood. Word was that Willie would lock Nikka in the house when he went over to Seventh Street to work at one of the pallet factories. He didn't trust her to be faithful, so he'd installed locks on the outside of the doors and windows. Before he left for work each morning, he would sprinkle flour around the windows and in the doorframe to make sure he'd know if she left him.

The word on Firestone, Manassas, Tully, and Marble was that Bone was a bad man with an angry .38, and Willie Coleman was just two steps from a regular cotton-pickin' fool.

Willie snatched up his wife and started to drag her outside, but she tore away.

"I told you, Cole. We done. I'm sick of being with you. I'm not yo' slave or yo' child. I'm—I *was* yo' woman. But we done."

"Oh, so that's how you wanna play it?" Willie snarled. "You bad in front of all these peoples, huh? Fine then. When this nigga use you up and toss you out on yo' ass, don't come sniffin' up 'round me."

Willie moved toward the exit, his shoulders slumped despite his hot words. Jackie captured the man's defeat. He twitched again, noticed that Bone was going into his jacket. Jackie tried to yell, but he felt like his words got caught in a tornado. His skin tingled with the same chill that jumped through all the folks gathered inside Fat Red's.

Willie frowned, turned, his snarl betraying a desire to

plant his steel-toed boot in Bone's gut—but a snub-nose .38, blacker than the fingers that held it, stopped him cold.

"You betta not move, mothafuckah," Bone said.

Nikka leapt on her lover. She ripped the gun from Bone's hands and jabbed it at her husband like a black-bladed knife.

"Oh—" was all Willie got to say before two pops from the gun opened two dark holes in his blue work shirt.

Jackie's hands moved on their own, snapping up, camera ready, the all-seeing eye drinking in the violence.

Willie ragdoll-jerked, then stiffened. It was kind of like in the movies, Jackie guessed, because when the shots hit, there was no blood. But by the time Willie landed on the sticky floor, his work shirt was half-black.

"Goddamn!" Fat Red swore, slicing the silence. Folks split like ants hit with bleach—everyone except Tabitha, who just stood staring at Willie's body, the rose to her chest. Jackie grabbed his camera and made for the back door. It was bad luck to step over a dead body.

The thumping in Jackie's ears wasn't his heart, like he thought. It was his boots on Fat Red's raggedy wooden floor, and as he scrambled down the darkened back hallway, Fat Red jumped out of the shadows and pressed his sour-smelling body up against Jackie.

"Here," he huffed, slapping a slimy something or other into Jackie's palm. "Don't say Fat Red ever did you wrong."

Money in Jackie's pocket made him feel like the walls were closing in. He nearly fell out of the door escaping into the North Memphis night.

The night was black, black as the scum between a bum's toes, and Jackie's camera was an anchor weighted by death. There were no stars. The hundred dollars in his pocket sent poison through his legs, slowing him down.

Young folks over from a nightclub run by Fat Red's cousin lined the street outside Fat Red's, armored in the swagger and invincibility of youth. Their pants sagged, their shirts and heels glittered, and their teeth gleamed, shot through with gold.

Jackie stumbled down Tully. His thoughts were mechanical: right foot, left foot, breathe, blink, sweat. The blood money in his pocket wasn't even enough to cover the backdrop and equipment that he left behind while Willie Coleman bled out onto Fat Red's floor. Half his livelihood was gone. His legs itched to go back to the scene of that killing, but he forced the urge away.

Sirens announced the police blaring down Firestone as Jackie passed shotgun houses. Something moved in the tall grass. Jackie fought to regulate his stride—the streets were hot, and the police were looking to stop any Negro moving too fast.

Across the street, the old Firestone plant was the darkened remains of some long-dead animal. A couple walking in the opposite direction caught Jackie's eye. The man had his arm flung over the woman's shoulder, but she supported him despite her own stumbling. As the couple passed, the woman seemed to recognize Jackie. His skin tingled. He could feel her eyes boring into him, and when she yelled out, his bones rattled. Jackie picked up his step.

He hadn't been to a church since his grandmother dragged him to her little house church when they lived over in Molen Town. He'd even let his grandmama force him up into the choir, where he'd lent his voice to the chorus of "Jesus on the Mainline."

"*Jesus is on the mainline, tell him what you want . . . Oh the line ain't never busy, tell him what you want,*" the old folks had crooned, and when Jackie saw the small white cross on the roof of Grace Baptist, he swore with relief.

Grace Baptist was an old-time church flung out of place. Its brick was painted the color of Christ's blood. Worn-out green carpet lined the steps and fuzzed around the wrought-iron railing on the wheelchair ramp. A gold mail slot had been cut into the storm door so the church could gather after-hours donations. Jackie opened the slot, dropped in the hundred, and prayed.

"Lord, I know I ain't been much for visitin' before now, but I feel the foulness comin', and I need you around me and mine. I—I don't know what else to say. I need help. Please. Amen."

Blue light pierced the night. Jackie realized that he had fallen to his knees. His camera lay beside him, that eye yet staring.

"Stay down there!" the cop's voice boomed. A white cop. Jackie's heart fell to his ass, bounced back to his chest.

Hands on head was standard operating procedure if you didn't wanna get shot and written off as an accident. Jackie stepped outside of his body, wondering if he would die before police got him down to 201 Poplar. Other realizations filled in the scene. Boots—two pairs—on the ground. The burned scent of the police car. Flashing blue light. Strong hands grabbed his wrists, hauled him up.

"The hell are you doing out here this time of night, man, with all this stuff going on up the way?" This voice was different. It rolled in a way that Jackie's ears found acceptable. He turned, eyes meeting a pair similar to his own atop a black mustache. The black cop turned his mouth into a sneer.

"Leavin' work," Jackie replied, apprehensive. Skinfolk wasn't kinfolk, especially when that skin was covered by a white man's uniform.

"Where you work at?"

Jackie pursed his lips, then said, "Fat Red's, up the street."

The look the cops shared turned Jackie's bowels to mush.

"You got some ID?"

"In my wallet, yeah."

The white cop patted Jackie down with half-hearted slaps against his torso and legs. The black cop walked over to where Jackie had been kneeling. Jackie felt thick fingers in his pockets, clumsy against his buttocks.

"Jackie Gerard?" the white cop asked. "That's the name your mama gave you?"

"Last I checked, sir."

"Found something, Brown." The black cop was holding Jackie's camera with the tips of his fingers. "What is this you're carrying around?"

Jackie wanted to punch him in the mouth. Instead, he answered, "It's a camera, sir."

"You some kind of photographer?"

"I take pictures up at the club—Fat Red's."

"Anything on this camera that we oughta see?" Brown asked, all business, like he was buying a pound of pecans.

Jackie peered at the ground. He felt Brown's eyes roaming over him. The black cop sighed, then stood on his toes and passed gas.

"Shit, Decroux," the white cop said, waving his hand in front of his face.

"No sir. No. There ain't nothing on there but pictures from the club. Folks posing. Maybe a couple of shots I thought was interestin', stuff like that. Nothing special."

Decroux dug his hard fingers into Jackie's shoulder, pulling him forward. Jackie pulled back. But Decroux was like gravity.

"What you know about Willie Coleman getting shot?" he asked. "Come on, nigga, I know you know something. Tell me or I'm gonna take you downtown and beat the black offa yo' ass."

"Let him alone," the white cop said in a whisper.

"What the fuck, Brown?"

"He don't know nothing. You shake him any more he's liable to shit himself, and then I'll have another stinking nigger on my hands. Let him go on home."

Decroux released Jackie's shirt. Brown tossed the camera at Jackie like it was a live grenade. Jackie caught it, steadying it against his chest. Decroux spat at Jackie's feet, headed back to the car.

"Don't let me catch you out in these streets no more!" Decroux said as the cops sped off, lights still flashing.

Jackie sat down on the curb. He looked at his camera, the plastic and glass and metal that may have been his name or may have been his soul. Something pulled in his chest, like a string reattaching itself.

"Thank you, Jesus," he said, and smashed the camera against the curb.

ABOUT THE CONTRIBUTORS

RICHARD J. ALLEY is a reporter, columnist, and editor from Memphis, where he lives with his wife and four children. His short story "Sea Change" won the grand prize for fiction in the 2010 *Memphis* Magazine Fiction Contest and his first novel, *Five Night Stand*, was published in May 2015.

JOHN BENSKO'S books include the short story collection *Sea Dogs* and several poetry books: *Green Soldiers*, winner of a Yale Younger Poets prize; *The Waterman's Children; The Iron City;* and *Visitations*, winner of an Anita Claire Scharf Award. He was a Fulbright Professor at the University of Alicante in Spain, and coordinates the creative writing program at the University of Memphis.

LAUREEN P. CANTWELL grew up in eastern Long Island and, after living in Astoria, Philadelphia, and Iowa, found her way to Memphis—"the rock 'n' roll side of Tennessee." She lived in Midtown for two years while working as a librarian at the University of Memphis and grew to love the darkness of the city—and Elvis.

STEPHEN CLEMENTS left his beloved city after graduating from the University of Memphis to serve in the US Army and take an extended, unpleasant vacation to Iraq. When he got out, he met a beautiful and mean woman, and they fell in love, so things definitely improved. He has three other books, loves foreign travel, and is an avid wine maker and political junkie.

ARTHUR FLOWERS is the author of several books, including *Another Good Loving Blues, Mojo Rising: Confessions of a 21st Century Conjureman,* and *I See the Promised Land: A Life of Martin Luther King Jr*. He is a Delta-based performance poet, webmaster of Rootsblog, and has been executive director of various nonprofits, including the Harlem Writers Guild. He currently teaches fiction in Syracuse University's MFA in creative writing program.

DWIGHT FRYER is a writer, speaker, and storyteller living in Memphis. His historical novels, *The Legend of Quito Road* and *The Knees of Gullah Island*, were both critically acclaimed. *The Legend of Quito Road* shares the tale of a religious man who taught his only son to make white lightning whiskey in 1932, and *The Knees of Gullah Island* follows the struggle of a family trying to reconnect in 1884 Charleston, South Carolina, after being separated in the slave trade.

Ron Whitfield

KAYE GEORGE, a national best-selling and multiple-award-winning author, writes several mystery series: Imogene Duckworthy, Cressa Carraway, People of the Wind, and, as Janet Cantrell, Fat Cat. *Fat Cat Spreads Out* was published in 2015, as was the second Cressa Carraway mystery. Her short stories have appeared in anthologies, magazines, and her own collection, *A Patchwork of Stories*. She reviews for *Suspense Magazine*, and lives in Knoxville, Tennessee.

Larry Kuzniewski

LEONARD GILL was born and raised in Memphis and today writes about books for the *Memphis Flyer*, the city's alternative newsweekly. He also spotlights local writers for a monthly book feature in *Memphis* magazine.

JAMEY HATLEY is a native of Memphis. Her writing has appeared or is forthcoming in the *Oxford American, Callaloo, Long Hidden: Speculative Fiction from the Margins of History,* and elsewhere. She has attended the Callaloo Creative Writing Workshop, VONA/Voices Writing Workshop, the *Oxford American* Summit for Ambitious Writers, and the Bread Loaf Writers' Conference.

Rhonda Cosentino

CARY HOLLADAY'S seven volumes of fiction include *Horse People: Stories* and *The Deer in the Mirror*. She has received an O. Henry Prize and fellowships from the Pennsylvania Council on the Arts, the Tennessee Arts Commission, and the National Endowment for the Arts. A native of Virginia, she teaches at the University of Memphis.

EHI IKE published her first novel, *Taken Away*, at age fourteen and its sequel, *Hidden*, at eighteen. She has been given the opportunity to speak at the University of Memphis, Jackson Library, along with other events for organizations. She has received the Creative Writing Award from Hollins University and the 2014 Best Literary Artist FACE Award. She is currently completing her BA in creative writing at Columbia College Chicago.

LEE MARTIN is the author of the novels *The Bright Forever*, a finalist for the 2006 Pulitzer Prize in Fiction; *Break the Skin; River of Heaven*; and *Quakertown*. He has also published three memoirs, *From Our House, Turning Bones*, and *Such a Life*; and a short story collection, *The Least You Need to Know*. He teaches in the MFA program at Ohio State University.

SUZANNE BERUBE RORHUS attended the Squaw Valley Community of Writers, served as coordinator for the Short Mystery Fiction Society's Derringer Awards, and is a member of Mystery Writers of America and International Thriller Writers. Her published short fiction has appeared in *Ellery Queen Mystery Magazine*, the anthology *Moon Shot*, and in various online and print publications, including *Norwegian American Weekly*. She recently won a Hugh Holton Award for an unpublished mystery manuscript.

ADAM SHAW and **PENNY REGISTER-SHAW** have collaborated on several books, including *Bloodstream* for Image Comics. Adam's resumé includes murals, illustration, gallery art, and concept design for film and games. Penny is an attorney and writer of children's books and scripts for television. They spent most of their childhoods in Memphis where they currently live with two canine daughters and receive occasional visits from their human daughter, Sophie.

SHEREE RENÉE THOMAS, a native of Memphis, is the Lakes Writer-in-Residence at Smith College. A Cave Canem and NYFA fellow, her work has appeared in *Callaloo, Transition, storySouth*, the *New York Times*, the *Washington Post, The Moment of Change, 80! Memories & Reflections on Ursula K. Le Guin, Mojo: Conjure Stories, Bum Rush the Page, Bronx Biannual No. 2*, and *So Long Been Dreaming*. Thomas edited the World Fantasy Award–winning *Dark Matter* anthologies and is the author of *Shotgun Lullabies*.

TROY L. WIGGINS is from Memphis, Tennessee. He was raised on a steady diet of Spider-Man comic books and Japanese role-playing games. His short fiction has appeared in the *Griots: Sisters of the Spear* and *Long Hidden: Speculative Fiction from the Margins of History* anthologies. He lives in Memphis with his wife and their two tiny dogs.

DAVID WESLEY WILLIAMS is the author of the novel *Long Gone Daddies*, a Gold Medal winner of the Independent Publisher Book Awards' Best Regional Fiction. His short fiction has appeared in the anthology *Forty Stories* and in such journals as *The Common* and *The Pinch*. Williams, a veteran Memphis journalist, is a two-time winner of the *Memphis* Magazine Fiction Contest. He lives in Memphis with his wife Barbara and two retired racing greyhounds.

Also available from Akashic Books

NEW ORLEANS NOIR
edited by Julie Smith
288 pages, trade paperback original, $15.95

BRAND-NEW STORIES BY: Ace Atkins, Laura Lippman, Patty Friedmann, Barbara Hambly, Tim McLoughlin, Olympia Vernon, David Fulmer, Jervey Tervalon, James Nolan, Kalamu ya Salaam, Maureen Tan, Thomas Adcock, Jeri Cain Rossi, Christine Wiltz, Greg Herren, Julie Smith, Eric Overmyer, and Ted O'Brien.

"It's harrowing reading, to be sure, but it's pure page-turning pleasure, too." —*Times-Picayune*

"It's a vivid series of impressions of the city . . . as part of the first wave of fiction to arrive in the wake of the storm, it's a thrilling read." —*Gambit Weekly*

CHICAGO NOIR
edited by Neal Pollack
258 pages, trade paperback original, $15.95

BRAND-NEW STORIES BY: Neal Pollack, Achy Obejas, Alexai Galaviz-Budziszewski, Adam Langer, Joe Meno, Peter Orner, Kevin Guilfoile, Bayo Ojikutu, Jeff Allen, Luciano Guerriero, Claire Zulkey, Andrew Ervin, M.K. Meyers, Todd Dills, C.J. Sullivan, Daniel Buckman, Amy Sayre-Roberts, and Jim Arndorfer.

"No stretch of the imagination is required to place Chicago among the burgs of *noir* . . . Corrupt preachers, desperate drug addicts, infamous murderers, cunning bluebeards, cuckolded pugilists, legendary drag queens, doomed assassins, and yes, existential Packer fans. Each, in his or her own way, is as representative of Chicago as Oprah, MJ, and a Gold Coast hot dog." —*Chicago Sun-Times*

RICHMOND NOIR
edited by Andrew Blossom, Brian Castleberry & Tom De Haven
248 pages, trade paperback original, $15.95

BRAND-NEW STORIES BY: Dean King, Laura Browder, Howard Owen, Mina Beverly, Tom De Haven, X.C. Atkins, Meagan J. Saunders, Anne Thomas Soffee, Clint McCown, Conrad Ashley Persons, Clay McLeod Chapman, Pir Rothenberg, David L. Robbins, Hermine Pinson, and Dennis Danvers, with a foreword by Tom Robbins.

"*Richmond Noir* touches on something unattainable by a singular author. Its collection of diverse voices, interests, period pieces, present-day reflections, architectural insights, cultural commentary, and the pervasive sense of mortality that characterizes an urbania so bound to inherited nostalgia, capture the indefinable nature of what it is to live in Richmond." —*RVA Mag*

MIAMI NOIR
edited by Les Standiford
332 pages, trade paperback original, $15.95

BRAND-NEW STORIES BY: James W. Hall, Barbara Parker, John Dufresne, Paul Levine, Carolina Garcia-Aguilera, Tom Corcoran, Christine Kling, George Tucker, Kevin Allen, Anthony Dale Gagliano, David Beaty, Vicki Hendricks, John Bond, Preston L. Allen, Lynne Barrett, Jeffrey Wehr.

"Variety, familiarity, mood, and tone, and the occasional gem of a story, make *Miami Noir* a collection to savor." —*Miami Herald*

"This well-chosen collection isn't just a thoughtful compilation of work by some of South Florida's best writers. Each story is also a window into a different part of Miami-Dade and its melting pot of cultures." —*Sun-Sentinel*

DALLAS NOIR
edited by David Hale Smith
288 pages, trade paperback original, $15.95

BRAND-NEW STORIES BY: Kathleen Kent, Ben Fountain, James Hime, Harry Hunsicker, Matt Bondurant, Merritt Tierce, Daniel J. Hale, Emma Rathbone, Jonathan Woods, Oscar C. Peña, Clay Reynolds, Lauren Davis, Fran Hillyer, Catherine Cuellar, David Haynes, and J. Suzanne Frank.

Part of "Year in Review: Why the Eyes of the Book World Were on Texas in 2013." —*Dallas News*

One of *Texas Monthly's* "5 Things You'll be Talking about in November"

LONE STAR NOIR
edited by Bobby Byrd and Johnny Byrd
284 pages, trade paperback original, $15.95

BRAND-NEW STORIES BY: James Crumley, Joe R. Lansdale, Claudia Smith, Ito Romo, Luis Alberto Urrea, David Corbett, George Weir, Sarah Cortez, Jesse Sublett, Dean James, Tim Tingle, Milton Burton, Lisa Sandlin, Jessica Powers, and Bobby Byrd.

"The biggest state in the Lower 48 . . . just means more places to bury the bodies. This isn't J.R. Ewing's Lone Star State. This is the Texas of chicken shit bingo, Enron scamsters, and a feeling that what happens in Mexico stays in Mexico . . . you better pray that blood doesn't stain your belt buckle." —*Austin Chronicle*

A world to win
Life of a revolutionary